ALICE'S COALITION

THE RATHE CHRONICLES
BOOK FOUR

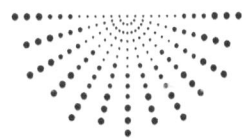

ALEXANDRA K MARTIN

"No one can make you feel inferior without your consent."

— ELEANOR ROOSEVELT

FOREWARNING

Please be aware that I'm an Australian writer, therefore this book is written with British spelling in mind.

This is also an RH Epic Fantasy/PNR novel, with adult content, and is recommended for the mature audience. Please note that there is extreme violence, explicit sex scenes, body image shaming, male victimisation of sexual assault, and female-on-female bullying in this novel.

Please keep this warning in mind going forward, and feel free to message me if you need extra information on any potential content issues you might be worried about. I'm happy to help.

Enter at your own risk...
*Insert evil laugh

To every person out there that doesn't think they're good enough. Stop it, you're perfect just the way you are, and don't let anyone tell you otherwise. X

GLOSSARY

KINDREDS & KIDS

<u>Summer</u>

Blayze (Phoenix)

Salvatore (Dragon)

Reid (Alpha Wolf)

Baine (Omega Wolf)

    Kids

- Meaghan (Human Female)
- Lawson (Human Male)
- Llewellyn (Human Female, Twin set A - Identical)

- Cheyenne (Human Female, Twin set A - Identical)
- Mina (Phoenix Female, Twin set B)
- Demetrius (Dragon Male, Twin set B)

Janice

Keneth (Grizzly Bear)

Anton (Grizzly Bear)

Kids

- Pregnant

Havana

Hermes (Drake)

Kids

- Brenda (Leviathan)

MHANU

Shifters
Phoenix (Rare and Powerful/ most feared shifter)
Dragons

- Dragon (fire Dragon/most powerful)
- Leviathan (Water Dragon)
- Drake (Earth Dragon/ no wings)

Wolf
Grizzly Bear
Shark
Cheetah
Griffin
Owl
Eagle
Panda
Panther
Polar Bear

Sorcerers

Fae

Elves (Earth)
Fairy (Air)
Siren (Water)
Wielders (Fire)

Downworlders

Vampyre
Demon
Gremlin

DIVINE ORDER

Guardians

Angel
Valkyrie

Celestials

Catholic/Christian God
Norse Gods
Azraelle (Goddess of Rebirth)

PLACES

Rathe (Parallel world to Earth)

   Threshold (Holding facility for human women stolen by Rathe for reproductive purposes)

   Downworld (World of darkness below and connected to both worlds)

   Bermuda Triangle (Door between worlds)

PROLOGUE

ALICE

e finally get to our destination, and I'm so done with walking. I didn't get this amazing plus-sized physique by working out, I tell myself bitterly.

My weight has always been my biggest flaw, but I don't seem to be able to stop eating. I love food, and I hate exercise; that's just the way it is. I want to be better, but I also don't want to have to change who I am and what I love, food.

It certainly doesn't help my self-love when I'm surrounded by a world filled with supermodels and bodybuilders. What a way to fuck with me.

I turn and look at my travelling companion, Mischa; she's a real piece of work. She has nothing to say to me other than how fat I am and how I should be disgusted with myself. To make matters worse, she's probably the hottest chick I've ever seen, and she's human.

"You're gonna love it here," Derryn tells us in his thick Scottish brogue as we approach the gorgeous, wooden village in the middle of a wide, grassy plain. Wildflowers grow all around and the whole place looks like a cute, old western. "The Cheetahs are proud males, and they take good care of their own, and while you're here, you'll be treated like kin."

He looks darkly at Mischa. "Dinnae be a cock up while you're here. They dinnae deserve your special brand of sass."

She gives him a fake smile that instantly turns into a real one when a blond, Henry Cavill in the Witcher look-alike, and Salem, the receptionist from the doctor's office in Threshold, stride over to us. The two of them take my breath away; they're so fucking pretty.

Great. More pretty people.

Mischa slows down, drops back to where I'm walking, and smirks at me cruelly. "Well, well, well. Look at the men here. Aren't they something? I think I'm going to like it here. I bet I'll find my Kindred with a sexy Cheetah." She looks me up and down in the way she does which tells me how ugly she thinks I am. "Sucks to be you. It's a shame there's no one in Rathe suitable for someone like you. You never know, maybe there are mole shifters. Then you don't have to worry about them seeing you."

With a boisterous laugh at my expense, she speeds up her steps, putting an exaggerated sway in her small hips, and says in a loud, saucy voice to the approaching men, "Hello boys, I'm Mischa, and it's a *pleasure* to make your acquaintance." She pronounces pleasure in her sexy Russian accent, extra thick, and I want to gag.

Unfortunately, I also want to hide because both sets of the Cheetah's eyes ignore her and fall solely on me. Their focused gazes trailing my body from top to bottom, and my stomach drops at their attention.

Please don't notice how fat I am.

"Alice?" Salem asks, recognising me. "I thought that was you. This is Baxter. Welcome to your new home."

Home? Yeah right, with the dirty look that Mischa just gave me for stealing her limelight, I doubt very much that this is going to be as simple as that.

CHAPTER ONE

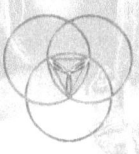

SALEM

*H*oly shit! I can't believe it's her! My gaze falls on the voluptuous creature that I've been dreaming about every single night since she was carried into the medical centre at Threshold.

I remember the moment I saw her with her cute little ears and cheeks bright pink with embarrassment when she was placed in the chair right across from me. My whole world fell into place, and it was like breathing in fresh air for the first time in my long life. I knew right then and there who she was to me and that my world would never be the same.

Unfortunately, I also knew that I couldn't do anything about it because at that time the females were all still in the dark, not to mention Alice was uncomfortable with my attention. Now that so much time has passed, and she's used to the idea of why they're here, hopefully, Alice will be open to accepting my affection.

When I heard that two new females were coming to stay with us for a while and that one of them was called Alice, I knew it was her because she was the only Alice at Threshold, but I didn't believe it until this moment.

Baxter's hand suddenly grabs my arm, halting my excited step, and pulls us to a standstill. Turning to look at him, his massive grin and wide eyes focused solely on Alice gives me pause.

"That's Alice?" he asks quietly, with more than a little awe in his words. His eyes shift to mine and his smile falls slightly as he asks me, "Would you hate me if I tell you she's mine too?"

Unexpected pride swells in my chest at the idea of sharing Alice with Baxter. I couldn't think of a better male to have protect and love her along with me, than him. Cheetah Shifters have always been more affectionate and prone to sharing than most other Mhanu, so in my mind, the more, the merrier. As long as they are good males that will help hold our family together and worship her the way she deserves to be worshipped.

My arm goes around my lifelong friend and I whisper in his ear, "I am honoured to have you as my future kin." I quickly add, "You will find her more distant than some of the females you've come across thus far. When I watched her at Threshold, she seemed to pull away from the male guards. It's best if we approach the subject carefully and let her settle in first."

Baxter pulls back and nods with understanding as the other female calls out to us for our attention, but when we turn to address it, all we see is *her*.

With swift feet, we catch up to their approaching party, my eyes never leaving Alice's face. Her cheeks and ears flame bright pink in the way I adore, and my heart skips a beat when her scent washes over me with a strong breeze, and I hear the sharp intake of breath when Baxter catches it too. Ylang-ylang, gardenia, and jasmine.

With a deep inhale, I catch the sharp, unpleasant tang of strong citrus coming from the other female that makes my nose crinkle with distaste. It's such an overpowering smell that it takes away the purity of Alice's.

As we step up to the group, I address the Goddess before me and welcome her home, praying inside that she will never leave.

Derryn steps forwards and introduces us to the other one that keeps stepping in front of Alice, and I realise I'm being rude. "It's lovely to meet you," I tell her honestly, reaching my hand out to shake hers the way that humans like.

Mischa takes my hand, not letting go, and steps way too close to me for my comfort. "Aren't you a handsome man? I think I'm going to like it here," she says with a different accent than I've heard in quite a while.

Baxter comes to my rescue and reaches out his hand to her so that she has to let go of mine. While they exchange pleasantries, I take a long step towards Alice and try to breathe in her comforting scent, but the overpowering citrus burns my nose instead, and I have to cover my mouth and nose with my hand to try to avoid its harshness.

Alice puts her head down, taking a small step away from me, and starts to fiddle with her backpack, a bead of sweat trailing down her neck. My eyes follow it like I'm in the desert, and it's my only answer for survival. It takes *all* of my willpower not to lap it up.

"Why don't we take the lasses to their cabin, so they can get comfortable before you show them around?" Derryn recommends, cutting off my intense gaze and bringing me back to sanity again.

With a smile, I reach out and grab Alice's hand automatically, pulling her back towards the village with a spring in my step. "Of course, let's go. I hope you like the cabin we picked out for you both. Summer and her friends stayed in it the last time they were here and seemed to like it. Of course, if you don't, we can find you a better one or build one for you." I ramble on, slightly nervous.

All the other males are in the main lodge where we are always convened as a group. Even though we have our own homes, we tend to eat as one big family in the hub, as we've dubbed it. The room is large and open with three long, bench-lined tables down the centre, an open-style kitchen and bar at one end, and a stage set up on the other for entertainment. We love music, dancing, and pretty much anything fun that we can do as a group. Cheetah Shifters are known for being a coalition. We do everything together and live as a democracy-based village.

While we have a small council, every voice here counts. We're also very touchy and that can make other Mhanu a bit uncomfortable at times. It's unusual to go long periods without giving each other affection in one way or another.

Baxter talks away with Mischa and Derryn as I pull Alice along with me, excited to show her the world that I want to gift her. I turn to look back and see that she looks visibly upset. Stopping, I ask if she is okay as she lets go of my hand and bends over, clasping at her side and panting heavily. "Are you hurt? Did I pull you too hard?"

Mischa laughs as she catches up to us and puts her hand on Alice's back in comfort. "Don't mind Alice. She's not used to movement. Why don't you just show her our house, so she can have a lie down? I'm sure she's dying to wash off all this sweat and eat before having a big sleep." She removes her hand from Alice and wipes it on her shorts with what seems like disgust.

I crinkle my forehead in confusion at the action as Derryn pipes in. "We've been walking for quite some time, and it's taken a toll on the poor lass. You dragging her behind you like your ass is on fire surely didn't help any."

Horrified that I've made her so uncomfortable, I reach forward and sweep her into my arms to carry her the rest of the way. Alice yelps, and I fear I've hurt her again and freeze.

"Oh my gosh. Put me down. Please," she squeals in a high-pitched, frightened voice, flailing her arms and legs.

I pull her in tighter. "Don't fear. I would never drop you." I try to console her.

Derryn scolds Alice, "Stop wriggling. You're gonna hurt the poor Cheetah with one of those rogue limbs flying about."

It takes everything in me not to growl at him for using such a harsh tone on her.

"He's right, Alice," Mischa says in a much happier tone. "Stay still, so he doesn't break anything, and be grateful that Salem is so strong." Her hand squeezes my bicep, and I have to suppress a shudder, and not a good one. Since I have a Kindred, it's really off-putting having another female in my vicinity. It almost makes me feel sick.

Picking up the pace, I carry the now quiet and still Alice the rest of the way, trying not to focus too hard on how amazing her soft curves feel in my arms and the rise and fall of her large breasts right below my gaze. *Gods give me strength.*

Baxter jogs ahead of me as we reach the front door and opens it with a flourish, a grin spread across his face as he looks down longingly at Alice. "Welcome to the female cabin. Your home until you find your own." Giving me a quick conspiratorial wink.

Stepping inside, I make my way straight to the couch and lower myself into the seat, placing Alice squarely on my lap. Knowing it would have been more appropriate to just place her there, I couldn't resist the temptation of holding onto her for a little longer.

She wiggles a little in my lap, probably from the discomfort of me not letting go straight away, and I have to mentally keep my body in check, stopping myself from purring or *rising to the occasion*.

Alice clears her throat, and Baxter chuckles under his breath before taking a seat close beside us on the couch. "Would you like something to drink, my queen?" he asks her, placing her feet on his lap and massaging her calf.

"I'd love one," Mischa chimes in across from us. Somehow I keep forgetting she's there. I need to make more of an effort to make her feel at home here, too.

With a huge dose of reluctance, I slide Alice over onto Baxter's lap and rise from the couch, heading towards the open kitchen. "Of course. Let me get some refreshments for everyone. I'll hold off on the food," I say as I reach into the fridge, bringing out a tall jug of cold water. "The other males are almost done with lunch and are waiting to meet you both. That's why you didn't see anybody in the village as we walked through." I grab three glasses for the travellers and hand them over one by one, noting that Alice was now beside Baxter and, by the looks of it, squishing herself as far away from him as possible.

I give him a questioning glance and receive a small shrug, some of the earlier excitement gone from his eyes.

"How about we give them some privacy, lads?" Derryn offers, getting up from his couch. "I'm sure they'd like to freshen up before dinner."

Alice seems to flinch, looking away and down. Maybe we've been a bit too handsy and are making her uncomfortable. I make a mental note to tell the other males not to touch the females too much. I'd hate for them to feel disrespected.

Leaving them to their own devices, we walk out the front and Baxter lets out a massive breath. "Fuck in hell. I need a shower too. Between wanting to wash away Mischa's nasty smell and rub myself all over Alice's juicy curves, my senses are super overwhelmed."

Derryn laughs outright, crossing his arms and shaking his head at us. "Do I sense a Kindred coupling or two? Being around you two in there was like suffocating on testosterone and lust. Fucking gross." He pushes out a big breath before turning more serious. "I'll give you a word of advice, Alice likes plenty of space and doesnae fair well with being stared at like she's meat. I thought she was gonna do a runner when you put her on your lap. Gods, what were you thinking? Cannae you see, she's like a deer thinking she's prey. If you're nae careful, she'll be out of here before you can say, 'ah fuck.'"

I know he's right because I've seen it before back in Threshold, but I just couldn't contain my excitement at her being here, in my village. I admittedly got carried away, even after I told myself not to.

Feeling dejected and annoyed with myself, I agree with him and promise myself, once again, that I'll behave.

"What's with the other one, Mischa?" Baxter asks, putting his long white hair into a braid. "She seems... extra."

With a scoff, Derryn growls out, "She's getting exactly what she deserves." His words are confusing and when I question him about it all he says is, "You'll see."

CHAPTER TWO

ALICE

$\mathcal{M}$ischa barks out a laugh at me as I awkwardly peel myself off the leather couch, my sweat leaving wet spots.

"Jesus, you're pathetic," she mocks me. "Look at the way those poor Cheetahs had to carry you and treat you like a sad little animal that needed fixing. They must think little of you. It's a shame that none of them will ever see you as a woman, because they are stunning. Why don't you go and put some dry clothes on after you wash off that stench? Did you see the way they kept covering their noses?" She laughs hard at that. "It was so sad that it was hilarious."

Without replying, I head down the hallway to find a bathroom. The first door on the left is a massive room with a big bed and beautiful wooden furniture.

Mischa pushes past me and into the room. "I'll take this one," she announces, diving onto the bed with a sigh. "Oh, so comfortable."

I turn and leave because I know she's trying to get a rise out of me, and I'm not in the mood to play after the embarrassment that has been my day. I wouldn't be surprised if the guys are all laughing at my expense outside. *What a fat bitch. She can't even walk without me having to carry her. I hope she doesn't eat all of our food.*

Tears fill my eyes at the thought, and a rush of relief welcomes me as I open the next door to a bathroom. Knowing I don't have time for much because everybody is waiting on me to be clean and not gross, I pull my small backpack off and take out the only other change of clothes I've managed to get while here.

Stripping down to bare skin, I use a wet face towel to quickly wipe down my body to get the sweat off, not forgetting the pool under my massive tits that's accumulated. The consequence of having too much boob is too much boob sweat.

I quickly pull on my underclothes, shirt, and pants, check myself in the mirror, and sit on the edge of the tub to put my sneakers back on when Mischa knocks on the door hard.

"I know you have a lot of ground to cover, but I'm hungry and want to meet the males. Quit making everyone wait for your fat ass and get out there. So selfish," she mutters, the sound of her footsteps retreating.

Another hot flush burns my cheeks and ears. Doing my laces up quickly, I shove my dirty clothes and bag in the corner of the room, deciding I'll wash them in the basin when I get back. I leave the bathroom with a sigh, trying to find the courage to face a whole village.

When I get to the lounge, I can't help but notice that Mischa has changed out of her walking shorts and shirt and into a much shorter skirt and tank top. Her still feminine abs and flat stomach are on display, not to mention her legs that go up to my armpits. With a deep sigh, I go to the front door and open it, the leggy goddess at my heels.

I almost walk into the tall Adonis that is Baxter as I pull open the door. The man in question practically fell inside, as if he was putting his ear to the door.

"Whoops," he says, smiling down at my much shorter frame of five foot five. "Caught red-handed. Shall we?" he asks, not looking the least bit sorry at having been caught eavesdropping.

He offers me his elbow like a gentleman, and I'm so startled by the whole thing that I just look at him like a goldfish gasping for air.

Mischa, being the Russian princess she is, sweeps past me, happily taking the offered arm, and smiles up at him hungrily, "I do love a gentleman," she practically purrs, and I have to fight the urge to roll my eyes at her sweet facade and batting eyelashes. What a snake.

Baxter and Mischa head off in front of me while Salem looks expectantly at me, Derryn nowhere to be found. "Hey, I'm really sorry about what happened before," Salem starts, gesturing for me to walk with him. "You'll figure this out sooner rather than later, but Cheetah Shifters are really touchy-feely, and we sometimes forget that others aren't like that. I will try to respect your space better in the future. I hope I didn't make you too uncomfortable. It wasn't my intention."

Feeling grateful but still uncomfortable, I answer quietly, "That's okay. I understand. Thank you for telling me." I look down at the ground as we walk because looking at these guys directly is like staring at the sun, very pretty but terrible for you. I know I can never touch that kind of beauty because all it will do is burn me and leave me scarred.

Unlike most of the girls here, I don't actually expect to find a

Kindred. I know what I look like, so even if for some reason I have one here, I have no doubt that they would be disappointed and not accept me. It's been like that my whole life. I've only ever had sex once. I thought I'd found a boy who liked me for me, but it turned out to be one big game. At school the next day, every corridor was filled with snickers and stares. It wasn't until Omar shunned me at lunch in front of everyone while laughing about what it's like to fuck a whale, that I realised what was happening. The rest of my senior year, I was nicknamed Tide because Omar told everyone that during sex my 'waves' just kept on rolling. It was then that I realised I was destined to be alone in this world. I'm twenty-four now, but the humiliation of those days still haunts me.

Snapping me out of my sad reverie, Salem gestures to the large double doors that Mischa and Baxter walk through, and my stomach rolls with nervousness.

I step inside just as three long tables filled with drop-dead gorgeous blond gods rise from their seats, a hushed tone taking over the whole room, and all eyes land on me. *Fuck!*

Run. Run. Run. My mind keeps repeating, but my fat legs don't move, refusing the exercise. My weight in this athletic land once again garnering everyone's attention. I have yet to see an overweight native to Rathe.

Baxter breaks the silence. "Males, these are our esteemed guests, Mischa," he gestures to the woman scowling at me by his side, "and Alice. Please be respectful of their personal space, and remember that this is probably a scary position for them to be in."

Mischa plants on a fake smile as she turns away from me and tries to call attention to herself, and I deeply hope that she does. "Thank you so much for having us. While I am outgoing and looking for love and friendship, Alice here prefers to be left alone. It's best to just feed her and leave her to rest alone."

I'm not sure if I'm grateful or pissed off that she pretty much just reminded them that I'm a slob that just lies around and eats all day. I decide to go with gratitude as *most* of the eyes turn to her, except for a few, including a very angry man sitting at the back with a brutal-looking scar across his face, scowling at me. He appears to be a lot larger than the other men here, not so much in height because they all appear to be tall, but in width. His broad shoulders and bulk are decidedly more intense than the model-type bodies the others seem to possess.

With a hard gulp, I drop my gaze from his immediately, the clear disdain for me evident in the depths of his stare, even from this distance.

I focus on the food lining the tables instead of the men surrounding it, and my mouth waters. Along all three tables is an endless supply of different types of meat, vegetables, salads, breads, and other miscellaneous yummies. I haven't eaten for hours and after that walk, I am *starving!*

Obviously noticing my look of intense hunger, Salem leads me towards the empty two chairs at the head of the middle table, gesturing for me to take one and Mischa to take the other. Both men sit at the end of the benches on each side of us with expectant smiles.

Mischa sits down with absolute grace and smirks at me when my ass doesn't fully fit in the chair underneath. *Why do people make such small fucking chairs? Some of us need more support.* It irritates me every time I go somewhere that gives me narrow seats. It feels like a personal offence.

"Do you want to swap?" Salem asks me. "I forgot how wide your hips are."

Just kill me. Right here, right now!

Mischa takes this moment to laugh out loud with no discretion, and I truly want the world to swallow me up as all the occupants of the room turn to look my way. Can this day get any worse? *Yes.* The answer is yes as I watch Baxter grab my plate and pile it up so high with so much variety that it's a mountain of food. *How much do these people think I eat?*

"Will that be enough?" he asks me, sliding it down in front of me.

Salem takes it and swaps it with his before getting up and standing behind my chair. "She can always grab more if she's still hungry," he replies on my behalf before turning to look down at me. "Please take my bench, I insist."

With as much courage as I can muster, I carefully lift myself from the small chair and slide into the bench seat. To my continued horror, the whole row of men get up and move down to give me more space.

The particular tall and lean gentleman at my side offers me a glass of what I think is milk. "Hi Alice, I'm Ture, one of the council members here. We are absolutely delighted to have you and Mischa join our village. I speak for everyone when I say that we hope you stay for a long time. There's too much testosterone around here, and having lovely ladies such as yourselves here will be a breath of fresh air."

Mischa answers before I get a chance. "I knew this place was going to be nice when we saw it, coming through the trees. What a cute little village and what a bunch of handsome men. To say I'm happy to be here is an understatement." I find it fascinating that Mischa's accent seems to come and go. I've found myself on more than one occasion wondering if she puts it on and is as American as I am. It wouldn't surprise me because she seems to do a lot for the sake of attention.

I just nod with a half smile and decide to focus on my food. The first bite of roast beef is like heaven in my mouth, it melts on my tongue, and I close my eyes, savouring the taste as I accidentally let out a small moan.

The clatter of utensils has my lids popping open to see what's happened when I once again find myself the centre of everyone's attention.

"Do you, um, like the meat?" Ture next to me asks, his eyes half-lidded and his tone huskier than it was a second ago.

I swallow and clear my throat, utterly embarrassed at my own lack of self-control around good food. "Yes. Thank you. It's really juicy, and I haven't had meat this good in a long time."

I watch in fascination as his pupils dilate, and his lips part slightly. With a hard swallow, his Adam's apple bobs before he replies, the silence in the room aside from Mischa chattering away to Baxter is ridiculous, and I decide that I'm going to eat in our cabin from now on because I can't handle this kind of judgemental scrutiny. "I will be honoured to give you my meat anytime you want it."

My eyebrows raise instantly at what sounded very much like an innuendo. Salem coughs, choking on his food beside me. "What Ture means," he starts, swallowing his bite whole. "Is that he cooked the beef and would be happy to make it for you again if you like it. We really like cooking here, and everyone has their own speciality meals. Sorry, we aren't used to conversing with outsiders much." Salem's eyes go wide, giving Ture a 'shut up' kind of look, and I have to stifle a laugh at the verbal slip-up.

Baxter doesn't have an issue hiding his outburst, as his and a few others' laughter echoes throughout the room.

"Ah, yeah, sorry about that. I'm just nervous, I guess. I'm not normally that foot-in-mouth. In fact, I'm usually the Cheetah's spokesperson. I don't know what got into me." Ture fidgets uncomfortably and focuses on his food, looking uncertain of himself.

Needing to get the fuck out of here as soon as I can, I set out to smash my dinner down, nodding and replying only when required, letting Mischa take control of the situation, pulling most of the attention away from me, and I've never been happier to have the snake by my side.

Before I know it, my mountain high plate is clean of every morsel, and I bow my head in shame because I had no intention of showing this room how much of a pig I actually am.

Baxter leans over and takes my plate, I pop my gaze up as he says, "Don't be sad, I'll get you more. Do you want the same, or do you have a preference? Perhaps Ture's meat," he finishes with a joking wink, but all I feel right now is the need to leave.

"Fill it up," Mischa adds. "Trust me, Alice can eat way more than that. She's like a bottomless pit, except for the fact that she clearly has a bottom that holds it all." She picks deftly at her plate, consisting of salad and a small piece of chicken that she's barely touched.

I raise my hand as Baxter reaches for the beef again. "Please no more. I'm actually tired and would like to lay down for a little while if that's okay?"

Baxter places my empty plate under his and rises from the seat, coming around to my side with a hand out for me. "Let me escort you back to your cabin. Rest is very important after such a long road travelled. Would you like me to carry you?" he asks after I let him help me to my feet.

My ears burn with heat, and I pull my hair in front of them so nobody sees. "No, thank you. I can walk," I stutter out quietly.

As we leave the room, I can't miss Mischa telling the room about how I can't stand for too long without needing a nap because of my size, and my feet walk me out of there faster than I've ever moved before. My insecurity screams at me that everyone is watching how big I am as I waddle away.

Baxter stays by my side all the way to the door, his body so close to mine that I can feel his heat radiating off me. *Maybe he's worried that I'll fall?* I think to myself, because why else would he be so close?

Before I get to open the door, he steps forwards, opening it for me, ushering me ahead of him but promptly following me inside, which is unexpected because I thought he'd just leave straight away. Instead, Baxter goes straight to the kitchen, turns on the kettle, and sets up a large mug with a tea bag.

"How do you like your tea, my queen?" he asks me with glittering eyes and a kind smile. *What's with the 'my queen' business?* That's the second time he's called me that.

"You don't have to do that," I start, but promptly change my answer as his eyes and smile dim. "Ah, just one sugar and black please."

With renewed vigour, Baxter continues making the tea while humming an unknown tune quietly, looking completely content in the kitchen. Perhaps they like doing acts of service here. I've never seen men so happy to cater to a woman before, except for maybe the Kindreds I've seen so far, but this is obviously different. The whole village acts this way. I can't even imagine how lucky a girl would be to have one of the Cheetah men as a Kindred. She'd never have to do anything for herself again. *Heaven!*

A yawn has my mouth opening hideously wide, and I try in vain to cover it as Baxter brings me my tea. With a small smile, he asks, "Which room is yours? I'll take your tea in there for you."

"I haven't picked one yet. I just left my bag in the bathroom and went to lunch," I tell him honestly. "Mischa has taken the first room, though."

I walk down the hall and go straight to the last room, wanting as much space between Mischa and me as I can get. As I open the door and step in, heat crawls up my back, and I know without turning around that Baxter is close behind me. Not wanting to check, I step to the side, putting my back to the wall.

Baxter strolls right past me and puts the tea on the side table of my twin bed. "There you go. Make sure you drink it while it's warm. And I promise that no one will enter your cabin without either your or Mischa's consent. You are safe here and the cabin is right in the centre of the village, so no one from the outside can come near it without alerting everyone. We have a very, very," his eyes seem to glaze over a little bit, "strong sense of smell. We know everybody's scents here and yours is very noticeable. There's no way anyone could take you without us all knowing."

Great. Not only am I the fattest, but also the smelliest.

With a sigh, I thank him and walk over, sitting on the end of the bed in defeat from the longest day ever, and I've had some long-ass days here. I'm starting to think that Rathe isn't for me and that it might be best if I just go home with the next lot of women.

"Are you alright?" Baxter questions me softly, sitting beside me. Once more, much closer than I'm used to. "Have we done anything to upset you or make you not feel safe and welcome?"

Feeling like an ungrateful bitch, I plant a smile on my face. "Not at all. You have all been wonderful. I'm just exhausted, and I'm finding Rathe a little overwhelming at the moment. I don't really fit in here, and I'm emotionally exhausted with it all," I admit, wanting to be somewhat honest.

Baxter reaches out for my hand but stops before he touches me. "May I?" he asks, seeming out of his comfort zone by having to hesitate.

I nod and give him my hand, not wanting his smile to ever dim. He's much too pretty to be sad.

"I want you to promise me that you will always be honest with me. I want you to feel welcome because we are genuinely so happy that you're here with us, and I'd like to be your friend, someone you can confide in when things get rough. Everybody needs someone, and I get the feeling you and Mischa aren't the best of friends." Baxter holds my hand softly, stroking his thumb gently against the back of my hand, and I like the intimacy of it way more than I'd like to admit.

Even though I know I could never have a guy like this as my Kindred, maybe I could be lucky enough to have his friendship like he's offering. Dare I wish for that much? What if he ends up just like Omar, and this is all some big joke that they'll laugh about behind my back?

My hackles instantly rise at the idea, and I close down a little bit more. "Thank you," I say, pulling my hand away. "But I really do need to rest."

Jumping up, Baxter backs out of the room with apologies and wishes for a good rest. When I hear the front door close, I get up and close my bedroom door, making sure to lock it. It's not that I don't want to trust them, but they *are* strangers to me, and I've met some bad guys since being here. The idea of being kidnapped again is way too prevalent in my head still. Plus, I know for a fact that I don't trust Mischa. She might just come in and shave my fat blond head while I sleep. *Bitch.*

CHAPTER THREE

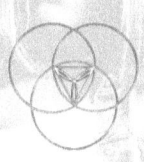

BAXTER

*C*losing Alice's cabin door, I take a moment to lean my back against it, needing a chance to breathe and calm down. My heart is racing and pounding inside my rib cage as if it's trying to escape the overwhelming emotions that today has flooded through my veins.

I woke up this morning excited about meeting the female that has so effectively encompassed Salem's heart. The one whose beauty he has raved about since arriving back from his duty at Threshold. I, however, was not prepared for the moment I set *my* eyes on her and how her scent would wash over me, instantly bringing me a level of home that I didn't know existed.

Alice.

My Alice.

Our Alice.

I'll never be the same again because I can never undo my now first-hand knowledge of what it means to find your Kindred in a world that so rarely gives you an opportunity to. We're all taught that it's a powerful thing, that it's the most special feeling to find the one that's meant to be yours; but those words don't mean anything any more because there are no words that could possibly describe the very moment your heart cracks open and then rearranges itself to change the very centre of your being, the reason that your heart beats. It's phenomenal; it's also terrifying.

What I can't understand is why, no, how, some males can either ignore the pull, fight the pull, or not understand its significance in the first place. You would have to be in a really deep hole of denial to be capable of that. I've heard of others that have rejected their Kindreds or mistreated them, but I, for one, will cherish every single breath that I am gifted to breathe with her by my side. I know one thing for certain, no matter how long it takes, no matter how worthy I must make myself, I will be with Alice. I will fight for her until my last day on Rathe, I swear to the Gods.

With a deep shuddery exhale, I push myself off the door and head over to the hub, hearing the gaiety produced from within. I ignore my still-thumping heart and push forward, regaining some of my self-control and ignoring the big part of me that wants to run back to Alice, fall at her feet, and beg her to accept me. I have to remember the warnings of her being skittish, or I might frighten her away.

"Thank you for walking me back, Salem. I really appreciate it," Mischa says coming out of the large double doors, her body pressed way too close for either of our comfort by the look on his face. Her strong citrus scent makes my nose twitch with discomfort. "You're so strong," she continues, her small hand squeezing Salem's bicep in way too obvious appreciation.

He looks at me with wide, pleading eyes, and I find myself

smothering a laugh. Deciding to leave him to his unfortunate fate, I nod as I pass them, with a smile I know I'll get my ass kicked for later, plastered on my face. "Have fun, you two," I add, unable to help put a little fuel on the fire.

Ture greets me at the door, and we both watch the other two walk off towards the females' cabin. Turning to me, Ture laughs, "You're such a shithead. Have you smelt her?" He visibly shudders. "It's going to be tough having her in the village and not being obvious about how terrible she stinks. Why did they send someone with such a sour, sharp smell to felines? Fucking rude much."

"Honestly, they probably didn't realise." I want to give others the benefit of the doubt if I can, but that gets shut down instantly when Derryn pipes in. "Nae, we just dinnae care. Trust me when I say that there's nae a soul who wants her stench around. It's your turn."

I didn't realise that other Shifters had the same issue with strong citrus scents that we do, but if that's the case, then I can understand why this particular female has been moved around a lot. She must be feeling terrible over having so many moves. I'll have to go out of my way to make her feel welcomed, my nose be damned. Hopefully, she'll find a Kindred with a different breed of Mhanu like the Fae or the Sorcerers because I wouldn't wish that smell on a Shifter for a lifetime.

"Perhaps her next move should be into the Fae lands instead," I recommend it for everybody's benefit. "I've heard that they have been in talks with Blayze about taking some of the responsibility to give their own people a chance to find their Kindreds, and honestly I think that's only fair."

Derryn scoffs and says as he turns to walk back inside, "Poor feckers."

I don't understand what his issue is with the female, but

clearly, they don't get along. Mind you, Derryn can be a surly son of a bitch at the best of times. Walking inside the great hall, I know that a meeting has to be held, and instant relief fills me as Salem enters behind us, a quick playful scowl for me for leaving him high and dry.

"I think we need to make this public while the females are gone." My hand lands on Salem's shoulder.

"Agreed. Before everyone is gone."

Ture gives us an odd look but gestures for me to step up to the stage before everyone. With a few large strides, I centre myself on it, garnering everyone's attention.

"While I have you all, I want to make an announcement that needs to stay between us until Salem and I choose to make it public knowledge." The silence in the room is expected, as we as a coalition have always respected the words of each other. "Alice is both mine and Salem's Kindred. While some of you already knew that Salem has been waiting for his female, the fact that she is also mine came as quite a surprise. So please, out of common courtesy, unless Alice is also your Kindred, do not pursue her in that way. We will take great offence and have to take the matter into our own hands, causing a rift that should by all means be avoided. The peace and tranquillity that our village offers should remain intact. Is there any question or concerns that any of you would like to address on the matter?" I speak plainly and with purpose, wanting there to be no confusion on the subject. Honesty is always the best policy.

Ture takes a step up the stage in askance, and I usher him forwards. His long fingers brush through his shoulder-length gold hair somewhat nervously, piquing my interest. "And if she has another Kindred here? Will that claim be accepted by the two of you?" he asks us both, Salem at this point standing beside me.

"Of course," Salem replies in my stead, his voice as important on the subject as my own. "We will honour the sanctity of Kindredship in all of its forms. Do you know of another?"

Clearing his throat deeply, he shocks us with the reply, "Myself, actually."

For a moment, we stare at him in silence, but before anything can be said, another voice chimes in from the tables. "I, um, actually need to put myself in that group as well. I knew when she walked in, but I was too afraid to say anything."

We turn to see Navy, half standing in the middle of one of the long tables, his uncertain fluttery gaze makes my heart hurt. Navy was born different from the rest of us, his birth was complicated, resulting in the death of his mother and father. He was born blue, and we all feared the worst for him, but his older brother Abel managed to bring him back from the other side. The age gap between them is great but destined him to be the saviour of the poor male.

However, as he grew into a child and then a man it was clear that he was not quite like the rest of us, no less important but his understanding of things was different from ours. Sometimes he sees and comprehends things that we all miss while having difficulty with some basic social etiquette. His empathy and intelligence are great while struggling with filtering his words and thoughts the way another would automatically do. He is by far the kindest of us all, with a constant desire to save the little creatures of the forest and make everything all better again. We as a village are proud of him, but I'm not sure how he will manage to be a Kindred or understand the responsibility of what that means.

"Are you certain, Navy?" Abel asks at his side, the concern for his youngest brother's welfare evident. "It's normal to think that the female is pretty."

Navy flops on his chair and picks up his fork, "Don't be condescending, brother. I may be different, but I'm not stupid. My heart doesn't work the way it should any more."

While Abel looks at him in confusion, Salem, Ture, and I give each other understanding glances because that's the God's honest truth. Our hearts will never be the same again.

With a slam of the back door, we turn our gazes to the back of the room, the parting scent of Alexion, a dead giveaway of who left the room in such a sudden show of force. I'm honestly surprised he even came to lunch today. It's not exactly like he's known for being anything other than surly and distant, with the little he chooses to mix with the rest of the coalition despite decades of us all trying to help him assimilate. He was never going to accept our female visitors anyway, our biggest hope is that he chooses to stay away from them without causing them any harm. The newest addition to our village, and not the most stable. His aggression is well known throughout the land.

Focusing back on the issue at hand, I smile down at Navy and tell him, "I am absolutely honoured for us to share a Kindredship. You too, Ture." I face my lifelong friend. "I am sure there is a full and wonderful life ahead of us all, but I would like to share with you both the importance of understanding where Alice is coming from. We have been warned to give her an abundance of space and understanding because she is not one to appreciate a lot of attention. That being said, Salem and I have decided that the best course of action is to slowly win her over, instead of ploughing her with the heavy responsibility of Kindredship so early in her moving here. It may be too much for her to handle, and I think that is the right thing even more now that she has four Kindreds in this one village. As I'm sure you may have noticed, Alice comes across as more conservative than most of the females we have been blessed to meet thus far."

"I one hundred percent agree," Ture chimes in. "The way she took my comment about the meat was charming, while different than I'm used to. I will have to make a concerted effort to really step back on my usual banter. I didn't mean to cause her discomfort, but I must say that she turns an impressive shade of pink, and it's utterly adorable. It took all of my strength not to kiss her warm cheeks."

With that, Abel stands and claps his hands together once. "And on that note, I think it's time for us unfortunate folk to head back to our duties while you all gloat over such a fine Kindred match. You, Navy, are coming with me. I think it's time we had a little chat about the birds and the bees."

"I don't know what they have to do with Alice being my Kindred, but whatever, brother," Navy scoffs, getting up from the table. "But for the record, I don't lie and will tell Alice when given the chance of my own sudden affections. Your own secrets are not mine to disclose." Without another word, he walks out of the room, his brother, Abel, hot at his heels with pleading words of reason. I have a feeling that he will say what he wants regardless of our wishes because it's just in his nature to speak his mind, consequences be damned.

"While we're on the subject of Kindred's, does anyone have a link to Mischa?" Ture asks, and the room goes utterly silent again. "I didn't think so, but I just wanted to make sure before we all head off."

I'm secretly glad because I don't know if I could handle a scent that strong forever.

Derryn chimes in from the side of the large room with a chuckle. "I was gonna leave in the morrow, but now I ken I might stay a few days. I have a feeling that this is gonna get good, and I dinnae want to miss Mischa's face when it all comes out."

I never took Derryn as nasty before, but the side smile he's wearing shows pure distaste for the female. I can't help but wonder how she got the pleasure of Derryn's displeasure.

CHAPTER FOUR

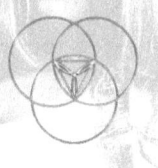

ALICE

Shrill laughter pushes through my sleepy haze, rudely dragging my slumber from me and instantly making me grumpy. My growl of displeasure is lost in the fluffy pillows as I turn my head to hold it tightly onto my face, deeply trying to deny needing to people again.

Another laugh has me wincing, a deep sexy baritone laugh that has to belong to one of the many surfer-looking pornstars in this Godforsaken village. *Why me?* Why of all people did I get stuck in this place full of guys so sexy that I can't even show my own face? Especially with Cruella De Vil. What a terrible person. If her outside matched her inside, she'd look like one of those terrifying creatures that Janice told me about.

A gentle knock raps on my door, and I quickly sit up, straightening my hair in a panic because there's no way that witch would knock with so much respect. "Hold on a second," I squeak out awkwardly.

Cringing at my own voice, I jump out of bed as fast as I can and frantically try to pull my pants back up. I fell asleep in my shirt and underwear after lunch without much thought because I honestly didn't expect anyone to knock at my door so soon. How long was I asleep?

I grab the door handle and pull it open at the same time that I remember that my girls are free-range because my bra is on the floor by my feet after throwing it across the room in protest of its very being.

"Oh, God," I mumble, looking up at the absolutely drop-dead gorgeous face of Baxter.

His lips turn up into a side smile and to my great horror he says, "I didn't know it would be that easy to get you to say those words." Seeming to instantly regret his words, he steps back with his hands up in surrender. "Sorry, that just came out. What I meant was, I've brought you a hot breakfast and I would hate for it to get cold. I thought you might like to eat in your own space after such a big introduction yesterday, especially after such a long sleep."

"Yesterday? Long sleep? What?" My words are as jilted as my confusion.

Baxter's laugh is deep and rumbles in places it shouldn't. "It's tomorrow, my Queen, you slept yesterday away, but I don't blame you after such an eventful day and long journey."

My stomach chooses that moment to sing the song of its people and growls like it's going to war. I swear I shrink at least a foot as he laughs again, jovially. "Let's go to the dining room, shall we?" He takes my hand and pulls me down the hallway where another three Cheetah Shifters are sitting in our lounge room as Mischa delicately picks at some spinach and mushrooms, while an entire breakfast feast is displayed along the centre of the dining table.

"Do you often not wear a bra?" a guy I've never seen before asks me, and I want to shrink yet another foot. "I thought all the females wore them, especially when they have such large breasts?"

Salem smacks him on the back of the head, mumbling under his breath about watching what he says, but the new guy just looks confused as he rubs his head, frowning at Salem. "What? I like it. I can see them much better this way. I don't think the females should even wear them in the first place."

"Oh my Gods! I'm so sorry, Alice. Navy doesn't have a filter, and he's not about to find one anytime soon," Baxter moans beside me, rubbing his face hard with his hand. "Just ignore him."

Navy stands and puts his hands on his hips in what seems like outrage. "Excuse me. Don't teach her to be rude. I was complimenting her. I heard that the females like compliments." Walking towards me and past the gaping Mischa who is just as shocked as I am about his blatant disregard for normal pleasantries. "Anyway, hi. I'm Navy, and you're my Kindred."

The air whooshes out of me at the same time that Mischa starts to choke on her food. "What?" I practically scream, and Baxter grabs my arm. My body apparently tried to escape the situation.

"You don't need to be scared, there's nothing wrong with me. I was just born different, but I'm still a very strong Shifter, and I will protect you from the other faction if they try to take you away," Navy tells me as a matter of fact, and I realise as I look around that the other men in the room are looking really nervous. *What's so wrong with this guy that the others are freaking out?* "Would you like me to shift for you and show off my prowess?" he asks, starting to take his shirt off.

"No," I squeal, because even though he's clearly weird as fuck, he's still just as pretty as the rest of them, and I don't need to faint in front of everyone because of his abs. "I need to go," is all I come out with as I pull myself from Baxter's grip and stumble my way back to the bedroom, slamming the door behind me.

My stomach growls again, but that bitch is gonna have to wait until the gang of Cheetahs in my cabin has left because there is no way in hell I'm going out there now.

I place my ear on the back of the door with my hand pressed hard against my wildly thumping heart, listening to the sounds of goodbye. I don't let myself relax until I hear Mischa cry out that they've gone, and I can stop being so pathetic now.

Sliding down the door to rest on the floor with my head on my hands and trying to comprehend that someone here has told me that I'm their Kindred. Never in a million years did I expect that to happen. Even though he's clearly a bit odd, which honestly doesn't bother me at all, how on earth am I supposed to let someone like that touch, let alone see, my body? We are very different types of people, and I don't want to gross him out with my rolls. Mind you, he's so honest that he'll probably just tell me outright that I look disgusting and make him sick.

What am I going to do?

Maybe I can stop eating so much and limit myself to less food so that I'm not *as* fat. I can't bear the thought of him mocking me and telling everyone else how revolting I am to look at. I wouldn't be able to show my own face in public, and it's such a small village that it'll spread fast.

I can't do this! I have to leave! I have to go back to Earth, where I can be invisible again. Too many people here see me. Too many hot people.

"Are you going to eat all this food or are you going to waste it?" Mischa calls from outside my door. "I'm going out to find myself a worthy guy, you can have the retard." Her shrill, unkind laugh has me clenching my teeth. How dare she talk about him like that. I don't care what she says about me, but all the guys here have been nothing but nice; but by the time I get up enough nerve to tell her off, I hear the front door close, and I know I'm alone. At last.

Picking my bra up from the floor, I redress myself properly in case I have another unexpected visitor drop by. Once I'm completely dressed again, I make my way down the hall and sit at the dining table, desperately trying to tell myself not to eat it but already knowing that I'm going to fail. With quick movements before my better judgement can stop me, I layer my plate with eggs, toast, refried beans, bacon, and mushrooms.

With more than a little self-loathing, I shovel the food in my mouth, but the taste of the delicious meal rids me of any feeling other than pure bliss and appreciation as the full flavour overtakes all of my brain power. The crispy bacon and the perfectly cooked eggs are my total undoing as I dive even deeper into my feast and have not one, but two, full-sized plates before my stomach complains and only then do I realise how much food my fat ass has devoured again and the ever familiar shame kicks in.

Why can't I be like a normal girl and eat a small plate of food? Why do I have to be this way? What's wrong with me? I just want some freaking self-control!

Slowly, I begin to clear the table, putting away the uneaten food and washing the dishes left behind. My mood rapidly declines the more I think about the situation I'm in, and guilt builds at the thought of leaving Navy behind without claiming him. Does it hurt them to be denied? I don't see a way for him to get out of this situation unscathed because if I stay then he's stuck with me but if I leave then I'm rejecting something that is important to the people here and from Janice telling me the last time I visited her, it's an unbreakable bond. Either way, I'm wrecking the poor guy's life.

Deciding on a shower to wash away my blues, I head to the bathroom, my steps heavy and laden with unworthiness. To my surprise, when I open the door, the clothes I discarded yesterday are nowhere to be seen and my bag is neatly stored in the corner of the bathroom bench. With a frown, I zip it open and find only my spare underwear, bra, and shoes. My other change of clothes is missing. *What the heck?*

I try to think back, but I'm certain that I left them in here because I was in a hurry. I start to change my undergarments with my head filled with questions, but the only thing I can come up with is that Mischa took them out, but why would she clean them for me when most of the time she spends her energy making me feel shittier than I already do. Maybe she's thrown them away or something else just as heinous? Honestly, it wouldn't surprise me. It'll give her a reason to call me dirty if I can never change out of my current clothes.

A light tapping comes from the front door as I re-enter the hallway, my mind concerned with possible outcomes. "Alice?" I hear in the now familiar voice of Salem. "May I speak with you a moment?"

I quickly smooth my blond hair down and straighten my shirt before going to the front door and opening it to find Salem and Ture at its threshold. "Uh, hey, what's up?" I ask timidly, noticing straight away that Ture is holding some kind of fabric bundle.

"We wanted to come and lend you some assistance. We couldn't very well leave you alone with all of that mess to clean up," Salem offers. "Besides, I think it's time to show you around your new village. Mischa has been out and about, making friends, and I'd hate for you to miss such a pleasant morning." Noticing my eyes shifting to the parcel, he adds, "Oh, this is for you," and nods in Ture's direction.

CHAPTER FIVE

TURE

 inhale deeply as Alice's full attention lands on me, and the weight of it almost brings me to my knees. My hands tighten slightly around the gift, as unfamiliar nerves overcome me. *What if she doesn't like it?*

"It's lovely to see you again. I'm sorry about this morning. Navy can be quite forthcoming sometimes." I notice Alice winces slightly, and I decide to change the subject straight away. I don't want to ever make her uncomfortable if I can help it. "I wanted to give you a welcoming gift to show you how happy we are to have you live in our village with us. I hope it's to your liking. I stayed up all night trying to make it perfect for you."

Her soft, rounded cheeks pinken beautifully and so do the tips of her delicate ears. It makes me want to touch her, to feel the warmth undoubtedly radiating from her. I reach my offering out to her, careful not to step forwards in case I make her feel smothered by my presence. I'm very aware that while I'm not as wide as some of the males here, I most certainly tower over most, and Alice seems so small compared to me. I find myself slouching slightly around her to make myself appear less intimidating.

With slow, cautious movements, she accepts the gift from me and looks down at it in confusion. "Just unknot it and the present is inside," I offer in explanation.

"Come inside," Alice tells us softly, and we follow her as she stops at the pristine table, placing the parcel down and unwrapping it to find the two dresses that I spent my evening creating for her.

It's a good thing too because earlier this morning when I gathered her dirty clothes from the bathroom, I was shocked to find that she had no more outfits inside her bag to wear. I was going to wait until I had a few more dresses made before handing them to her, but with this new information, it was imperative that I gave her what I had already fashioned.

"I hope they fit you well," I tell her, noticing Salem beside me frowning at the surrounding room. "I didn't want you to be without suitable attire, and your other clothes were much too dirty to wear again. I'll make sure to return them to you when they're dry."

Alice gasps, her head whipping up to look at me before she even had a chance to look at what I'd made. "*You* took my clothes?" I watch in horror as mortification covers her usually soft features.

I don't understand her reaction, and I find myself frozen and without words. Did I do something wrong?

"I'm sure Ture was just trying to help," Salem volunteers in my stead. "Right?" He looks at me with widened eyes, pleading for me to say something in my own defence.

I lick my suddenly dry lips. How can one small person make me so anxious? "I, um, well... When I used your bathroom, I couldn't help but notice that your clothes from yesterday were very dirty and had too much of your scent all over them. I didn't want anyone in the village to smell so much of you if you wore them again."

I'm not sure why, but she looks even worse, even taking a step back from the table. "I assure you that I will bring your clothes and undergarments back this afternoon. They will be fresh and clean. Does that not make you happy?"

"I think you should stop talking now," Salem whispers to me quietly, then with a louder voice asks her, "What do you think of the dresses? Ture has always been exceptional with the needle and supplies many of us with quality clothes, but to my knowledge, he hasn't made dresses before yesterday."

Alice looks down, with her features an even deeper tone of red, and carefully picks up the first dress, a halter-neck, tie-up, white ankle-length dress that I attached extra fabric to so that it should flutter nicely on a windy day. She studies it carefully and gives me a small smile and nod, still avoiding eye contact with me.

"This is very nice, thank you," Alice says softly before picking up the second dress, also white but this time a strapless, knee-length dress that was pulled in just under the breast. I hope I left enough room for her boobs to fit in, she is very blessed by the Gods in that department. Alice will be very good at child-rearing with her ample chest and wide hips.

I shake a mental image of my hands running over her thick luscious hips, the desire to taste what's hidden below them, making my mouth water. Salem nudges me, and I realise that he can scent my growing arousal, and I breathe out slowly, controlling my body so that it doesn't respond physically. The last thing I need right now is for her to get an eyeful of just how much I want her and with my loose comfortable pants, it would become very obvious, very quickly.

Alice folds both dresses up and places them neatly on the table again. "These are very lovely, but I'm not sure if they'll fit me," she explains, but I attempt to put her mind at ease straight away.

"Don't worry, they will fit your body well. I took a good amount of time studying all the curves on your body last night to make sure I measured correctly." I smile reassuringly at her. "I also designed them so that you didn't need to wear the bra contraption to bring you more comfort."

With a sharp inhale, Alice brings her arms up to cover her breasts, and I have the distinct feeling that I've said something wrong again. How on Rathe do I keep getting my words so wrong? I am the chosen spokesperson for our coalition and the deciding vote within our counsel, but whenever I'm around this female, every word I say seems to offend Alice or make her so uncomfortable that she can't even look at me. How am I meant to win her over at this rate?

I think, to save me from myself, at this point Alice thanks me quietly and says she'll try them on later. Salem then takes that opportunity to change the subject, but I'm left feeling disappointed in not only myself but also because I don't think she liked my gift very much. I spent so much time on it and wanted to give her something that she may cherish. Perhaps I can come up with a better gift instead, and decide to focus on new options later.

"Who came and cleaned your cabin, if you don't mind me asking?" Salem walks into the kitchen and looks at the neatly dried and stacked dishes from this morning.

Alice shrugs, turning to face him, her back to me. "What do you mean? I just cleaned up after myself."

"You didn't need to do that," Salem says, frowning. "I am here to serve you in any way that I can, Alice. You aren't here to work but to relax and let us take care of you and Mischa. Did you both eat all the food? I can make sure your next meal is larger if that would suit you?"

"No. Thank you, but no. That was plenty. I placed the leftovers into the fridge to snack on later, if that's alright?"

Salem smiles his warm, friendly smile at her, and I step around Alice to see her pinken at it. He seems to be doing better with her than I am. I'm not jealous, but I do find myself envious of the ease with which he communicates with her and how responsive she seems to be with him over any of the rest of us. Thinking back, I realise that Baxter too seemed to garner a positive reaction from Alice as well.

Stepping forwards, Salem grasps Alice's hand and tells her, "Today we're going to show you around, and you are going to be happy. Deal?" To my surprise, instead of pulling away like she normally seems to, she smiles up at him and nods sweetly. How I wish that was my hand. "Let's go and show her how wonderful it is to be a part of this coalition, Ture. It's about time that she gets to see all the beauty this place has to offer."

With a smile at me and a quick wink at her, Salem pulls her to the front door, throws it open with his spare hand, and a gentle warm breeze filters through bringing with it hints of Alice's floral perfume as it brushes past her, to me. There is nothing more divine than the scent of this woman. Yesterday, when I held her discarded garments, the overwhelming scent of them almost drove me mad with lust, and I knew I had to wash them before any of the other males smelt them. Even though she has Kindreds here, it wouldn't be unheard of for other males to attempt to form bonds of their own, and the possessive male inside me is not going to let that happen. I'd hate to fight with any of my brothers here but for her, I would. Kindred being the only exception.

Alice's response to Navy's declaration earlier only reinforced that we need to take our time courting her before revealing how significant she is in our lives and our hearts. She appeared utterly petrified of him, and I don't think it was because of how he said it but the fact that it was said at all.

We walk into the sunshine together. Alice pulls her hand out of Salem's instantly, and we go on to show her our fire pit, where everyone lives so that she knows how to find us, and where the animals that we live off of are kept. However, before we can show her any more, we're interrupted by a wide-eyed Derryn.

"Sorry to cut your sightseeing short," he directs to Alice. "But would you be bothered if I borrowed Ture and Salem for a moment? A quite urgent situation has just arisen," he says the last bit to me with a pointed stare.

"Not at all," Alice says, seemingly relieved. "You guys go. I'm just going to walk around for a bit."

Deciding that she must need space at this point, I nod to Salem and say to Alice. "We'll be back shortly to walk you back. Enjoy."

After we walk far enough for her to not hear us, I warn Derryn, "This had better be good."

"Well, you see, Mischa, the nasty piece of work, is lying in the sun topless next to the lake, and it's causing a bit of a stir among the males here, and I'm a tad worried that there is gonna be a fight and dinnae kin what you'd want me to do about it."

"Holy shit," Salem swears, starting to jog in that direction with me and Derryn hot at his heels.

Well, this isn't how I thought the day was going to go today. Mind you, it's been a mess from the start.

CHAPTER SIX

ALICE

*W*atching them jog away, an immense sense of relief fills me because the closer they are to me, the less oxygen I can find. As if their very presence sucks it out of a room and considering we're outside, that's a big feat.

I walk further through the stunning village and can't help but admire the beauty of the place. Every wooden lodge is made with obvious painstaking perfection. The time, effort, and love that has gone into the creation of this place are astounding, and I can certainly think of no better place to live. The rolling hills of wildflowers and the luscious thick forest surrounding them are an incredible sight. There's apparently even a lake nearby.

I let my mind wander as I stroll lazily along, deciding to focus only on the buildings and surroundings and not the men littering the place. Everyone here is hard at work on one thing or another, but all of them apparently have time to stop and gawk at me as I pass.

A smaller cottage-type building further off in the distance catches my eye at the treeline, far away from the bustling village. A barely used path is evident in the ground between the two places, and with my curiosity getting the better of me, I follow it. The serenity of the small abode pulls me forwards and invites me to know more. Why would somebody live so far away from the others? If it wasn't for the clothes flapping on a makeshift clothesline right outside it, I would think it was unused because of lack of any other movement.

As I approach, the wind seems to pick up around me, as if it's warning me to turn back, but the draw of the unknown pulls me forwards with every step. The skin on my arms prickles with goose pimples and the feeling of being stalked suddenly fills me, halting my steps immediately.

My gaze shifts from side to side looking through the trees that I now find myself very close to, trying to find the source of my unease, and all of a sudden it doesn't feel so smart of me to walk this far away from the village. I want to look behind me to see how far I've come, but fear has me frozen to the spot. The sense that if I turn my back on the trees, I might regret it.

A flicker of movement catches my gaze, and I find myself staring into the dark eyes of a large man with long, unruly hair, staring at me from the trees. A large, menacing scar is torn through his face from the centre of his hairline, through his right eye, and down below his ear. From this distance, I can make out that the darkness of his right eye seems to be cloudy and not as sharp as the other. His massive bulk is in major contrast to the rest of the men here, and my heart begins to pound hard and fast in my chest, the fear I felt rising as his penetrating stare only seems to sharpen.

With a heavy foot, the large man steps out of the tree line, towards me. I let out a small gasp, my instincts screaming for me to run when suddenly a hand grasps my upper arm, and I squeak out a small terrified scream, spinning to see a wide-eyed Navy before me.

"Whoa!" he cries out, taking his hand off me and taking a step back. "I'm not going to hurt you." Navy looks as terrified as I feel.

My hands clasp my chest and I turn my head back to where I saw the scarred man but find nothing there but trees. *What the fuck?* I scan the forest wildly, but I don't find any sign of a person there. "Did you see him?" I ask breathily, my previous fear is still very prevalent.

"Who?" another man asks, coming to stand beside Navy, and I can instantly see a resemblance, even though Navy is noticeably smaller, barely six feet, unlike the rest of the guys here.

I look between him, Navy, and the treeline and decide I don't want to seem crazy. "No one, don't worry. Why are you here?" I ask Navy.

He beams a giant smile at me, and his eyes light up with happiness at my attention. "To see you. I missed you, and I was looking for you for ages. You can't come down here."

"Why?" I ask, genuinely curious.

"Because Alexion wouldn't like it. This is his house and he won't like you down here. No one's allowed down here, especially not you. When he saw you at the hub, he left looking angrier than normal, and he's always angry. I don't know what you did to upset him, but if I were you, I'd stay away," Navy explains, and I remember the man that left the building and wonder if he's the same man that I just saw in the trees. I hope not because he's terrifying.

I start walking back towards the village, with one last look back. "You don't have to tell me twice."

"I'm Abel, by the way, Navy's brother," the new guy says,

introducing himself. "I thought it would be prudent to stay with Navy when he came to meet you again."

"I don't need a babysitter, and you can't have her because she's mine." Navy pushes his body between ours and slightly shoves his brother away. "Find your own female." His words come out like a low growl, and I'm not really sure how to take it.

Abel sighs heavily. "Stop embarrassing yourself. This is exactly why I came with you. For once in your life, will you be careful about what you say, or you're going to scare her away again like you did this morning."

"Yeah, hi. I'm standing right here. You guys shouldn't talk about me like I'm invisible." It annoys me when people do that, and I don't feel as nervous around these two as I do the others. Maybe it's because Navy always seems so blunt. "Either way, Navy, you can't just *have* me. I'm not a possession."

Abel tries to hide a small laugh, but I catch it as Navy grumbles. "But why? That's not how it works. You're my Kindred, and I know you're not a possession, but you're still mine."

I roll my eyes at his stupid assumption that anything is that cut and dry and try to walk faster. Of course, that doesn't work because they have long legs and my short chunky stubs don't take me anywhere fast. Before I know it, I'm huffing and puffing embarrassingly.

Having to catch my breath, I stop and close my eyes with my head back and my hands rubbing my lower spine, focusing on my breath and trying to get my stitch to recede. I hear a weird sniffing noise and open my eyes to find Navy smelling my neck, his nose so close that it's almost touching me. His brother has his hand covering his face, shaking his head.

I step back and stare at Navy in horror. "What are you doing? Were you just... sniffing me?"

"Mmm. Yes. You smell really good, and I like how your breasts stick out when you do that. I can see your nipples."

Um, okay. Can you say creeper?

"Look, you seem nice and everything, but you're kind of freaking me out," I explain, taking another step back when he reaches out for me. "You can't just go around smelling people and saying things like that."

Navy looks at me with a confused expression, his head tilting to the side. "Yes, I can. I just did."

Abel steps in to help. "Navy, she's human, not a Cheetah. It's not the same for her, remember. You need to take your time and win her over properly before you can go around sniffing or touching her. And for all that's holy, will you think about what you're saying."

"Does that mean I can't lick her either?" he asks innocently, and I almost laugh at the disappointment on his face.

Yes, Navy is a little far out, but I have to admit, he's freaking adorable. I decide to cut him some slack because I've realised that nothing he's saying to me is meant as an insult or to make me uncomfortable. He honestly just doesn't seem to realise. "How about you take me to lunch?" He starts nodding emphatically, and I add, "But you can't touch, sniff, or lick me without my permission. Understood?"

With a step back, he smiles at me with stars in his eyes, and I can honestly say I've never had anybody look at me as though I hung the moon before, and it makes my heart do a little skip. *Maybe, just maybe, he will like me just the way I am?*

I turn back to the village and find that we've garnered a few spectators. "What are they looking at?" I ask Abel quietly but of course Navy answers.

"You're boobs, of course."

"Navy," Abel reprimands quickly.

After clearing his voice and squinting his eyes in deep thought, Navy says slowly, "I mean, your pretty face." He looks at his brother in question and after Abel gives him a quick nod, Navy smiles brightly at me. Triumph written all over his gorgeous face.

I stifle my laugh and let them lead me to the hub, where others are also slowly converging. I choose to sit in the same place I did yesterday, and Navy sits proudly by my side, looking as though he's won the lottery, and I'm worth a million dollars. I decide to talk to Abel later on about Navy and find out exactly why he seems to behave differently than the other Cheetah Shifters. I want to understand him, and I'm going to try not to let his words offend me as much as they did. Everything he says and does looks as though it comes from a place of love and happiness, not sexism or anything untoward.

"My queen," Baxter says happily as he sits at the head of the table to my other side. "How has your day been? I was hoping to hang out with you for a bit later and play chess or something. Would that be alright?"

Before I can answer, a commotion near the doorway gets my attention. Mischa comes through it with several different males at her tail, undressing her with their eyes. She walks past me with her nose in the air and swaying her small hips more than necessary with each step. She only stops once she reaches the other end of the table and a large group of guys from the village sit as close to her as possible. *Figures.*

Salem, Derryn, and Ture choose that time to come and join us, sitting directly across from me, their faces with matching frowns as they look down at Mischa lapping up as much attention as she can.

"Get used to that," Derryn says, grabbing a piece of bread from the centre of the table. "Dinnae worry too much, lads, it will nae last long. Mark my words."

Abel comments oddly, "How can they stand it?"

Derryn scoffs. "A good pair of tits will do wonders on a starved male, and she made sure to show all of her *assets* if you ken what I mean."

With rounded eyes, I look down at her and realise that all the guy's eyes are laid directly on her chest, and I don't know what she's talking about down there, but I have a feeling they're not listening. "What happened?" My curiosity is piqued.

"She was sunbathing topless by the lake, and it stirred up some issues with the males," Salem informs me, and Baxter's eyebrows shoot up.

Baxter laughs low and says, "Yep, that'll do it."

A surprising feeling of jealousy burns through my veins at Baxter wanting to see Mischa's boobs. I know he'll never look at me like that, but he doesn't deserve to be stuck with an awful person like her, and my words slip out before I can take them back.

"At least my boobs are real." All eyes pop up to me, including hers, and I realise that I spoke way too loud. Whoops.

CHAPTER SEVEN

ALICE

*L*unch passes relatively quickly after that, with the odd random stare from the males around the room, but I'm getting used to them now and just choose to ignore it.

A glass of orange juice appears in front of me, and I look up at another new guy. "You looked thirsty." He squats beside me, his hand on the back of my chair. "I just wanted to introduce myself and let you know that I am interested in getting to know you, if that's okay with you? I've never met a female as curvaceous and beautiful as you are, and I wanted you to know that you are exactly my type."

Absolutely shocked, I just stare at the honesty shining back at me from his eyes. "But I'm too chubby," I whisper, unintentionally.

"No. You are perfect just the way you are. Plus, I love your extra curves, they are so much sexier than Mischa. She's too skinny and needs to eat more." His smile is small but sweet as he stares into my eyes. "I know that I'm not your Kindred, but I also know that I would regret it forever if I didn't tell you how I felt."

Low growls erupt around the table, making me jump in my seat. I turn to see that all of my new friends, bar Derryn and Abel, have eyes filled with fury directly at the sweet man beside me, growls rumbling low from their chests. Derryn winks at me and continues eating his burger like nothing's happening.

"What are you doing?" I quip at them. "Stop that."

One after the other they cut it out except for Navy, who I nudge under the table with my foot. Surprised, he looks at me, stopping his growl. "Did you just kick me?"

"No. I nudged you," I scoff. "Regardless, you are being unreasonable and rude."

Navy suddenly stands violently. "I am not. You are my Kindred, not his, and he has no right to make an advance like this. What kind of Kindred would I be if I didn't protect your personal space from would-be suitors? No! I am right this time. I know I am."

I mean, he has a point but still, it seems rude. I look at the other guys around me that were growling and wonder if they are all trying to stick up for Navy's right as my Kindred. I don't exactly know how the politics of all this works, but I imagine that my friend's Kindreds would kill someone for trying to flirt with them.

I inwardly sulk at that because I realise that I might be the one in the wrong here, but that's not fair because this guy seems so nice and genuinely comes across as though he finds me beautiful.

Baxter must read my face because he says, "It's ultimately your choice at the end of the day but" he pauses with a deep breath, "Navy has every right to threaten Cloud for coming over here and propositioning you in front of him. It's very disrespectful, whether he finds you attractive or not."

Cloud. Oh man, he even has a cool name. *Fuck my life.* I know I have to do the right thing because I can clearly see the hurt in Navy's eyes as well as the guys around me on his behalf. *Goodbye, Ryan Gosling look alike that likes chubby chicks.*

"Thank you for your interest, Cloud, but I'm afraid that I'll have to pass. It doesn't seem right, but I do appreciate your kind words. It meant a lot to me," I tell him honestly and regretfully.

Navy sits with a loud huff and starts eating, looking irritated and flustered, even though I said no. What does he want from me?

Cloud stands and gives me a slight bow. "Thank you for listening, and I hope you find true happiness. If you ever change your mind, I'll be here."

Salem growls again and Cloud walks away with his head down, and I have no doubt that if he was in Cheetah form, his tail would be between his legs.

"Why did his words mean so much to you that you looked at him like that?" Salem asks grumpily.

His tone of voice takes me by surprise, and I note that the males around me still look angry, but this time at me. "It was nice to be told that I'm beautiful, even though I don't look like Mischa," I say into my cup before I drink, too embarrassed to say it louder than that and unable to meet anyone's eyes. I don't need to see pity in their eyes when I was just given such a nice compliment.

Salem's fork clatters to the table in frustration. "But you are beautiful. If I knew that all I had to do was tell you the obvious to make you smile, I would have done that the moment you walked into the village."

"To be clear," Navy says, chewing on his steak, "I did tell her, but she doesn't like it when I tell her that."

I've had enough. "Stop talking about me like I'm not here, Navy, and you don't tell me that I'm beautiful. You just keep talking about my breasts. It's not the same thing."

"You have beautiful breasts. That's why I keep looking at them, but you are beautiful everywhere else too. You have juicy thighs, a round bottom, and hips that I would very much like to grab," Navy lists off shamelessly, and I realise that I shouldn't have baited him if I wanted to avoid such an obviously intimate answer at the dinner table with every Cheetah here to hear. "And I know you're here, but I was talking to Salem, not you, because you keep getting angry with me every time I tell you something nice, and I'm tired of it. I'm doing my best, but you are always disappointed in me, and I don't want to make you upset any more."

Navy drops his cutlery and storms out of the room, with his big brother right behind him. Now I feel like shit, but I also feel like I have the right to be put off.

I decide that Navy had the right idea, and I calmly excuse myself from the table, take my dishes to the kitchen, clean them, and put them away. The whole time, I'm aware that most of the eyes in the room are on me, again. As soon as I'm done, I get the hell out of there, walking back to my cabin with my head down and my heart in my throat. This place is way more overwhelming than any of the other places I've stayed since being here, except for when we got kidnapped last year.

When I reach for my door handle, a big hand covers mine, and I look up to see Baxter by my side. He turns me gently and then wraps his strong arms around me, holding me tight. I usually wouldn't like it, but as the sadness creeps in, I decide to relax into it, accepting the comfort he's giving me.

"Let's go inside, and I'll make you a cup of tea." His warm breath brushes through my hair as he speaks, and I try to keep the tears that want to escape inside. Without being able to speak, I just nod into his chest and let him guide me inside and to the waiting couch.

I kick my shoes off, pull my knees up and sit on my feet,

making myself into a comfortable but small ball on the couch while Baxter makes us tea. Closing my eyes, I let my head rest on the back of the couch and focus on breathing through my emotions.

The cushion dips as Baxter sits close beside me, his hand gently lifts my head and guides me to his shoulder. "It's okay to cry, little one. I'm here as your friend, and I'm not going anywhere while you need me."

As if on cue, my tears flow freely as I silently cry on his shoulder, his big arms wrapped around me, stroking my back and hair without another word and some semblance of peace finds me there; safe and cared for, for the first time in a very long time.

When my tears subside, I stay like that for a while, not wanting to move, but the call to drink my tea is just too strong. Pushing off Baxter, I lean forwards and pick up my cold tea, taking a sip.

The cup gets snatched out of my hands. "No. You're not drinking cold tea." Baxter takes it back to the kitchen along with his own and makes a fresh batch, which makes me smile. He really is a good friend, and I've really needed one lately.

Passing me a steaming hot cup, Baxter sits back down and turns to me, sipping on his own before saying, "I really wish you weren't offended by everything that the males are saying to you. We are all trying to adapt to what you need from us, but we also need you to understand that we aren't used to conversing with human females. We only mean kind, nice things, but I understand that some of it is making you uncomfortable. Help us to understand what we're doing wrong so that we can fix it and be better males for you. But in saying that, it would be nice if you also tried to meet us halfway."

Everything that he says to me, I already know, and I'm fully aware that I'm being completely unreasonable by expecting them to all conform to my comfort zone when I'm not taking into account that they have their own too. What gives me the right to expect everything, but give nothing in return? Just because I'm a woman and they are men? No. That's preposterous and underhanded. I will make more of an effort to understand the people around me and know the difference between when something is said as an offence or if it is their way of trying to reach me.

"I know and I'll try. I'm sorry for the way I've been behaving, but I'm honestly feeling super overwhelmed by all the attention. I'm used to being invisible." I decide on honesty.

Baxter brushes my hair out of my eyes and strokes my cheek gently. "You could never be invisible, Alice. You're much too special."

Before I can think of a response, he gets up from the chair and heads to the wall closet, opening it and pulling out a chess set. "Now, what do you know about chess? I've heard that it's just as popular on Earth as it is here."

"I happened to be in the chess club all through school, so you'd better know your stuff mister because I'm not afraid to whoop your butt." I smile up at him and move my tea to make room for the chessboard.

Baxter laughs loudly as his eyes sparkle in a way that makes my heart pitter-patter, and sits across from me, beginning to set the board up. "You're in for a treat then because I'm not going to take it easy on you just because you're a female. All is fair in love and war, after all."

"Bring it on."

CHAPTER EIGHT

NAVY

I longingly stare through Alice's window as she laughs freely, playing in obvious comfort with Baxter. Her face glows with happiness and her bosom bounces with every funny joke between them. Alice's beauty is more than I could have ever imagined, and it's beyond clear that I am not good enough to be around her, and I don't know what to do about that.

Stripping my clothes off on her front porch, I let my beast fill me and take over my form with pure fluidity. Being in my Cheetah form always makes me feel like coming home. I find comfort in it more than the others do, I believe. There are no societal rules, no pressure to say and do the right thing, and no words that I can spew out that bring such discomfort to those around me.

I'm tired of being in my Mhanu form. All it ever does is bring displeasure and unhappiness whenever I open my mouth. I decide then and there that I'm going to stay by her side as my beast for a while. If I can't make Alice happy, the least I can do is keep her safe because no matter how much she fights it, *Alice is mine!*

CHAPTER NINE

ALICE

Mischa's scream has my head whipping to the front door and Baxter jumps up, running past me, and rips the door open, almost taking it off its hinges.

Confusion hits me when I see the back of Baxter start shaking with laughter before he says, "What are you screaming at, female? You knew we were Cheetah Shifters, didn't you?"

"I didn't expect a giant Cheetah to be sleeping at my front door, though." Mischa's voice once again loses its accent, and I squint in suspicion. "Shoo. Shoo. Scat cat."

Baxter shakes his head, and I walk up behind him to find a massive but, incredibly, beautiful beast curled into a ball on the front door mat. It lifts its head only when I approach and seems to look directly into my soul.

All of a sudden, the big feline starts to purr so loud that it vibrates along the floor, and I feel tempted to pat it, which is probably super offensive. Also, I have no idea who this dude is.

"Navy, why are you sitting here like this?" Baxter asks putting a name to the cat before me.

Obviously, he doesn't reply but just gives Baxter a passing look before settling back on me, his purring increasing even louder than before.

Mischa looks down at Navy like he's some kind of dirty rat and stupidly says, "Ach, I hate cats. Nasty things."

Both Baxter, Navy, and the Cheetah Shifters passing by all stop to stare at her in shock and I gasp, "Mischa!"

Immediately, she seems to notice what she's said and tries to hide her previous scowl of disgust with a fake as fuck smile. "Obviously, I don't mean Cheetahs, only house cats. You are all very incredible creatures, but I would really appreciate it if you could let me inside. This Cheetah is scaring me, could you make it move, Baxter, darling?"

"Navy can hear you," he replies flatly, not at all impressed with Mischa right now. "Ask him yourself." Turning to me, he gives me a quick squeeze. "I'd say Navy might be here for a while. I have a sneaking suspicion that he's feeling down after what happened today and wants to protect you. I'll get going but if you're uncomfortable, just talk with him about it. Please remember what we talked about earlier. Navy won't take too much rejection well."

The man, or should I say the cat, in question swipes his large paw at Baxter's leg, but he jumps out of the way in time with a chuckle. "Calm down mate. Take good care of her." With a wink at me, Baxter steps over Navy and walks off towards his own cottage.

"Oh, well, I guess I can do that," Mischa says nervously, but when she steps towards the door, Navy growls low at her, his eyes trained on her legs, and she takes three steps back. "That's not fair. I have to get inside. It's my house too."

I cover my mouth with my hand in an attempt to hide my smile at her discomfort and Navy's funny behaviour.

With an angry huff, Mischa turns around and stomps away, mumbling to herself but by the hiss that Navy gives out, not quiet enough. I get down on my knees, just out of reach of Navy, and he turns his massive head to look at me.

"You're beautiful." The awe in my voice is one hundred percent real because his animal is like nothing I've ever seen before. Navy makes a choked sound, and I rephrase with a flourish at the end, "What I meant to say is that you are *magnificent*." With his nod of approval, I let out a little laugh. "Are you going to stay out here all day?" Another nod. Feeling brave, I ask, "Can I touch you? It's alright if you don't want me to."

Navy purrs softly and leans his head towards me about halfway, letting me choose whether I want to close the distance. Carefully and with more than a little dose of fear, I stretch my hand out until I touch the fur on his head, and it's surprisingly soft. I expected it to be more like hay for some reason. His eyes close and Navy nudges my hand for more. I scratch behind his ear like I would a large house cat and his purring increases until all of my fear melts away, and I end up rubbing my hands all over his muscular cat body, seeing how much he enjoys it.

Since I was a little girl I've always loved cats and past me would have thought this was a dream come true. I find myself relaxing as I cross my legs to sit more comfortably, and Navy stretches out, resting his massive head on my thick thigh. Stroking his soft fur, I enjoy the soft lulling sounds of his purr and close my eyes, leaning against the door frame behind me.

I don't know how long we sit like that but after a while, the familiar voice of Abel shocks me back into the moment. Clearly Navy heard him coming because he doesn't even flinch.

"I was wondering where you got off to. I'm glad to see you're both getting along," Abel says as he approaches us.

I look up at his friendly face and smile. "I just found him here like this."

"How did you know it was my brother?"

A small giggle accidentally pops out of me at the memory. "Baxter told me after Navy gave Mischa a heart attack. It was actually kind of funny, but don't tell her I said that."

I try to push Navy's head off my lap, but he scoffs and wriggles closer to me before putting his nose way too close to my crotch for my liking, so I give him a much harder shove until his head falls off, and I quickly make a move to stand before he tries it again. It takes me way longer than I'd like to admit getting up because my legs are stiff and sore from being in the same position for so long. Navy bounds up and leans his body against me, trying to help me stand. I tell myself it's not embarrassing but if I'm being honest, that's a total lie.

"I was on my way to dinner and thought I'd check to see if Navy was here on my way through. You gonna shift, bro?" Abel asks, scratching at his short beard.

Navy turns and nudges his brother until he is off the front stoop before coming back to my side and sitting down at my feet like a dog. "I take that as a no." Abel frowns down at Navy. "Alice is going to need to eat, you realise that. You can't keep her here."

In response, Navy stands and leans his body against me, pushing me all the way inside, using his paw to close the door on a shocked-looking Abel, his eyebrows so high that they're almost touching his hair. I listen as Abel shuffles around on the porch and looks through the window to see him pacing and scratching his head in clear confusion.

I look over at Navy as he gracefully steps onto the couch and settles down in obvious comfort. "I take it we're not going to dinner?" I ask, knowing he won't answer me, but I'm hungry. I scowl at him and place my hands on my hips. "You remember me telling you that I'm not a possession, right? I'm hungry, and I'm pretty sure that as my Kindred you're supposed to make sure that I'm fed." My stomach chooses the perfect time to growl out in hunger. "See?" I point to said stomach.

A knock on the door gets my attention and I open it to find Ture, Salem, and Baxter with plates full of delicious-looking food, including what looks like the same beef as last time.

"Oh, my heroes," I cry in delight. "Did you hear my stomach from the hub?" I ask with a small laugh.

Ture steps forwards and passes me a plate. "Baxter told us about Navy, and we assumed that he would want to keep you here."

"How did you know?" I ask, eagerly taking my plate and sitting at the dining table.

"It seems he's gone into protective mode," Salem adds, sitting to one side of me and Ture taking the other. "It's not that unusual for Cheetahs to want to separate their Kindreds from other males before they have been claimed. I'd want to do the same thing." The guys go silent and give each other weird looks that I can't decipher. "If you're comfortable with it, maybe we can have breakfast and dinner here as a small group and just go to the hub for lunches? It'll put Navy at ease, and I suspect also make you feel more comfortable while you get accustomed to the village."

Relief floods me at that idea. I'd been wanting to opt out of those public meals anyway but didn't really know how to ask without sounding rude. "Sounds like a great idea. Thank you for thinking of it."

Salem reaches over and takes my hand softly, surprising me. "My absolute pleasure."

I look down at my meal and feel the heat rise on my cheeks and ears, these guys sure know how to make me hot, and not just my face. Trying to get the focus off me, I take my hand back and start eating my food, asking, "What do you all do around here anyway?"

Baxter puts a plate of food on the ground for Navy as Salem explains their roles within the coalition, which is what they call their community. Ture works on intercommunity relations, including bartering and stock exchange, as well as helping to bring peace within the village with any disputes that may arise.

Salem is the closest thing to a healer in the village from getting years of experience working for Dr. Orion in the past after their old healer died in a tragic landslide accident. He says he still has quite a few things to learn, but for now, he's needed at the village and has been working closely with Ture on intercommunity relations lately due to the changes that having new females in flux has brought.

To my surprise, I find out that Baxter is in charge of security and defence here because he is known as the lead warrior with exceptional fighting skills. He also does a lot of hunting and gathering in the outskirts to provide everyone with extra meat and herbs while keeping others out of risk.

"Well, what does Navy do?" I wonder as I look down at him licking his plate clean.

Salem smiles down at him. "He and his brother are in charge of what you would call accounting. Navy has a way of saving our resources and paying for new ones at a reasonable cost. He's saved us quite a lot of hassle since he took over the position."

"He's also an exceptional fisherman," Ture adds. "Navy goes off by himself a lot to the lake and comes back with more fish than

I've ever seen anyone else come back with. Maybe if you're free tomorrow, you will allow me to escort you to the lake. It's really beautiful there, and it's a great place to swim. Maybe you can try on one of the dresses I made for you?"

Not wanting to be rude, even though I'm a little worried about how those dresses are going to hold up my tits, I agree. "That would be nice, I've always liked water. I assumed you guys wouldn't being Cheetahs and everything." After I say it, I can't help but wonder if that was a rude question, but they all laugh and smile at me.

"We are men, too," Baxter chuckles. "Otherwise we'd be a pretty smelly lot, don't you think? I might come along if that's alright with you two? I could use a nice swim, and I have a feeling tomorrow will be a beautiful day."

I feel myself gaze into nothing as my mind starts flickering with images of Ture and Baxter shirtless and dripping wet in the sun, glistening and sexy.

A purring Navy nudges my thigh under the table, seeming to sniff at my private area, and I swat him away, my cheeks flaming red for sure. Oh my god. I hope he can't smell how turned on I just got. I'd be mortified.

Clearing my throat, I tell him he's more than welcome to join and spend the rest of dinner staring at my plate. While they chat away with each other, I focus on my food and try to ignore the images flooding my mind. I find out that Derryn left earlier this morning, and I'm a little disappointed that I didn't get to say goodbye to him, but he's not exactly the sentimental type, unlike his twin Baine.

Mischa bursts through the front door as we finish up, and before she's about to spew some kind of ugly hate, she realises that I'm not alone and her face changes from a twisted scowl to a sweet smile in seconds, only reinforcing my belief that she's a sociopath and full of shit. Why couldn't Derryn have taken her with him? I suppress an eye roll.

"Oh, hello handsome visitors. I didn't know you were here, or I would have stayed to eat with you all," she starts but steps back as Navy rounds the couch and stalks slowly towards her. "Good kitty, I live here," she says to him shakily, sidestepping towards the hallway in order to escape him, I'm sure.

Navy lets out a low hiss, his long teeth on display, but he lets her slide away until she reaches the archway and fake pounces at her. With a squeal, she takes off and runs down the hall, her door slamming behind her as she reaches her room.

"That wasn't nice Navy," Baxter scolds, folding his beefy arms. "You know how scared of you she was today. Yes, she is super rude sometimes, but she's still a human female that we have to protect and help feel safe. This is her home while she's here, and you are trespassing on it without her permission."

Ture turns to me. "If Navy does that again, let me know and we'll make him leave. This is your house, and he knows better than to behave that way."

Navy makes a scoffing sound and then goes back to the couch he was on earlier, closing his eyes and choosing to ignore everyone around him. The other guys get up and gather the dishes with them.

"I'll take care of them," I protest, standing up, but Salem just takes my plate out of my hands with a smile and wink. "Really. I don't mind. It's the least I can do since I haven't exactly been contributing to the village yet."

Ture wipes the table down with a cloth he got from the kitchen, saying, "Don't be silly, you're our guest, and we get a great thrill taking care of you. Please let us spoil you."

He places the cloth back in the kitchen as Salem steps up to me, kissing my cheek so softly that it takes a second for me to realise what he just did. "Have a good sleep, Alice, we'll let you rest now but if you need anything please don't hesitate to ask. Anytime, day or night. I live next door, after all."

"You do?" I ask softly, touching my cheek where he'd kissed me. I notice him watching my movement, and I quickly drop my hand. Sometimes their focused gazes make me feel like I'm being stalked, not in a bad way, but I feel very much like I'm the centre of attention in a way I've never felt before.

"I do. Just call and I'll come." Is it just me, or did that sound kind of suggestive? "For you, I'll always come." Yep, there was definitely a hint of something in the way Salem's voice almost purred when he said that.

My cheeks heat once again, and I look away from his deep gaze. "Um, thank you. Are you all going?" I try to move on from the moment, feeling uncomfortable.

Baxter comes in for a quick hug after giving the dishes to Salem. "Almost all of us. I think you've got a visitor for the night," he laughs, pointing to the giant snoring cat sprawled on my couch. "No point trying to move him, he's made up his mind to stay but don't worry he won't move from there. Plus, as Salem said, we live right next door if he bugs you."

I didn't realise that they lived together, I think to myself when it hits me. Of course, they must be a couple. One thing I have realised since being on Rathe, there are a lot of male couples because of the lack of females. I look at them both as Baxter gives Salem the finger and laughs playfully as he walks past him holding all the dishes. Salem tries to kick him and fails, chasing him out the front and feeling myself smile wide, they're a gorgeous couple and seem really happy together.

"Good night, Alice, it's been a pleasure spending time with you," Ture says sweetly at my side, and I look up at him, a smile still on my face, and he sucks in a sharp breath. My face drops at his reaction, not sure what I did, but he steps closer, completely in my personal space, and says in a raspy voice, "Never stop smiling, you're so breathtaking when you smile like that."

He was doing so well until he says, "The only thing better is seeing your lips around my meat."

Baxter runs back into the house and grabs Ture's arm, pulling him out the door with an apology on his friend's behalf. "He meant the beef," is the last thing I hear before a loud thud and cursing as they disappear into the night.

CHAPTER TEN

*A*fter a deep and dreamless sleep, I wake up feeling refreshed and excited about the day ahead. I can't wait to see the lake that I've heard so much about.

A squeal and a curse from Mischa about "that fucking cat again" really sets my good mood, and I have to bury my face in the pillow to smother my laughter as her overly loud grumbling continues until she leaves the house. I could really get used to having Navy's Cheetah around.

I roll out of bed and pick up the two dresses that Ture made me, trying to figure out which one would be better for the lake and most likely to keep my ladies in place. Deciding on the shorter of the two, so I can put my feet in the water, I get out of my pyjamas and pull the dress over my head, surprised at how perfectly it fits. Ture really has an eye for this kind of thing. I test the fabric encasing my rounded breasts and decide that it's holding fairly well considering the style and the size of my chest. I'd still prefer straps on it, but I want to show Ture that I'm grateful that he made me such a thoughtful gift.

I put my dirty sneakers on and wish that I had some slip-on shoes to wear instead. It seems like such a shame to wear something so pretty and then ruin it with these shoes. Maybe I can ask where I can get some new ones, but I'm not sure if I feel comfortable asking for anything when they've already done so much for me.

A knock on the door gets my attention, and I quickly finish tying up my laces calling out, "I'm coming," and bound towards the door, almost tripping over the large cat lying across the floor. "Oh, shit. Sorry, Navy. I didn't see you there. Are you coming to the lake?" I ask, reaching for the doorknob. In answer, he stretches his body out and glides over to me, rubbing his body along mine with a small purr. "I'll take that as a yes."

Opening the door, I find Ture and Baxter smiling from ear to ear with a few towels and a picnic basket. "Shall we, my queen?" Baxter asks, giving me his spare arm, and I take it happily, feeling even more comfortable in his presence now that I know he's with Salem. It takes a lot of pressure off me about worrying what I look like around him, but when I look up at him and Ture, I can't help but get flushed at how incredible they look in the morning sun.

"You look beautiful in that dress. Are you happy with it?" Ture asks as he closes the door behind Navy and me. I nod shyly, and he steps in beside me, so close that his arm brushes mine as we walk along.

We head towards where I saw the lone cottage at the edge of the treeline, and as we approach it I ask, "Why is this house so far away from the others? I noticed it the other day too and have been curious about it."

The guys look across me at each other and towards the

cottage on our left before Ture says, "It's best if you steer clear of that house. Not that you're in danger or anything, but that's Alexion's place, and he likes his home to be as private as possible."

"Why?" He's only making me more curious.

He huffs out a big breath and bites his bottom lip in thought before answering, "It's not our story to tell, but I can say that he is the newest member of our coalition and that his last home was wiped out by a fire. Alexion was the only survivor, and since then has decided that he would prefer to be left alone."

"I think it's because he's afraid of losing any more people, but everyone here has their own theories about him and what happened. Unfortunately, no one really knows the full story, but we give him his space while letting him know that he's welcome to join us whenever he wants," Baxter adds as we walk past the cottage and into the tree line. "I will say that he's a grumpy old guy, and I can almost guarantee you won't enjoy his company, not that you'd see him for more than a minute or two at a time."

Ture scoffs, "Honestly, we go weeks sometimes without him talking to anyone for anything. You may not see him at all for quite some time." He stops, seeming to think of something before adding. "You should be aware that he has a vicious scar across his face and eye. It can be quite shocking for new people when they come across him. Try not to stare at the scar or his eye if you can, he won't like that at all."

I nod, remembering. "I saw him the other day in the woods, watching me." They both stop walking and stare at me in shock. "I wasn't quite sure if I was just being paranoid and seeing things, but I remember his scar. I couldn't see him properly through the trees, though. Is something wrong with his eye? How did it happen?"

"He was staring at you?" Ture asks nervously, and I nod,

confused at why he looked so worried. "Are you positive he wasn't just looking around, and you were just in the way?"

I shook my head and tucked loose strands of hair behind my ear. "No. He was definitely staring, but he was hidden in the trees. It was kind of creepy actually but when Navy," I nod at the Cheetah waiting ahead for us, "and Abel found me near his house he seemed to just disappear." I shrug.

Still quiet, Baxter takes my hand and continues walking on, but I notice that both he and Ture seem to be focused on the woods now surrounding us as if they're looking for Alexion. It makes my skin rise with goosebumps.

Navy all of a sudden takes off down the track faster, leaping playfully, and the men beside me relax, smiling as we turn a corner and the lake comes into view. The vast open space of glistening water sparkles in the morning sun, the surface smooth and velvety.

"Here we are," Baxter proclaims happily, his steps speeding up, dragging my slow self behind him. I almost trip over the root of a tree, and he realises what he's doing with an apology. "I just got excited."

I let go of his hand and gesture for him to go ahead with a smile, and he takes off running barefoot, as usual, taking his shirt off as he goes. God damn, that man is pretty!

"Careful, you're drooling," Ture teases, and I smack him gently on his rock-hard abs with a laugh. "Here, let me give you something else to look at." Ture drops the towels and picnic basket, strips his shirt off next to me, and throws it to the ground. He flexes his abs and biceps, winking at me before following his friend.

The two of them go crashing into the water, splashing and laughing playfully, trying to grab and dunk each other under the water's surface. I swear the scene before me is like porn for women, and if I wasn't drooling before, I am now. I look for Navy and see him above the water to the left on some high rocks, lazily lying in the sun on his back, and it's immediately obvious that the spot is a favourite of his.

I pick up the discarded things and step onto the smooth, warm stones that lead into the water. Placing the stuff back down in a neat pile, I sit down to take my shoes off because there's no way I can be here without feeling that water between my toes.

Getting up, I hold on to the top of my dress so that it doesn't fall and half jog to the water's edge. Laughing, I step into it and feel pleasantly surprised by how warm it is and wish that I had swimmers too. Not that I'd ever be comfortable enough around these guys to wear any.

I hear a big splash and a roar of laughter and look up to see Baxter running back towards me with Ture breaking the surface of the water with a curse.

"Haha. Catch me, motherfucker. I am the best warrior after all, remember?" Baxter calls over his shoulder after doing a wet hair movie flick, his abs tight and flexing as he runs back to me. "Ready for a swim, my queen?" His cheeky smile tells me to turn and run.

Knowing there's no way to outrun this guy, I put my hands up in defence. "No, thank you, Baxter. I just want to relax today. Maybe another day." Total lie.

His face drops slightly but nods as he reaches me. "Are you having fun?" He goes to put his arm around my shoulders, but I step back and push it away.

"Yes, thanks, but you can keep your wet self away from me," I reply with a chuckle. "I'm going to sit up there with Navy and watch you guys play, if that's alright?"

With a movement too quick to stop, he gives me a quick peck on the cheek. "Whatever will make you happy, my queen." Baxter smiles radiantly at me, then turns to run back to Ture. "The female wants a show of our prowess, shall we wrestle?"

I shake my head with a laugh at Baxter and Ture as they collide in the water like two titans. I love watching how happy they are, and for the first time in a while, I feel like maybe I've found a place I can stay. I look up at the Cheetah lying on the rocks, now eyeing me, and wonder if he and I really can have a relationship. It's a bit of a weird thought when he looks like a cat right now, but I'm kind of glad that he's been shifted because it gives me a chance to get close to him without feeling as self-conscious as I have been. I logically know it's still him, but for some reason, I just feel more comfortable.

Deciding that I'm going to be open-minded about getting to know him, I start to, very awkwardly, climb the large boulders up to where he is. I keep freaking out that I'll slip and fall, but at least it's only water below.

Navy gets up and rubs his head on my leg once I get to the top with him. He sits back down where he was, but leaves room beside him for me to sit as well. I look around before I do and take in the breathtaking scenery around me. The beautiful lake sits before large wooded mountain peaks, with the plain visible to my right beyond the trees we came through, the village easy to see. I turn and peer into the trees directly behind me, but don't see anything but more trees. I decide then and there that Navy is right, this spot is perfect.

Lowering myself beside my Kindred - that feels weird to even think about - I let my feet dangle off the edge and lie back against the smooth stone and close my eyes, feeling the breeze tickle my skin softly and my chest rise and fall with slow deep breaths. I let relaxation take over, even as I feel Navy rest his head on my hip, I refuse to feel self-conscious about my rounded tummy and love handles, instead, I just let it go and breathe in the fresh forest and lake air.

CHAPTER ELEVEN

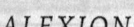

ALEXION

Fresh gardenia, midnight jasmine, and ylang-ylang float along the breeze as it brushes off the female's large breasts and into the treeline where I hide, looking on like a complete creep.

I hadn't planned on watching her, but as I saw them disappearing down the track, I found my feet trailing along quietly, unable to take her out of my vision for even a second. My heart racing and my palms sweating as she bounced along with every step, her hips, breasts, and ass moving to the beat and hypnotising me.

With absolutely soundless movements, I stayed downwind to keep the other males unaware of my presence. Navy noticed me straight away but unlike the other males here, he doesn't bother me, never has.

Stalking effortlessly, I watch as they leave her unattended on the shore, oblivious to me creeping in behind her, only metres away now. It would be so easy to slip in and take her away without them noticing. Very careless!

I move along the woods, staying hidden as she climbs the rocks, her movements awkward and strained. Clearly, she has no wildlife skills. How has she lived so long? How long will she remain alive? Not long, of that I'm sure.

With a smooth step closer, I glide in as she lies with her eyes closed, completely oblivious to the threat right behind her. Her mortality never more clear. Navy opens one eye and watches me approach through the trees, alert but not worried. He should be, they all should be.

A small stick crunches under my foot, and I flinch at my own lost focus, her heaving breasts having caught too much of my attention. What would she taste like? Salty? Sweet? Should I find out?

"Alice?" Ture calls out from down below, and I cringe back slightly at the sound of his irritatingly joyous voice. What is there to be *that* happy about? She opens her eyes and sits up, looking down at the Cheetah. "Do you want something to eat? You didn't have breakfast this morning. I packed some nice wraps, fruit, and muffins."

Navy sits back on his haunches, looking at me instead of down at the others, and I scowl deeply at him in warning. *Don't blow my cover, kid!* He sees the threat and pokes his tongue out, showing his age. Little punk, I'm half tempted to push him off the ledge.

The female stands up, just as awkwardly as before, and leans over the edge. "Sounds great. If I stay up here any longer, I'll burn anyway. I'll be down in a second."

Her round ass calls to me, and I unconsciously step forwards and accidentally catch Baxter's attention from below.

"Shit," Baxter calls out pointing at me, fear for the female evident because I'm the resident Cheetah boogie man after all. "Alice, watch out."

She turns too fast as I take a step towards her, Alice spots me straight away in her space, but before I can grab her she steps back in fear. Of me or of my scar, I'm not sure, but she steps into the air, falling off the ledge and into the placid water below, a short scream in the wind.

Without thinking, I dive in after her because I have no idea if human females can swim. My body collides with the water, and it embraces me warmly like an old friend, and I open my eyes in its depth, spotting the female straight away. My arms grab around her thick waist and I pull her into me, reaching the water's bottom and pushing us both up to the surface.

Breaking through, we both breathe in the fresh air, and I hold her tight against my body, her squishy flesh feels amazing in my hands, I want to touch her all over. My dick hardens instantly, and I swim us to the rock edge immediately, using my large body to cage hers against it to keep her still, keep her in my arms.

A low rumble builds in my chest, and she looks up into first my good eye and then the grotesque one that showcases my shame, my guilt, my failure. I turn my head away, so she can't look at it, remembering at that moment who and what I am. My impulsive move to jump in after her and hold her so close feels ludicrous now, and I can't believe my own lack of self-control. After everything I've been through, I let my dick decide my actions like a fool.

I let her go almost at the same time that Ture growls low, "Let her go and move away, Alexion. You're scaring her."

I feel both males right behind me, but neither of them is stupid enough to lay a hand or paw on me for fear of my temper. Baxter may have been the greatest warrior here in the past, but we both know that if he fights me, one of us will die, and it most likely won't be me.

With one more look at the creature before me, I take in her soft rounded features, soft blue eyes, and pinkened cheeks. Her beauty is one of legend, one I don't deserve to touch, and I force myself to get away from her as fast as I can, diving under the water and swimming in the other direction. I hold my breath for so long as I swim under the water's surface that my lungs scream in pain, and I let it burn because I deserve it.

If I'm not careful, I will be the ruin of that female. She will scream, she will burn, she will die. Just like all the others.

* * *

SIXTY YEARS *earlier*

THICK, intense smoke licks at my skin, my eyes, and inside my lungs as I breathe. Fire is everywhere, and so are the screams. Blood-curdling screams that set my hair on end and turn my stomach.

I watch on as the village that I was born and raised in, lights up the sky with the embers of the homes and people within. The rising lit ash floating away on the wind, as weightless and carefree as my childhood was.

This is all my fault! I did this.

Above all the other screams, I hear a sudden cry of a voice so familiar that nothing could hold me back. My little sister screams; she screams for me, my name joining the ashes in the wind. With no regard for my own safety, I run into the flames, my feet scorched from the burning earth below, but I feel no pain, only adrenaline, fear for my family, and hope that it's not too late.

I stop before my home, the wooden walls ablaze, the screaming louder within. Running forward, I crash my body into the door, again and again, as the fire burns away my clothes. The door knob is gone and all I can do is bash into it with all my might. Open, god damn it.

"Alexion." My beautiful sister screams in agony one final time before silence reigns, and I roar into the night. I go to ram the door once more refusing to give in, but the roof collapses in on itself sending a shocking wave of heat, fire, and blazing debris, throwing me far from the house.

Closing my eyes, I let the heat take me, but something or someone lifts me into the air and away from the heat. Just before I lose consciousness, I look up into my big brother's eyes. At least he lives, I'm not alone.

How wrong I was.

"WAKE UP," Jamal's voice cries to me from outside the pain of my feet and back. "You have to be okay." His little voice cracks with sadness, and I open my eyes slowly to find his chubby face wet with tears.

As I lift my hand to touch his face, I stop as I take in what they look like. My palms look like they've melted, and I remember. I remember everything and my heart screams.

I look up at my little brother and know I have to keep it together. He needs me, he needs us. I look around for my eldest brother, Kessar. I know he took me to safety; I saw his face.

"Calm down, boy, I'm right here," his deep voice says slowly from behind me. "Jamal, go and fill up the water bottle, I have to talk to Alexion."

Unable to move because of the intense pain radiating all over my body, I lie still, closing my eyes to deal with it quietly, until I know Jamal is far enough away. He is only five, and I can't lose it now. He must be so scared.

Kessar comes into view as I open my eyes, his body leaning over mine. "Let it out, boy. He won't be gone long, and I need to tell you what's happened while you cry."

He's never been a loving brother, but Kessar is great in a crisis. I allow my tears to fall silently as he explains how we are the only three left in the village. Everything is burnt and gone, and we're going to start new elsewhere. Apparently, he knows people nearby that can help me heal.

Kessar tells me slowly that I have burns to my hands, feet, and back from falling on the burning ground. I'm lucky that was all that got burnt, besides a small burn here and there on my chest from my clothes burning off.

My mind goes back to my sister screaming my name, and I choke on a hard sob, my throat burning with the movement. "Phillis," I manage to get out, my voice husky and pained.

"I know," Kessar sighs deeply. "She was meant to stay with us. She shouldn't have run home like that. If you hadn't let her go back, she would still be here. Next time, when I tell you to do something, listen."

Guilt assails me, and I choke on it, bile rising at the truth of what he said. *It's my fault.* Why didn't I just listen?

"No point crying over it now. Jamal is on his way back. Get your shit together because we're going to have to keep moving if you want to get medical attention for these burns." Kessar stands up and grabs me under my arms, lifting me effortlessly and placing me on a nearby rock. I cry out from the pain, unable to keep it in. "Shush," Kessar reminds me, and I seal my lips together. Turning around, Kessar tells me to get onto his back and he'll carry me because my feet won't be able to walk.

Jamal stands beside me quietly, looking terrified, and I rasp out, barely audible, "It's alright buddy. I'll be fine. We all will."

I've been wrong about a lot of things in my life, but I've never been more wrong about anything than that because we would never be fine again.

CHAPTER TWELVE

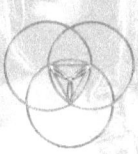

ALICE

The heat from Alexion's large, rough hands remains on my skin as he swims away, disappearing beneath the depths of the lake. I watch in fascination as he doesn't come up for air until he's almost at the other side when his head breaks the surface, and he pushes himself out of the water, running first in human form before shifting into a massive Cheetah, his clothes tearing, and his cat disappearing within the brush. The memory of his cloudy, almost white eye, will forever stay with me. *What happened to him?*

"Alice?" Ture is in front of me, and it's only then that I realise that they've been talking to me.

I shake my head slightly, "Sorry, what?" I ask, bewildered by everything that just happened and, if I'm honest, kind of turned on.

Alexion is both terrifying, and dare I say, sexy? I'm not quite sure what, but when he held me in his arms and pressed my body against the wall, I wanted him. The hard cock I felt pushing against my stomach certainly didn't dissuade me. I know it's wrong. I know his actions are kind of scary, but there's something about him. Every time I see him, I want more. I can't help but wonder when he was so close to me, why at the last second he went from fierce and strong to - scared?

"Are you alright? Did he hurt you?" Ture asks, and I don't think it's the first time he's asked me.

"I'm fine," I tell him honestly and push off the rock face, swimming back to shore with ease. I love the water, although it's a little less comfortable in a dress. I'm glad I didn't wear the floor-length one today.

Baxter and Ture swim by my side, as though they're afraid I might sink or something. When it gets shallow enough, I stand up and put my head under to sweep my hair back so that it's not in a clumped-up mess.

I flick it back and wipe my face, looking up to see two very stunned men staring at my chest. Looking down, I find that my dress did not stay up after all, and now I'm high beaming the world, or more specifically the two sexy men gawking at them.

With a quick movement, possibly the quickest my fat ass has ever moved, I spin in the water to put my back to them and pull up my dress, only to find Navy staring at me on the rocks. Great. Why not share them with the whole freaking village while I'm at it?

I squeeze my eyes closed and am completely frozen on the spot. I have no idea how to come back from that, so I choose to pretend like I'm a mannequin and hope that I just disappear. You know, the adult choice.

"Shall we eat?" Baxter croaks awkwardly behind me. "I'll go set up the picnic blanket."

Grateful that they're giving me space to soak in my shame, I turn back around, realising there's no hiding from this, but I'm happy to pretend it didn't happen.

To my absolute horror, I turn my body right into Ture's. I look up at him in shock and find his eyes half-lidded and his not-so-little Ture pressed against my stomach. That's the second dick against me today. Well, at least I'm a turn-on and not a turn-off.

"Um, sorry," he almost squeaks out, and it's so funny coming from a grown man. "I can't control that. I've never seen anything like your breasts before, and they're way better than I ever imagined. Not that I imagined them. I mean, I thought they would be good, but I didn't know they would be that good. I didn't dream about it, though, I just was thinking. Not thinking, um wondering. Well, not rudely, just sort of... I'll stop now. Sorry," he rambles on quickly, clearly embarrassing himself whenever he opens his mouth. It's actually freaking adorable, and he goes almost as pink as I do.

"It's alright," I reassure him, now pretty sure he's more embarrassed than I am, which helps. "Let's go and eat."

Exhaling in relief, he walks beside me as we leave the water, and I hold back a smile when he walks with his hands covering his manly salute. My dress is plastered to me like a second skin, and I just know it's got to be see-through because it's white. I decide to cut him and myself some slack, pretending that this is totally normal, and sit down where Baxter indicates, his eyes firmly on the food below respectfully, and I appreciate it.

"May I have a towel?" I ask as calmly as I can, and Baxter passes me one that I wrap around my shoulders, attempting to cover my chest the best I can.

Ture picks up a blueberry muffin, breaks it in half, and passes me one of the halves. "Want a nipple? They're really delicious."

Baxter whacks him in the arm and looks at me apologetically. "He meant nibble. What's wrong with you, man?"

I look between his and Ture's horrified expressions for a second, then laughter explodes from my mouth without warning, and I can't control it. I laugh so hard that I fall to my side, clutching at my stomach, and can barely breathe. *Nipple.* I know I'm acting like a child, but apparently, hysteria has a hold of me and it's not letting go.

Joining me in temporary madness, Baxter and Ture crack up laughing right beside me, successfully popping our bubble of awkwardness and breaking the tension. I come back to myself and sit up, wiping rogue tears away to find Navy sitting beside us looking between us. If I didn't know better, I would say his cat face looked concerned.

I stroke his face. "It's alright, Navy, it's just a little insanity amongst friends." Picking up the piece of muffin, I take a bite and smile wide at Ture. "You're right, it is delicious. Thank you."

He smiles right back, and we proceed to enjoy the rest of our morning tea, laughing and getting to know each other better. It ends up being a really nice start to the day, but I have questions and on the way back from the lake when we're all dry again, I decide it's the best time to ask.

"Why did you look so freaked out when Alexion was at the lake? You scared the crap out of me, the way you called out." I look over at Baxter and see him rub the back of his neck nervously, his wet, long white-blond hair in a messy bun.

He kicks a rock in thought before looking back at me. "Honestly, I can't really say. He's just so different from the rest of us, and there are so many rumours about what happened to his old coalition and some of them make him out to be not a good guy. I just saw him sneaking up behind you, because he was sneaking, and I reacted on instinct. Then, when you fell in the water, I felt instantly bad as he jumped in after you."

"Yeah, until he plastered her against the rock like that," Ture interjects with a mumble. "What was with him today? It was weird. You've got to understand Alice, Alexion doesn't generally go near anyone but the way he behaved for you today and the fact that you've seen him staring at you from the woods is super out of character for him. It makes me nervous. Maybe I should go and have a talk with him later and see if he's okay."

Baxter nods in agreement. "That might be a good idea. He high-tailed out of here pretty quickly like his ass was on fire. No pun intended."

"How is that a pun?" I ask because that didn't make sense, but both guys pale and change the subject, starting to talk about a tennis tournament they want to organise for fun.

My hand reaches down to pat Navy beside me as the other two guys take off at a faster speed than I'm comfortable walking, and I have a suspicion it's to get away from my questions.

"You can tell me what that was all about later, deal?" I ask Navy, and he nods once, rubbing his body against my thigh with affection.

* * *

OPENING the bedroom window I let the cool night breeze in, the room feels stuffy and hot after an unreasonably warm day. I close the curtains to keep my privacy and then take off the new wrap dress that Ture gave me yesterday. I like this one because it feels more secure around my curves.

I let it fall to the floor and flop down onto the bed in just my underwear and bra because it's way too hot to wear pyjamas tonight. Arching my back, I undo the bra clasp and throw that horrendous thing across the room.

Even alone, I feel self-conscious, and I slide under the sheet on my bed, letting the blankets fall over the bottom. I won't be needing those tonight, or any night soon, I'd wager. Summer is now in full effect, and I can't stand it. I'm definitely a winter kind of girl.

Closing my eyes, I think about Salem's shirtless and sweaty body as he was chopping down the tree today, the sweat dripping down his rippling back that made me want to lick him dry. Then I picture Baxter and Ture splashing each other in the lake a couple of weeks ago, and how the water plastered their pants to them, giving me a generous view of the outline of their dicks. *Holy shit, they're hot.* Alexion's hard cock pressed against me in the water, has my hands softly caressing my aching breasts. It's been so long since that time I had sex with Omar, but I've never wanted to try again more than I have since that day. The memory of having so many hot guys so close to me is getting me hotter under the collar every day.

I suppose it can't hurt to just visualise them, even though they're way out of my league. It's not like they'll know.

My right hand slides slowly down my body as I picture Alexion rubbing up against me in the water, his hardness pushing between my thighs and rubbing over my most sensitive area again and again. I let my fingers slowly glide over the fabric covering my clit in time with the movements of my fantasy, picturing his dick instead.

My mind shows me Alexion's full lips closing down on mine so hard that it almost hurts, needing to take me, his hips moving faster with my fingers. I feel his fingers take over, sliding my panties to the side and sliding them through my swollen slit and my hips buck as I mimic the scene with my own digits, using my own moisture to circle my clit the way I want him to and let out a small whimper at how good it feels.

In my mind, Baxter swims in behind me, and I'm sandwiched between the two sexy men, one light and one dark. His hand reaches around to knead my breasts, pinching my nipples as Alexion pushes one finger inside me while using his other hand to stroke his own desire.

Fingering myself to the rhythm that my body likes, I envision Ture pushing his dick against my hip from the side, kissing and nibbling my neck as his finger slides between Alexion and me to roll and circle my clit in time with Alexion's finger thrusting, now with two of them filling me just right.

An aching moan rips out of me as my climax gets closer and closer, the overwhelming need of my fantasy pushing me to the edge quicker than ever before. Wet sounds fill the air because of how turned on I am, my sheet now mostly off me from the frantic movements of my desperate body, wanting more.

"Oh God, yes!" Slips out, quiet but uncontrolled.

CHAPTER THIRTEEN

SALEM

With my new normal routine before bed, I head out to do a perimeter check around Alice and Mischa's place next door. Ever since that weird exchange between Alexion and Alice that Baxter told me about, I've been on edge. I really don't like to think the worst of people, but this is my Kindred we're talking about, I can't risk anything happening to her.

Over the last few weeks, I think I've made some real progress with Alice, and I'm seriously considering asking her to let me court her properly, the way they do on Earth. I figure it will make her more comfortable to do it that way.

Alice and Navy haven't made any Kindred progress since he told her about their connection, but I think that's mainly because he hasn't shifted out of his Cheetah form since he first shifted for her. I'm not sure why, I've asked him a few times, but he just turns tail and stalks back to her. I hope he changes back soon before she can only look at him as a cat and not as a male.

Quietly, I walk around the first side of her cabin, sniffing and looking for any sign of Alexion being there now or lately but see nothing. No one has seen or heard from him since he took off from the lake, and I'm getting worried about him and his state of mind.

A small sound gets my attention, and I tilt my head trying to figure out what it is. I round the corner of the building and see Alice's curtain dancing in and out of the window with the wind. She must have left her window open because of the heat.

I take a few more steps but stop dead in my tracks as a thick, sweet scent of arousal pours from her room. *What the hell?* I take two more steps, unable to damper my curiosity, and when I reach it, the scent increases, and my cock hardens to the point of pain immediately at the sound of a low, needy moan coming from inside.

Wet rhythmic noises reach my ears, and I inhale deeply to catch who else's scent is with her but find none but Alice's. Is she? Do females do that by themselves? Curiosity and my raging sex drive have me pressing my back against the wall outside the window sill, my eyes closed, imagining what it would look like to see her soft fingers delving into the moist heat of her pussy, and I have to stifle a groan.

"Oh my god, yes!" three words that nearly bring me to my fucking knees. The desire, desperation, and ache of Alice's moaned words have me wanting to dive through the window and bury my face between those perfect thighs and taste every single drop of her sweet juices until she cums all over my face.

My hand reaches down and adjusts my pained cock, and I groan. I don't think it's possible to get harder than I am right now. I listen intently as her breathing picks up in tempo with the wet sounds of her fingers searching for release.

That's it, baby. You're almost there. I can hear her suck in a sharp breath and a trembling cry as she finds her release, and I almost cum in my pants, right then and there.

I exhale and realise I was holding my breath, and I instantly feel so guilty. I can't believe I just stood here listening to such a private act. I don't know what got a hold of me, but my shame is choking me.

Pushing my body off the wall, I turn to walk back the way I came and flinch at the Cheetah sitting at the corner of the building watching me. With a shake of his head at my disgusting behaviour, he turns and walks away, letting me know that he knows what I was doing and isn't impressed. Me neither, Navy, me neither.

Quickly, I return home and practically jog to my bedroom, needing to release my dick from its confines before it rips my pants open. With fast movements, I tear my pants down and grasp my hand around it, crying out as I squeeze my cock hard, precum already soaking the tip. Fuck, what is this female doing to me?

"Dude," Baxter calls from the other side of my bedroom door. "Are you alright?"

"I need a minute," I strain out, jerking my dick in my hands, unable to wait for him to leave. The scent of Alice's arousal and orgasm still in my nose, making me salivate and my hand increase in rhythm. "Fuck," I groan, jerking hard and fast, thinking of her moans.

My seed spills hard and fast in my hands and my head falls back, with me wishing I was spilling inside of her tight pussy. Filling her up again and again.

I look down at the mess I made on my hands and shirt and shake my head at my still-hard dick. That thing isn't going down anytime soon. I don't think any amount of jerking off is going to dampen down the need to fuck Alice now. Not after today.

I pull my shirt off and use it to clean myself up the best I can before putting on fresh clothes; but before I leave my room, I hear the front door slam, and Baxter's normally soft footfalls jogging to my room.

He bangs hard on my door, demanding, "Open this mother fucking door right now." Confused, I do and instantly see that Baxter's eyes look wild, his hair askew and dick bulging from his pants.

"Can you not?" I say, cringing at it. "I'd like to keep my eyes, thanks. The last thing I need is to open my door to that thing."

"Speak for your fucking self," he growls out, pointing to my own obvious problem. *Touché sir, touché.* "I was worried about your weird behaviour, so I took off around Alice's cabin, and holy mother fucking shit, her window was open and the smell coming out of there was... I don't even have words for how good that was. I think I jizzed in my pants a little bit. Is that what you were doing? What happened?"

I feel myself heat at being caught, and I tug on my earlobe. "I was just, you know, doing my rounds. I didn't expect," I pause and look away guiltily. "Her to be doing that while I was outside her window. It was an accident, but my feet wouldn't let me leave, and before I knew it, she was crying out, and I was trying not to jump through her window. Don't judge me, okay?"

"I am completely judging you," Baxter almost screams. "I would have been inside her juicy cunt quicker than she could say, 'What are you doing here?' How on Rathe did you leave? Did she know you were there?"

I shake my head and walk back to my bed, plopping down on it with a huff before burying my head in my hands. "No. Thank the Gods, but now I can't get my dick to go down. I've already cum, hard, but it didn't make a difference." I adjust myself again. "Bloody Navy caught me, and to say I felt judged is an understatement. Do you think he'll tell her? Do you think I should?"

Baxter pulls his hair out and re-ties it up. "I think I'm going to have to go over there now and say something because I wasn't the only male outside to scent her arousal. I noticed a few of the others lingering around the area. She needs to close her window."

Someone knocks on the door and we both walk down the hall, Baxter opens it to a distressed-looking Ture. "We know dude. Trust me, we know," he says to our guest because it's pretty damn obvious from the front of his pants why he's here.

I sigh, knowing what needs to be done and really wishing that wasn't the case, but since Alice moved here, everyone has been on the edge of their seat because she hasn't been claimed by anyone yet. Some of the males seem interested in Mischa, but only because she keeps taking her breasts out and rubbing herself against them. It's a shame she smells so bad, plus I don't think I like her personality. Sometimes she says things that I think might be mean to Alice, but I'm never quite sure.

"I'll be back," I tell Baxter, stepping onto the porch with Ture. "I was the one who noticed first, so I'm going to be the one that brings this up."

Ture tells me he's coming too, and I kind of want the backup because I'm pretty ashamed of the way I've handled the whole situation so far, and his presence can help me find my backbone.

When we approach the front door, I pause at Navy sitting on the mat, staring me down. "I know, okay. I'm here to tell her now. Cut me some slack, if you were in your man form you would have found it hard to walk away too."

The front door opens suddenly and Mischa smiles up at us. "Why hello boys, to what do I owe the pleasure of your gorgeous company?" She is wearing only her bra and underwear. At least I think it's underwear, the back seems to be missing for some reason. I bet Alice would look good in something like that.

"May we come in, I need to have a chat with Alice?" I tell her honestly, trying not to look at her exposed body because I'm pretty sure Alice wouldn't appreciate that. Not that I find Misha attractive, she's much too lean for my taste, maybe we should feed her more?

Alice must hear us because she comes out of the hall wearing the white strapless dress, ruffled like she quickly put it on. Her hair is mussed and looks wild, and her cheeks glow and glisten. From the heat or her orgasm, I'm not sure, but for certain her scent is still strong and sweet, and I have to swallow hard before I can speak.

"Can we have a word?" I ask at the same time that Ture asks, "Can I take you on a date?" I look back at him and mouth, 'What the fuck?' at him, so the females can't see, but he shrugs at me like it just slipped out.

Navy meanwhile starts wiggling excitedly, purrs, and rubs his body all over Alice's legs. I watch in horror as he nuzzles her way too close to her pussy for my liking, and she shoos him away, but I catch him lolling his tongue out, saliva obvious. "You're no better than me," I accuse out loud, pointing at him, forgetting that everyone is around us.

"What?" Alice asks, confused.

Ture takes that moment to step around me and up to Alice. "I know I say the wrong thing all the time around you, and you probably think I'm ridiculous, but I really like you and would like to start dating you. I will treat you well and Navy won't mind." He looks at the Cheetah in confirmation and Navy nods, nudging Ture a step closer to Alice in approval that he's finally making a move. *Way to steal my thunder dickhead, I was going to ask her that tomorrow.*

"Ah," Alice looks around nervously, her hand clutching her

throat, but the scent of her arousal grows thicker in the air. "Okay. I'd like that." Her response is quiet and cute.

Ture beams a smile from ear to ear and then adds, "Oh, Salem noticed your bedroom was open earlier when he was doing a sweep of the vicinity. I know it's been really warm lately, but I recommend that you keep it closed at night because you sleep alone. Just for safety precautions. If you are comfortable with it, maybe Navy can sleep on the floor in your room too."

I don't know why I didn't think of saying that. I could have really made a dick out of myself and made Alice feel vulnerable again when she's only just started to come out of her shell with us all.

He's a genius. Also, still a dick for stealing my idea. I'm going to have to wait now, otherwise, it will overwhelm her, which is annoying as fuck because I loved her first.

CHAPTER FOURTEEN

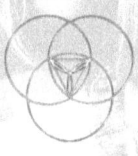

ALICE

I can't believe Ture just asked me out. The memory of me stroking my clit in the fantasy I just flicked the bean to, is still fresh in my mind and my core clenches as my imagination relives it again. *Focus!*

"Just out of curiosity," Ture asks me, rubbing his chin. "What exactly do people on Earth do on dates?"

Mischa sputters in laughter after getting herself together. Don't think I didn't notice her pale when I was asked on a date instead of her, and that neither of the men in front of me have even looked at her half-naked body. It's obvious why Salem hasn't because of his sexual orientation, but it makes me feel a lot better about Ture wanting to date me when I know he never gives her the time of day, and not once have I seen him checking her out. Come to think of it, Ture spends a lot of time hanging out with me, and he does all sorts of things for me, like make me clothes, baked goods, and recently even made me leather slip-on shoes that are so freaking comfortable. Dare I believe that he really is interested in me as a woman?

I shuffle on my feet nervously before answering, "Well, there are dinner dates, movies, dancing, and stuff like that but you guys don't have movies here."

"Dinner it is." Ture perks up. "Is tomorrow night good for you? I'll make a nice meal at my place and even make the apple pie you said you liked so much for dessert. How does that sound?"

My cheeks flush, and I smile at him, my heart racing. "I'd love that."

I look down at Navy, thinking about what Ture said before about safety, and decide that I trust him because he's only ever been amazing and protective with me. "Do you want to camp out in my room until you feel like shifting back? Only if you want to, of course." In true Alice style, I instantly doubt my words, thinking I'm being too presumptuous.

Navy walks past me and down the hall to my room. I guess I'll take that as a yes.

"Thank you for looking out for me, and I'm looking forward to tomorrow," I tell Ture, blushing again. "Would you like me to bring anything?"

"Just your body," he replies with a straight face and Salem facepalms. I can't help but laugh, used to his foot-in-mouth syndrome by now.

"You have got to think about what you say before you say it." Salem grabs the back of Ture's shirt and starts to pull him out. "Okay, we're off. Sorry about that, and don't forget to close your window in the future. Safety and all that. See ya." He closes the door behind him, and I hear a thud and Salem's mumbled, "Seriously? You couldn't wait?"

Mischa turns the lock on the door and then leans against it.

"Oh, isn't that cute? You get the retard that is always a cat and the guy who can't help but embarrass himself whenever he opens his mouth. You must be so proud?" She squints her eyes and purses her mouth in disgust. "At least you won't die alone now. I should have known you'd be an old cat lady." Her laugh is cruel, and I don't appreciate the way she talks down about the guys when they're not around.

"You can talk. No one even wants to touch you because they know your vagina will turn their dicks into bitter pickles after touching your dirty cooch." I have no idea where the nasty words come from, but after weeks of her constantly talking down to me and making me feel like shit, I'm over it.

Not even waiting for a reply, I storm back to my room and slam the bedroom door behind me, leaning on it with my hand on my chest, shocked by the toxic words that came out of my mouth. Maybe being a cuntbag is contagious. I hope not.

Opening my eyes, I find Navy sprawled across my bed like he owns it, rubbing his face all over and under my sheets. That's funny I remember saying he could sleep on the floor, not my bed, and even if I did, where on earth am I supposed to fit? He's huge.

Seeming to read my mind, Navy rolls over and onto his back, leaving one side free for me. At this moment, I'm glad he's not a Lion Shifter, otherwise, I'd be shit out of luck.

"You really think you're sleeping with me, huh?" I ask as I go over to the window.

I jump back in shock when I open the curtains, finding four random guys outside being ushered away by Baxter. "What the fuck?" I ask quietly, snagging Baxter's attention.

"Nothing to see here," he says with a smile at me while simultaneously shoving one of the men away. "Have a good sleep."

Oookay. That was weird, but alright. Navy makes this chuffing noise that I have figured out is his version of a laugh, and I scowl at him as I close the window and curtains. "What are you cackling about?"

I pull my dress over my head, turn away and bend over to get one of my shirts when I realise what I just did. I stand up superfast and spin to find a very naked, very human-looking Navy sitting at the edge of my bed, only inches away from me, and staring at my chest with his mouth open.

"If I knew it would be this easy to get you to accept my claiming, I would have come to your bed a long time ago," he says in a raspy, unused voice. "You are so perfect. Never change," he practically whispers as if in worship.

He reaches down and grasps his, holy fuck that's bigger than I thought, dick. The hard and pulsing appendage weeps slightly with pre-cum, and I can't stop staring at it. I've only ever seen one penis up close, and even then it was not standing at attention right in front of my face. I'm a bit star-struck by it, and my mouth opens and closes like a fish, with no words coming out.

Navy stands up, and I tear my eyes away to look up at him. I completely forgot how handsome he is, he's been a Cheetah for so long that I was starting to doubt he'd ever change back.

He reaches a hand for me, and I step back on instinct. Instant regret hits when I see him flinch and pull his hand back. "Do you only like me as a Cheetah? Will I never be enough for you as a male?" His pained voice stuns me. The tone is filled with rejection and despair that I know all too well. "Is it because I'm different from the others? Am I not enough the way I am?"

"I'm sorry, I," is all I can get out. My shock overwhelms my sense. Is it possible that he is as self-conscious as I am?

"I'm not a pet!" Navy's voice raises, his displeasure more than clear, and I know I've fucked up. "If you can't accept me the way I am, then I won't bother you any more. I thought I was going to be alone forever anyway. I couldn't believe my luck when I first saw you. It was like all the dreams I never dared to dream came waltzing into my life, and all of a sudden I could breathe when I didn't even know I was suffocating."

I step forward, but he sidesteps and starts to walk towards the door and away from me. "Wait," I cry out, a little too loud probably, but I'm a little overwhelmed and shocked by his words. "Please."

Navy stops before he reaches the door but doesn't turn around, his head hung low and shoulders slouched in dismay. I slowly walk up to him with every ounce of courage that I possess and wrap my arms around his waist, keeping them high, so I don't accidentally touch his dick. I'm not that courageous yet. I just know that I don't want him to leave, especially if it's because he doesn't think he's good enough when that is absurd.

I squeeze him tight, my bare breasts flat against his muscular back, and I murmur onto his skin, embarrassed with the honesty that I'm about to spill but deciding it's worth it to try. "I'm sorry. It's not you. You are so perfect and beautiful, and I'm just me, fat and ugly. I didn't want you to see me like this and then be stuck with me because the Gods decided to give you a dud prize. I'm so sorry that I'm not like the others, but I can't be anyone else."

My tears flow freely as I talk as if my inner pain couldn't be contained inside any more, but even though I'm making Navy's back all wet, I can't move, and I can't look up because I feel too ashamed and need to hide.

His hands grab mine around his waist and he sighs. "You shouldn't let Mischa make you feel that way. I hear the way she talks to you and about you when you're not around because she's too stupid to remember that I'm a Shifter. Honestly, how dumb can you be, and by the way, that bitch stinks. Can I move her out of here because I don't know how much longer I can deal with that smell? It burns my nose."

Navy tries to turn around, but I hold on tighter, not wanting him to look at me and see me so vulnerable right now.

With a sigh, he gets the hint and strokes my hands softly instead. "If I got to talk to the Gods and wish for the perfect Kindred, I couldn't even describe a female as perfect as you. Every time I look at you my heart beats strangely inside my chest, at first I thought something was wrong with me, but then I realised it's because my heart loved you straight away, and it's trying to jump out of my chest to reach you. I'm a very patient male, but I don't think I can sit by and watch you hate yourself any more. It hurts me because you are a part of me whether you like it or not." Navy grabs my hands suddenly, opening them and turning around, facing me in my imperfect glory, and asks me with his own eyes shining with vulnerability, "What do you want from me, Alice? Tell me, and it's yours, but please don't push me away any more. What am I doing wrong? I only want to love you."

A tear renders my heart and in that crack Navy slithers inside. His words battled my wall of defence and won. How can I possibly fight my feelings that have been growing for him when he says shit like that. "Don't hurt me, Navy, I can't take it if you hurt me," I whisper up at him, with more silent tears tracking my already-soaked cheeks.

"I'm not by any means dumb, but I'm admittedly not excellent at reading social cues or dissecting sentences that are anything but blunt. Does that mean you will let me be your Kindred because I promise you that it is impossible for me to hurt you without hurting myself, and I'm not a masochist?" Navy's matter-of-fact tone and straight face bring a wet smile to my face, and I reach up on my tiptoes to kiss him softly on the cheek.

"Let's do this," I tell him with my heart in my throat. "But you need to give me time to let you all the way in. I've been closed off for a long time, and I'm being as brave as I can right now, but I will accept you as my Kindred if you'll have me."

Navy frowns. "Didn't I already tell you that I want you?" He's serious, and I let out a laugh and nod. "Good. Can I claim you now because your breasts are distracting me, and I'd like to get inside you and bury my face in them. See?" He grabs his erect again penis with a cheeky smile.

I cover my breasts with my hands and step back.

"Hey! They're mine, you said so. Why are you covering them? I haven't even started playing with them yet."

"You can't just have sex with me straight away. I need time to get comfortable with that, and I'm not ready yet," I tell him, trying not to laugh again at his sulking face.

His eyes light up again, and he steps back into me, grabbing my hips and rolling his erection against my stomach. "Oh yes, you are. I heard and smelt you pleasuring yourself through the window with Salem. You are very ready for claiming. I can still scent it now, it's sweet on my tongue, and I'd very much like to taste you now."

With a swift movement like I weigh absolutely nothing, he picks me up and carries me to the bed, placing me down carefully with my knees over the end.

"Wh- what are you doing?" I ask breathlessly as my mind goes over what he just said.

Navy opens my thighs and licks up the inside of one of them with a deep, rumbling purr that vibrates right up to my sweet spot. *Oh, fuck yes.* Wait! What?

I sit up and gasp, enough to stun Navy into sitting back on his ass with confusion.

"What's wrong?"

My cheeks and ears get hot as I squeal, "Did you just say you were outside my window with Salem while I masturbated? The open window? The one that Baxter was shooing those men away from?"

"Yeah, why?" he answers innocently like he doesn't see a problem with that.

Mortified. Absolutely mortified!

How will I *ever* be able to show my face outside this room again?

"How many people were out there?" I shouldn't ask, but I need to know how bad this is.

Navy shrugs. "Just me and Salem but when he realised I was watching him after you came, he ran off to his own place to finish himself off. It didn't affect me as badly because I was in Cheetah form, but he was hard as a rock. That's gotta hurt. Now that I'm me again, though, your scent is really affecting me because it's so strong in here from your current arousal and your previous pleasure."

Salem was hard? I thought he was gay. Maybe he likes both, but I feel bad because that puts me in an uncomfortable predicament with Baxter. I'd hate to put a strain on their relationship just because I was horny and fingered myself. Not to mention how I can never look at Salem again without knowing he heard me cumming.

What a fucking day!

CHAPTER FIFTEEN

NAVY

eaning up, I take Alice's beautiful, rounded face into my hands and kiss the tip of her nose. Who knew that doing something even as simple as that would feel so good? I can't wait to taste her everywhere.

"Now I feast," I say simply, pushing her gently onto her back, then opening her knees for my viewing pleasure. I don't know why females insist on wearing underwear and bras. They only get in the way. I make a mental note to throw all of Alice's out later. She's agreed to be mine, and I don't want to see these any more.

I reach up and rip open the flimsy fabric, and a gasp comes out of Alice as she leans up against her elbows.

"Did you just tear my underwear open?" she asks when it's obvious that I just did that. Then she tries to close her knees for some reason, saying, "Oh my gosh."

Easily, I hold open her soft pale thighs and lean further in to lick up the inner seam of one of them. "Lie back now. I want to taste you, it smells so good down here. Keep your legs open, please."

My hands slide up her legs while still holding them open, and I knead her perfect flesh. I've never seen such a juicy, sexy female, and I can't believe that she's mine. I must have done something very good for the Gods to gift me such a perfect Kindred.

My mouth moves closer to her pink glistening lips, open for my view, with soft curly hair framing it, and I blow warm breath on her gently to see what will happen, and to my delight, she shivers all over, falls back, and groans in a good way. She liked that. I do it again but this time closer, her scent strong, and my mouth waters. Just one taste, I need just one.

Lowering my mouth, I tentatively lick at the wet slit. The powerful taste of absolute perfection lines my tongue and purrs of happiness erupt from me and with no self-control left, I dive in for more, needing to coat my whole mouth in the delectable taste that is my Alice.

My purring increases, and I notice that every time I slide my tongue across the small nub above the opening, Alice moans loudly and rolls her luscious hips to get closer, so I focus on it, circling and purring until her breathing gets really intense, and her legs suddenly clamp around my head, and she screams so loud that I'm sure all the others Cheetahs will hear. Her orgasm flows more delicious juices into my mouth, and I groan at the taste. Why didn't anyone tell me how good this tastes? I wonder if I can live off this nectar of the Gods.

"No more," Alice squeaks, trying to push my head away. "It's too much."

I raise my head with a big smile, to see her looking down at me. Her eyes are half-lidded, her face the beautiful pink flush that she gets, and her hair is all poofy. I lick my lips and ask, "When can I have more?"

Looking down at her swollen pink lips, surrounded by soft golden hair with a creamy filling, I can't help but lap it up a few more times while Alice wriggles beneath my face, saying incoherent words at first, but soon she grabs my hair and holds me even closer. You don't have to ask me twice. I focus back on her little nub again but this time, I slide a finger inside her. It's tight, wet, and warm, and I can't even imagine how good it would feel to put my dick in there. Will it fit inside this tight hole?

I insert another finger and thrust them in time with my tongue, following the cues of her writhing body, which tells me clearly what she likes and what she doesn't. I was worried I'd need a manual for this stuff, but Alice's body is so easy to read that it's like a problem-solving quiz that gives me a delicious treat at the end.

Working her over with my mouth and fingers she cums again, even quicker, screaming louder than the first time, calling out my name, and I find that I love that sound and want to hear her call my name like that all the time. I just found my new hobby.

When Alice's body goes limp I withdraw my fingers, giving her one last big lick so that I don't miss a drop of her, and then I stand up, looking down at her sexy body, licking my fingers clean. I think she's falling asleep. Her eyes are closed, and her engorged breasts slowly rise and fall in a soft rhythm as she breathes.

"Hmmm." I guess that's all the Alice I get tonight, but that's alright because she looks happy and satisfied and that is enough for me.

I carefully lift her, so that I don't disturb her too much, and I use my toes to pull her sheet down before laying her back on the bed, with her head on the pillow. Straight away she turns over, her back to me, and curls up in a cute little ball. Pulling the sheet up, I carefully cover her and look down at myself. *I'm going to need some clothes.* There's not a chance that Alice will want me walking around Mischa naked. Humans are not as liberal with their nudity as Mhanu are, I've figured that much out, at least.

Quietly opening the curtains and window, I slip over the window frame and outside to head back to my place to pick up some clothes and decide I can't be bothered going all the way there, and I don't want Alice to wake up alone.

Changing direction, I head next door and knock. Within seconds, Baxter swings the door open with an open-mouthed Salem behind him, the two of them looking downright stunned. I wonder what's wrong with them?

"Can I borrow some pants, please? I don't want that stinky bitch staring at my dick in the morning?" Instead of an answer, they just continue to stare at me. "Are you guys alright? Should I call someone?"

Salem pushes Baxter to the side and puts his face in mine, sniffing my mouth. "Did you - is that - the screaming was from you?" Salem's voice comes out a little tense.

"Didn't you hear her calling my name when she orgasmed?" I scrunch my face up. "I could have sworn it was really loud. I'll have to do better next time. I like the idea of everyone here hearing that Alice is mine and that they can't have her. Except for you guys and her other Kindreds, of course." I step past Salem inside their cabin and look around. "So, can I borrow some pants or not?"

Baxter pats me on the back with a huge smile. "Congratulations my friend. Did you get to claim her? I don't smell your release."

I explain what happened in great detail to them because they seem to be having a little bit of trouble following along and by the end of it, they're both groaning and complaining about why they can't taste her too.

"It's your own fault. I don't know why you weren't just honest with her in the first place. If she knew you were her Kindred, this wouldn't be such a big deal." Baxter grabs me a pair of pants and I slide them on. "Thanks, I'd better get back. I went through her window because I didn't want to run into Mischa. Speaking of, can we move her somewhere else because she stinks up the house? I had to spend most of my time out the front because I couldn't handle breathing it in. Now that Alice has said she will accept me as her Kindred, I'd very much prefer for that one to go away."

Salem and Baxter laugh. "It's not that easy, unfortunately," Salem tells me. "There are no other empty cabins for her to stay in, and we can't just give her one to share with other males because that wouldn't be fair to them and might make her uncomfortable."

I see the logic in that, but I don't have to like it. "Fine. Then you two or Ture need to hurry up and tell her, so you can give Mischa one of your houses. I'd take Alice back to my place, but I share it with Abel and as much as I love my big brother, I'm not having my Kindred share a house with him. I don't want to attack him if he looks at her in a way I don't like."

They nod, but I can see them both being cowards and don't expect them to come forwards any time soon. My money is on Ture after his declaration today, which is a surprise as Baxter was always the one I thought would jump in first with both feet. Who knows what's going on in his head? I really don't understand other people sometimes. I'm not even going to factor in Alexion, he's got his own headspace to deal with.

"Right. I'm going back to bed," I tell them heading out the door and I call back. "I'm hoping to have Alice for breakfast in the morning. She's really tasty. You guys should seriously hurry up. You're missing out. Night." I wave and head to the back of Alice's house, happy to see her bedroom window still open.

Climbing inside, I carefully close it behind me and the curtains as well. I turn, inhaling the overpowering scent of my

Kindred's arousal, and tell my dick to calm down because he's not getting any action tonight. My Alice is tired, and I will give her everything she needs from now on, and if that means she sleeps instead of letting me claim her, then that's what she gets.

I drop the pants I borrowed and lift the sheet. Taking a moment, I enjoy the view of her soft, rounded ass before sliding in beside her. Curling my body around her, I let myself give off a soft purr of contentment as she wiggles her body back into mine. My arm wraps around her tightly and pulls her in the rest of the way. "Sleep my Alice. I have you now, you don't have to be alone ever again. Neither of us does." Kissing her temple, I rest my head and close my eyes, having the best night's sleep I've had in a very long time.

CHAPTER SIXTEEN

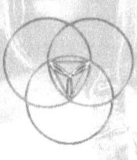

ALICE

*P*leasure shoots through me, waking all of my senses as something wet and rough slides through my folds, and I let out a small whimper. Opening my eyes, I look down to find Navy's face between my thighs, his grey-blue eyes looking up at me, dark with desire.

He laps at me again, starting up his purring motor at the same time, and my whole body shudders at the instant build in pleasure that it brings. It's hard to believe that Navy's never done this before, with the talented way he strokes me with his tongue and slips his fingers inside me, curling them just right. I feel like an instrument that expertly plays, bringing my orgasm quicker than I thought was possible.

As I scream out his name, my legs closing around him with the intensity of it, he chuckles against my folds, getting one more lick in then rising up and looking at me like the cat who got the cream. Then again, I guess he is.

"Good morning," he purrs out as he slides his naked body up mine, licking his lips. "Did you have a good sleep?"

Yep. I could definitely get used to waking up like this, except for how exposed I feel. I grab the discarded sheets and try to cover myself, wishing he would stop rubbing himself along my chubby stomach.

Navy flicks the sheets away and off the bed. "No. It's too hot for them, and I won't be able to see you." *That's kind of the point.* I wriggle uncomfortably a little, but he kisses both of my cheeks, before kissing the tip of my nose. "You know, I just realised that I made out with the wrong set of lips first," he tells me with a laugh.

Heat fills my cheeks and ears, and I try to look away from the blaze in his eyes and the blunt words he has no problem throwing around. Navy grabs my chin and turns me back to look at him. "Is something wrong? Did I not satisfy you with my tongue?" He frowns, lifts himself up, and looks back down at my very exposed body. "Would you like me to try again? I'll pay more attention this time, I must have gotten carried away with tasting you."

He starts moving back down, but I grab his shoulders, not wanting him so close to my tummy in the light of day. Earlier I'd just woken up, but now I feel painfully aware of our physical differences as I take in his long, athletic body, rippling abs, and complete lack of any body fat. I can't even see my own legs from this angle because my tits and stomach are too round. I feel disgusted with myself.

"Kiss me," I tell him, hoping he won't continue with his line of questioning. Plus, I'd rather have him up near my head.

With a face-splitting grin, he leans in and softly kisses my lips before deepening it, letting his lips caress mine like sealing a promise. I close my eyes and fall into the kiss, he feels like a drug and I don't want to come down. Navy's tongue tentatively licks my lips, and I let him in, using my own to return the affection he so freely gives me with his whole heart. Our kiss turns into a hot and heavy make-out session, one I've never before experienced, and we both get out of breath as we hold each other close, tasting and breathing in the other. It's both beautiful and messy, and I don't want to let go for fear that it's all a dream.

Navy's dick slides between my slightly open thighs and rubs against my still very sensitive clit, his hips gyrating back and forth through my wet folds. It pulls me from the moment because I know I'm not ready for more between us yet. I want to be able to enjoy this stage before my heart gets broken again, and I lightly push on his chest, to let him know to stop.

Parting his lips from mine and breathing heavily, Navy rasps, "What's wrong? I'll be very gentle. I won't hurt you or anything because I asked Abel how to do it properly and make it good for you." His hips roll again, and I almost change my mind.

"It's not, it's just that I'm not ready yet." My fingers softly stroke his jawline, hoping he'll understand, and of course, he doesn't by the look of his confused frown.

Navy rolls off me and rubs his face with both hands as he mumbles. "But that's what I'm supposed to do. You're my Kindred, and I have to claim you to keep you safe. It's the rules."

At times like these, it reminds me that he's different. I know he's not being a dickhead or disrespecting my opinion, he just, honestly, doesn't understand why I would want to wait. I try to think of a way to explain the way I feel so that he can be patient with me.

"Human females take time when it comes to sharing their bodies with men," I start, as I get up and quickly pick up the dress I discarded on the floor yesterday while he's distracted and not staring at me. "It's just the way it is. I want you to be patient with me while understanding that I have chosen to let you share this part of me but at a time when I feel ready and comfortable. Do you understand?"

He sits up in bed, looking at my boobs with a sulking face because they're already covered. With his eyes still focusing on my chest, he says with an almost whining tone of voice. "Fine. I want you to be happy but don't take too long because I can't keep you safe until you let me claim you. All the other males here think they can try to take you until then, and I don't like that."

"Don't worry about that. I'm yours. I'll let Ture know today that I can't date him any more." I sit down on the edge of the bed, slipping on my leather shoes, trying not to stare at Navy's penis.

Navy starts to laugh and jumps up, pulling some pants on that I don't remember him having earlier. "That would make him very sad," he laughs quietly again and kisses me on the cheek. "But much too mean, he is very excited about being your male. I think you should pick him too because he is your Kindred as well after all."

He opens the door and reaches out for me to take his hand with a bright smile. It takes me a minute to process what he says as I hold his hand, his fingers squeezing mine.

"He's not my Kindred."

With another, louder laugh, he walks me down the hallway. "Of course he is. Ture doesn't want you to know because he thinks it will scare you, so don't tell him I told you. It's a secret after all. I'm going to make you bacon and eggs, sit down and relax."

Mischa steps out of her room at the same time I sit at the table, and she openly scowls at me. She loses a lot of her looks when she screws up her face with so much distaste. "Did you need to make so much noise last night and this morning? You're not the only one who lives here after all," she whines, in her usual accent, which I no longer buy. Sitting at the table, she looks over to Navy as he hums happily at the stove, frying some bacon. "Did you fuck him as a cat to make him change back to a man? It wouldn't surprise me."

"Ew." I put my hair behind my ear and give Mischa a dirty look. "Don't be gross. You know I would never do that, and what I do in my room is none of your business." My voice comes out confident, even though I'm secretly wishing I had been a little quieter. I'm not used to cumming so hard, and I was definitely louder than I meant to be.

Navy comes over with two glasses of fresh juice, giving both of us one, and he scoffs as he puts them down in front of us. "I intend to make her scream louder when she lets me claim her. Would you like me to give you a warning so that you can go away and bother someone else?" he asks, completely serious, and I cover my smile with my glass.

I knew I liked Navy.

"Oh, so you haven't had sex yet. Interesting," is the only answer she gives, looking at me with a look that makes me more than a little uneasy. "Thanks for the drink, comrade. I'll have my eggs scrambled."

Why do I have a feeling that she's up to something?

THE DAY PASSES SLOWLY because I find out relatively quickly that every single Cheetah Shifter in the village is talking about the scent of my 'private time' last night. As well as the scent I had when I left the house with a very proud Navy. I practically ran back to the cabin to shower, and now I'm too freaked out to show my face.

Navy promises me that it's a good thing, but I'm a human and that's not freaking normal. I don't want random guys coming up to me and telling me how good I smell and how they would like to get to know me better. It's a very strange kind of day, and I'd like it to be tomorrow now.

My date with Ture is soon, and I'm nervous to see him now that I know he must have smelt me, but I'm also super curious to find out if what Navy said is true, and Ture is also my Kindred. He can't be right, though, otherwise, I figure he would have told me ages ago.

I tie up the back of my halterneck dress that he made me and look at myself in the mirror. The dress really shows off my breasts and a good amount of cleavage, which is why I haven't worn it in public yet, but Navy talked me into giving it a try. It's more than bizarre having the guy I'm kind of dating, tell me what to wear for a date with a different guy. I'm definitely not on Earth any more, that's for sure.

Navy goes to answer the door when we hear a knocking, and I tuck my hair behind my ears while fiddling with my dress one more time. I can do this. Ture is a nice guy, and I am worthy. Yeah, okay, I can tell myself that, but I'm still shitting myself.

I walk into the living room, and Ture sucks his breath in, looking me up and down. "You look beautiful. I knew that dress would look good on you." His voice comes across as sincere, and I feel myself relax a little.

"Alice's breasts look very sexy in that dress," Navy adds, nodding with his arms crossed, staring at my chest. "If you're lucky, maybe she will let you lick her. It's like nothing I've ever tasted before, especially when she climaxes in your mouth. Mmmm, yep. Maybe I can do it again before you leave?" he asks me with a hopeful gaze, stepping forwards.

Ture pulls him back by his collar. "Come on now, even I know you can't talk like that. Look how uncomfortable you made Alice, her cheeks and ears are all pink again."

"I like it when she's pink. It won't take me long, I just need to purr, and she cums pretty quickly."

Needing to get the hell out of there before Navy drops to his knees and starts trying to eat me out again in front of guests, I walk to the door and call back, "I'll be back later," and wait outside for Ture. Thankfully, he's right behind me and apologises for Navy. He doesn't have to, though, I truly do like him just the way he is. I just have to get used to his quirks.

Ture takes my hand, and I let him as he guides me to the other side of the village. I've actually never been inside his place, and I'm pretty keen to see inside.

I watch as the full moon glistens in the sky and enjoy the warm breeze floating by, making my floor-length dress dance. Turning my head slightly, I look up at the very tall, very sexy man by my side and sigh softly. My life is like a dream right now, and I'm in no hurry to wake up. Between Navy and Ture both wanting me just the way I am, I can't imagine my life being better.

I let my mind drift off to Baxter, Salem, and Alexion, but I shake it off, telling myself not to be selfish and to appreciate what I have before me, even though it feels like something inside me is still missing.

CHAPTER SEVENTEEN

TURE

Over the years I have faced enraged Polar Bear Shifters, Dragon Shifters on a rampage, Gremlins, the loss of my parents, and the fear that only a rogue Fae murderer can inflict, but nothing makes me as terrified as when I'm with this female. She has the power to make and break me with a single word, touch, or breath, and for some reason, everything that comes out of my mouth is either super inappropriate or downright stupid.

All of my knowledge, education, and political suave might as well not exist. Thankfully, Alice is very forgiving and hasn't judged me too badly for it so far, and I love her all the more for it. And it is love, not just Kindredship, not that I'd ever belittle the power of that bond but getting to know her since she's been here has me completely besotted to her in every way.

Alice has the most luscious curves, the sweetest personality, and a great sense of humour. The only thing I would change about her is that I wish she could see herself from my eyes. Her self-love needs work but luckily for her, I have enough love for everything she is for the both of us. My hope is to bring her so much happiness one day that she only ever views herself with the adoration and respect that we do.

Walking along hand in hand, I hope that my palms aren't sweating too much from how nervous I am. I briefly crinkle my nose in jealousy at the fact that Alice is covered in Navy's scent. I'm very happy that they found each other, and I have no problem sharing Alice with him, Baxter, or Salem, but I'm so desperately afraid that I'm going to say the wrong thing and push her away for good.

"Here we are," I tell her in a steady voice, trying to pretend I'm not shitting myself. "I hope you're hungry. I made some of your favourites especially."

I open the door for her and step back, letting Alice go ahead of me and hold my breath. *Did I go too far?*

Alice sucks in a sharp intake of breath and turns back to look up at me with her mouth open and her cheeks flushed a beautiful pink. "Holy shit, Ture. Is this all for me?" Her voice is a higher pitch than normal, and I'm not a hundred percent sure if that's a good thing or not. Does that mean she likes it? "This is like a film." Her tone is hushed and reverent, and I smile, letting out the air I was holding in my lungs with a whoosh.

Earlier today I took all the furniture out of my living space and laid down large soft cushions in a semicircle, with a short table in the centre. I made a path of candles and wildflowers along the floor and surrounding the arrangement, as well as a large bouquet of multicoloured gerberas from the side garden in the centre of the table. I set it out for two, with wine glasses and a small wooden box on one side.

Walking in beside Alice, I take her hand and lead her to her side of the cushions, helping her to sit comfortably before picking up a jug of red wine and sitting beside her. As I fill our glasses, I ask her, "Is this the kind of date you wanted? I did a lot of research and I really wanted to get it right?"

"I've never seen anything so beautiful, Ture, thank you." She leans over and kisses my cheek softly, and I almost spill the wine. "This must have been a lot of work for you. You didn't have to do all of this just for me."

My heart thuds inside my chest so loud that I'm worried she'll hear it, as my cheek burns from the contact of her soft lips. "I would do anything for you, Alice," I start, getting more nervous by the second. "I know that much of the time I don't say or do the right things, but I'm going to be honest with you tonight. You make me nervous. You did the second you walked into our village. We have been lucky enough to be able to host lots of your females here and keep them safe. It's been our absolute honour, but I wasn't prepared for how one female could quite literally take my breath away. You are so beautiful that you give the Valkyries and Angels a run for their money."

Alice looks down and wrings her fingers together, looking sad, and I'm not sure what I've said wrong this time. "I'm sorry." I grab her hands, intertwining my fingers with hers, and silently plead for her to look up at me. "Whatever I said wrong, I didn't mean it. I just wanted to be brave tonight and tell you how I've been feeling. I didn't mean to deceive you, but I wanted to give you time to get to know me as I am before I threw all of my feelings at you. Was it still too soon? When you agreed to go on a date with me, and I saw how well you and Navy had progressed I thought it would be okay, to be honest, but if you need me to back off again, I will."

I know I'm rambling, I can hear myself, but I just can't seem to stop. I have to be making an absolute fool of myself right now. Closing my mouth, I look down at Alice, but her face is so far forwards that her pretty golden hair is blocking my view, and I have no idea what's happening with her expressions right now. My stomach starts to flip at the idea that I've screwed this up already.

"Please speak to me?" I plead in a low tone. "Do you want to leave?"

Alice looks up at me then, and I'm trampled with guilt as silent tears glide down her perfect cheeks. *I've made her cry!* My own lip trembles of its own volition, and I try to beat back the burning behind my eyes. I can't believe I've hurt her so badly. I should have listened to the others and gone slower. What was I thinking? Maybe I'm a disappointment to her?

Alice tries to speak but her voice creaks, trying again she whispers, "Thank you for this, Ture. In my whole life, I've never had anyone do or say anything so perfect, and I don't know if I'm worthy of this, or you."

Her words shock me, and it takes me a second to wrap around the fact that she didn't just reject me.

"So, you're not upset at me?" I ask cautiously before I let myself get my hopes up.

Pulling her hands from mine, which I was apparently holding in a death grip, she lays a hand on each side of my cheeks, looking into both of my eyes as if looking for some kind of confirmation. I smile softly at her, hoping she's asking what I pray she's asking, and my dreams come true as she moves in, her plump lips brushing softly onto mine.

Without any tact at all, I pull her in and deepen the kiss as though I'm starving, and she's all the food I'll ever need. Luckily, she lets me and gives back as much fervour as I gave. I practically pull her onto my lap, my arms wrapping around Alice and bringing her as close to me as I can in this position.

We sit like that for what feels like both an eternity and no time at all, when I remember I have food in the oven. Not wanting to serve Alice something burnt, I slowly pull back, giving her one final kiss. "Give me just a moment, I have to get the food out. Hold that thought."

Hating myself a little bit, I pop up and go to the kitchen, my heart on my shoulder, my head in the clouds, and my dick as hard as a tree trunk. I take the food out and, carefully, adjust myself out of view, so I don't seem rude. This is going to be a long ass dinner if she kisses me like that again. Either very long or very, very short.

"I hope you brought your appetite," I call out, plating up our meals. I made the same beef that she had the first night, which almost killed me when she moaned at the dinner table. I'd never been so close to cumming involuntarily in my life. It was like an instant reaction, and then of course I opened my mouth and made myself look like a total tool. I add a fresh salad and my famous potato bake to it, excited to see her eat my meal.

Carrying them in, I'm happy to find her looking at my gift box with curiosity. "That's for you," I inform her, putting our filled plates down and handing her cutlery. "But you aren't allowed to open it until after dessert. Think of it as a reason to stay until the end."

Alice's smile beams at me with full force, and I have to remember to breathe. "Well, I better make sure that I eat it all, then," she jokes, putting the box down gingerly and picking up the cutlery. "This looks great, and you know how much I love your meat."

I choke on the bite I've just taken, and Alice laughs joyfully, patting me on the back. "Sorry, I couldn't help myself." I clear my throat and smile back at her while chewing. I'm glad she finds me funny and not a total sleaze.

We enjoy the meal and Alice tells me all about her upbringing, and how her family was small but not overly affectionate. Apparently, her parents cared more about her academics than her emotional well-being, which she said started her unhealthy obsession with food. I don't really get that though because aren't we meant to be obsessed with food? You eat when you're hungry, it gives you joy when you're sad, and it brings contentment when you're empty. Humans are weird, thinking that it's a bad thing.

Alice has an older brother that pleased her parents much more by going to some big school when she didn't want to. So when she graduated, Alice said she just faded into the background without any resistance, only to pop up on important holidays and such. I can't even imagine not being close to your family. Everyone in this coalition is a part of my family and their well-being would always be important, even Alexion. Whether he likes it or not. That reminds me.

"Just so you have a heads-up, Alexion was spotted back in his cabin this afternoon." I don't want her to be shocked if she runs into him. It was a very tense situation they got into, and I wouldn't blame her if she was feeling afraid. "Don't worry, I'm sure he'll leave you alone. Regardless, we will be available if you are ever feeling threatened or uncomfortable."

Alice finishes off her last piece of dinner and puts her fork down, her eyes on me. "I'm not worried about Alexion, but I do have questions about him that no one seems to be able to answer."

"Probably because he makes those answers none of anybody's business. Just be cautious, please, that's all I ask." I hop up and put both of our plates back in the kitchen. "How about I give you your gift early? I can't imagine you're gonna duck out on my famous blueberry cheesecake, are you?" I think it's a good idea to change the subject.

With an excited wiggle, Alice sits straighter on the cushions, eyeing up the little box that I made for her. I spent all morning making her gift and all afternoon making sure the box was right. I hope she likes it. I put so much time and effort into researching how to woo a female from Earth since Alice arrived. I wanted to give her something sentimental that a *human* female would appreciate, something that would help me to explain the depths of my feelings, but now that the time to give it to her has approached, I'm having second thoughts. What if I got it wrong? What if she doesn't like it?

Kneeling beside her, I inhale deeply and pick up the same box, facing her. Alice turns to me and claps her hands. "What is it? I'm so excited. I love presents. If it's another dress, though, I have to warn you, it's probably not going to fit."

With all of my courage, I open up the box and place it on the table before her and reach for Alice's hand. Inside, the gold ring I painstakingly made by hand sits in the centre of the box with three amethyst stones in the middle; to signify her past on Earth, the present that brought her to us, and the future I want her to share with us on Rathe.

She looks down at it confused and then looks up at me. Squeezing her hand, I pull it to my lips and kiss it softly. "The moment I met you, I knew you were my Kindred, and my whole world flipped upside down. I wanted to give you time to get to know me, and along the way, I fell harder for you than I ever knew was possible. You are my whole world, and I never want to spend another second of my long life without you by my side. I know that humans do marriage, but I'd like to offer you more, my very life force," Alice gasps, but I keep going, scared to stop, now that I've started. *Shit, I hope I'm doing this right.* "Alice? Will you accept me as your Kindred?"

CHAPTER EIGHTEEN

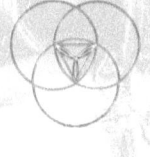

ALICE

I'm sorry, what?

My whole body freezes, and when I say freeze I mean, my face is stuck in place with a half smile, my breath no longer works, I can't swallow or blink, and for a moment there, I think my actual heart stopped.

Is Ture really proposing to me, or am I dreaming? Maybe I'm dead. Yep, I've had a stroke from all the sugar I've consumed and died. That's got to be it because there's no way I'm sitting here with Ture and a ring. No way.

"Alice?" Ture asks slowly, his nervous features changing to one of worry. "Alice, breathe!" His long hands clasp my face and bring it closer to his with wide eyes. "Breathe," he practically shouts, with a tinge of hysteria.

The shock of it has me sucking in a sharp inhale, and I blink rapidly looking around, my mind feeling super manic and the need to escape imminent.

Gathering myself internally, I go with a basic response that I can focus on, needing to move on from what just happened so that I don't have a full mental break. "So," I clear my throat, looking up at him, my mouth kind of squished between the tight grip he has on my face. "How about that cheesecake?"

Ture doesn't respond for a minute other than losing some of the light he had in his eyes, and I'm instantly swamped with guilt, but I'm too shocked to react any other way. He needs to give me time, but I don't know how to express that at this very moment.

Letting go of me and leaning back on his feet, Ture sighs deeply. "I'll get you some now." Within seconds, he disappears into the kitchen, and I'm alone, looking down at the prettiest ring I've ever seen. Tentatively, I pick it up between my shaking fingers, trying not to focus on what it signifies and more on the ring itself. It's delicate and yet sturdy, and I adore the soft purple stones. Wondering if it fits, I slowly slide it onto my ring finger and find a perfect match. Ture has an uncanny way of making every gift he gives me fit like a glove. I wonder how he does that?

"You can keep it, no matter what your answer is." Ture makes me jump as he approaches with his cake. I didn't hear him approaching. "It was made for you. No one else. Here," He slides me the cake with a fork but doesn't look at me. "I hope you enjoy it, the blueberries are extra sweet."

Leaving the ring on, I pick up my fork and play with my dessert, as I watch Ture out the side of my eye. His focus on the food is too precise, and I know my response has hurt him, he's too kind to say so. It's not that I don't want him as my Kindred, I was just taken by surprise with his grand gesture. It's the kind of thing that I have always dreamed of but never in my dreams did I fuck up the answer so badly.

"I'm sorry, Ture." My voice is quiet, but I know he hears me as I stare down at my own plate. "I was just surprised, and I'm not very good with surprises. It's not a no, please just give me some time to wrap my head around it?"

A slender but calloused hand covers mine, stopping me from fidgeting with my fork, but I can't muster up the courage to look up and see his disappointment in me. "Take as long as you need, Alice. I'm not going anywhere."

A sob gets stuck in my throat and my eyes burn with unshed tears. Ture's way better to me than I deserve. His voice holds no judgement at all, only understanding and patience. "Thank you," is all I can say, taking the first bite of what turns out to be a mouth-watering cake. *Is there anything this man can't do?*

The rest of dinner passes in relative silence, and not exactly a comfortable one. At this point, I kind of want to finish my wine and dessert and get out of here as quickly as possible, but that plan changes with Ture's next words.

"I have another surprise for you, but I'm a little nervous to give it to you now after how well the last one went down." Ture rubs the back of his neck, squinting a bit in discomfort. "It's nothing quite as grand, though, I'm afraid. Should I risk it and bring it out? I asked the neighbouring Sorcerer Bubba to recommend what kind he thought would be a good choice because he's been to Earth numerous times over the last few centuries."

Now curious, I nod and tell him I'm game, but I was not expecting him to walk away and come back with a small white glowing orb, somewhat similar to the lights they use here but with a more yellow tinge and smaller. Ture places it on the table before me and reaches out his hand for me to take.

Hesitantly, I let him take my hand and pull me up as though I don't weigh a thing. Something I'll never get used to. With a smile, he guides me to an empty side of the room and says, "Music on."

The romantic, soft sounds of Micheal Bublé fill the room as he sings, 'The way you look tonight.' I beam at the familiar melody I've heard a million times in a life that feels so long ago now.

Ture slowly pulls me into his arms, looking down at me for permission as he does so. Letting him lead, Ture surprises me by dancing beautifully in the candlelight, swaying me to the tune, and effectively sweeping me off my feet. We get lost in the music and I find myself leaning my head against his chest with my eyes closed.

I remember, as a young girl, dancing with my Grandmother to music like this and her telling me that one day a tall, handsome man would take her place and make me feel like the princess I am. She would hum the music under her breath, and I would dream of a day that I would be loved and cherished so much by someone who would care for and protect me, but he never came, until today. I miss my Grandma so much, I wish she could see me now. I know she would be smiling down on me.

A silent tear slides down my cheek and I let it, the perfect moment between us tattoos itself to my heart, and I know I will never forget the way it feels to be held like this by Ture. A man that seems to truly love me just the way I am and has never asked me for anything except for my heart.

In this utopian moment, I know without a doubt that I am going to be brave and let this man in because even though it will risk me feeling so much pain if it doesn't work out, the risk of happiness with him is worth it.

Leaning back, I gaze up at Ture, garnering his attention, and I entwine my hand with the ring on with his and pull it between us, kissing his knuckles. "If you'll still have me, I'd love to be your Kindred. I'm sorry I didn't say it sooner. I was just scared, I still am, honestly."

His white teeth shine in the candlelight because Ture's grin grows so wide, "Really? You will?" Before I can confirm, he picks me up by the waist and swings me around in the air until my legs wrap around his waist for purchase and his lips smash down on mine. He whispers sweet nothings to me in between each kiss, and I know I'm cherished. I just hope it lasts forever because now that I know I have him, I don't want to lose him or Navy.

CHAPTER NINETEEN

ALICE

*L*ying across the smooth stone, with my eyes closed and my loose dress fluttering in the wind, I smile wistfully, humming 'fly me to the moon' with the sweet memories of last night fluttering in my head.

Ture and I made out with each other for what felt like hours and unlike Navy, he was content to not push me any farther than that, and I appreciated him all the more for it.

Speaking of, Navy tried to eat me out again as soon as I got back to the cabin because apparently, he lives in my room now. I was pleasantly surprised when he was so excited about how I'd accepted Ture's advances and even went so far as to ask me when we're moving into his place.

Being around Summer and Janice, I've gotten used to the idea of harems being a normative around here, but it's still so bizarre to me. How can anyone be excited about their partner loving up to someone else, let alone multiple someones? Mhanu are a hell of a lot more advanced than Humans, that's for sure. I am absolutely certain that I wouldn't be alright with it.

"I'm going for a quick swim," Navy says, and I turn my head to see him bounding down the rocky ledge as easily as if he was walking on a flat path. He's so graceful, it's ridiculous. They all are. "Let me know if you need anything and don't freak out."

Don't freak out. What's that supposed to mean?

I hear a twig snap, and I sit up to see Alexion off in the woods, sitting on a downed trunk and watching me. Now I get the 'don't freak out' reference. Well, if Navy doesn't think that Alexion is a safety risk and is content with leaving me up here with him, then I need to give him a chance.

He might stay in the shadows because of his scar, and I want him to know that I don't care about it. I know what it's like to want to hide away from the world and hope that no one sees you, but I also know how lonely that kind of existence is. I know it more now that I'm surrounded by people who care about me, the contrast between the two is a canyon apart.

"It's alright to come and sit with us, you know?" My voice didn't come out as confident as I wanted it to, but I can't turn into a whole new person overnight. I'm still nervous as shit.

Alexion slowly rises, his focus never leaving me, but his body language makes it look like he's about to bolt. How come someone so huge and ferocious looking can also look like a deer caught in headlights?

"Don't be a chicken shit. No one else is here, and you won't normally get this kind of chance," Navy calls out from the water as he wades into the deep end, and I look down to see a cheeky smile on his face.

I smile back down at him before turning back. However, when I do, Alexion is gone. The woods are quiet and not a person can be seen. I'm about to call out when a deep, almost painfully raspy voice beside me says, "You haven't been claimed. Why?"

Jumping so far that I almost pull a muscle, I squeak in surprise at the massive man beside me. How the heck did he move so fast and without sound? Talk about a predator.

He doesn't move or look away from me as I hold my hand to my chest trying to slow my sudden heartbeat increase, his long hair hangs half over his face, but the top of the scar is still visible. I try not to look at it in case he's self-conscious about it. I focus on his visible eye. The deep forest green captures my full attention, and I can't help the thought that it's a shame what happened to his other one. Not because I pity him but because it's just such a pretty eye.

"Why?" he repeats, squatting to the side of me but still far out of arm's reach after I don't reply.

I look down to see Navy splashing away happy as can be, thinking about how to answer this man that I've never spoken to before.

A grunt has me turning back to Alexion, a frown marring his face. "You scent of Navy and Ture, but you haven't fucked them yet." His words come out as crude as his raspy tone. "What about Salem and Baxter, do you not want their dicks inside you? I've seen you with them, staring at their bodies."

For someone who never talks to anyone, he sure has a lot to say today. "I don't think that's any of your business. Who do you th..."

My words are cut off as he leaps over to me and grabs my chin, lifting my face up to his. With his hair fallen to the side, I can take in the severity of his scar, and he doesn't flinch away, as if daring me to say something. I don't, but I don't cower down from his pointed gaze either.

Without warning, he tilts my head to the side and rubs his nose from my collarbone, slowly up to my ear, inhaling deeply and then letting out a deep purr. What is happening right now? I have no idea, but my core floods and tingles spread all over my body. Alexion nips at my earlobe, and I involuntarily shiver at the contact and let out a small, needy gasp.

Alexion jumps away from me in an instant and disappears back into the trees where he came from, and all I can do is rub my thighs together, needing the friction, and stare after him.

"Well, that was hot as fuck," Navy says from the top of the ledge, his body naked and dripping, and his cock large and hard. He grabs himself and looks down at me with hooded eyes. "Open your legs for me. I need to taste how wet you are."

Feeling uncharacteristically brave, I turn my body so that I'm facing him and slowly open my thighs, pulling my dress up so that he can see my core exposed because for some reason I can't find any of my underwear. Which I suspect Navy has something to do with.

A growl rips from deep within Navy, and he practically dives between my legs like a starving man, taking my clit into his mouth and sucking. With perfect precision, he licks and sucks me until I'm shaking and screaming out his name, not caring nearly as much as I should that other people might be able to hear me. A forbidden part of me hopes that Alexion is watching out there somewhere, wanting to touch me as much as I want him to.

I don't know what Navy has done to me, but my insatiable appetite for him eating me is non-stop. He's just so freaking good with his mouth. It makes me almost scared to find out how good he's going to be in bed. Navy might just kill me from pleasure.

"I wish you would let me enter you," Navy croons as he slides up my body, taking me in his arms. "But I'm very happy that you never deny me such a delicious meal."

Navy nudges and rubs his face along me and my neck just like a cat, nipping and licking me as he goes, his purr a soft lull that vibrates along my skin, and I seriously consider letting him take me right here until I hear someone clear their throat.

Practically shoving Navy off me, I look down to see Baxter, Ture, and Salem staring up at us, my dress still above my waist and showing all of what I've got. I slam my legs closed, scoot back and pull my dress over my legs frantically.

"Way to ruin my fun," Navy grumbles, flipping them off, and I flush so hard that I wonder if I can spontaneously catch on fire.

I fix my hair a little and ask, completely embarrassed, "How long were you guys standing there?"

Ture steps forwards, eyes hooded. "Long enough to get very, very hungry." His innuendo is absolutely not missed, and I'm not at all mad about it. The way he's looking up at me makes me feel sexy and wanted. The inner vixen that Navy has awoken inside me is all for it.

Then, I remember that Salem and Baxter are here too. I don't want them to be any more uncomfortable than they probably already are, so I get myself together and stand up, making my way down to the group.

Exchanging pleasantries with them, I try to act normal, like the guys didn't just catch an eyeful of me that they weren't bargaining for. I find it surprising that Baxter and Salem keep staring down at me like they should have been looking at each other, but I just chalk it up to me being hornier than I've ever been before and my mind making shit up.

Ture comes to stand behind me and wraps his arms around me. I try not to be self-conscious of the fact that he's touching my stomach, and only focus on the fact that he's being sweet. While still trying to suck my gut in as much as I can.

With a kiss to the side of my temple, Ture whispers, "You look beautiful today."

It's amazing how four simple words can make me feel so warm

inside. Four words that I'd never heard before I came to this village but since being here, I hear them all the time. Except for Mischa, but she's a bitch, and I refuse to let her vile words hurt me any more.

"How about we head back?" Navy comes over after pulling his pants up, his smile wide. "I'm still hungry and if you're not going to let me eat you again, then you'd better take me to food."

Baxter laughs and puts his arm around Navy playfully. "Let's go stick some food in your mouth before you take Alice prisoner in the bedroom like you did this morning." His laugh is jovial and light, and it makes my mood lift even more.

Right! It's official, I'm never leaving this place. I'm much too happy here to leave. I guess this is my new home.

With a smile, I grab Ture's hand, and we follow the other three guys back to the village, laughing all the way.

CHAPTER TWENTY

ALICE

The day started off the same as all the others, but with the mid-summer festival coming up, the air is thick with excitement. Cheetah Shifters everywhere are building stalls, organising fun and games, and deciding what kind of feast will be had. I've got to be honest, I'm getting pretty excited about it.

The mid-summer festival has been around for as long as they can remember and no one seems to know how it originated, but what's abundantly clear is that it's beloved by all.

"What are you going to do for it this year?" Baxter asks Salem as they lounge on the couch. We've decided on a lazy day today because of the sweltering heat outside.

Salem picks at the grapes on the table, popping one into his mouth. "Mmm, I'm not sure. Maybe I could organise a three-legged race or a spoon race."

"Why does everything have to be a race with you people?" I ask with a groan.

They both laugh and Salem throws a grape at me, hitting me in the chest, and it goes straight between my breasts.

"Bullseye!" Baxter calls out on another laugh, high-fiving Salem, who then gives a mocking bow.

I roll my eyes at their childish manner and dig it out. I have to pull my shirt out a bit to get at it. As I go to put it in my own mouth, Salem leans over suddenly and takes it from me, sticking it in his mouth before I can object.

"That's *my* grape," he purrs, sitting back with his eyes going half-lidded.

I wiggle in my seat at the heated look. "Um, that would have been gross and sweaty," I complain, my face screwed up at the thought of how yucky it must have tasted.

Baxter scoffs and Salem says, "Nope. Salty, sweet, and delicious. I love the way you taste. It's a shame that only Navy knows just how good, though."

I almost choke on my own spit and splutter a bit. *What the heck?* I look between the two and don't see any anger from Baxter. If anything, he seems pleased with Salem's remark.

Alright, I'll ignore that. "Do you guys want a drink? I made some iced tea this morning." I get up and walk to the kitchen, turning for their answer, I notice both males' eyes on my ass. "Excuse you, there's no tea down there."

"Ha. Sorry. We'd love some," Baxter adds, not at all looking guilty for being caught.

What is these guys' deal? They live together, and I hardly ever see them apart from one another, but sometimes I'm sure they're flirting with me or checking me out. Maybe they have an open relationship and also like women. My curiosity starts getting the better of me and I decide to just be blunt and ask them. I hope they don't think I'm rude, but I'd like to think that we are good enough friends that they won't mind.

I set an iced tea down in front of each of them and then sit down with my own. "I have a question," I start with, continuing when it's clear they're waiting. "Do you two have an open relationship?"

"What do you mean by that?" Salem asks before taking a sip. "Oh, this is really nice. You should make this for the mid-summer festival. It would be great on a hot day like that."

Clearing my throat, I try to figure out how to word it so that they will understand me. "Uh, well, do you both date other people as well as each other?"

They just stare at me with wide and confused gazes. So I try again.

"You two love each other, do you also physically love others with each other's permission?"

Baxter frowns and points to Salem. "I'm sorry, do you think Salem and I are Kindreds with each other?"

"Yes, and of course, I don't think anything is wrong with that. I think you both make a very cute couple," I stammer out, a bit uncomfortable with the way he's looking at me.

Salem all of a sudden starts laughing his ass off, having to put his drink down, he's laughing so much. "Holy Gods above, that's funny. What made you think that?" he asks as he catches his breath again, while Baxter looks kind of offended.

I stutter a bit and wonder if I got it wrong. "You live together and are really close," I trail off and realise how stupid I sound. I've never once seen one of them be romantic or touchy with the other, maybe they just have an epic bromance after all. The idea of that makes me a little nervous because I've been way more relaxed and open around them, thinking that they wouldn't notice my body as much because of it.

Salem puts his arm around Baxter and pulls him in. "How about a kiss, babe?" he asks him, licking his face, and Baxter jumps off the couch horrified.

With his hands up in defence, Baxter looks at me wild-eyed. "I have absolutely nothing wrong with that dynamic, but I am most definitely not into males. I want a female, no, I want *my* female. Is this why you never look at me like that? Because of him?" He points accusatorily at Salem like he's got the plague.

Salem just starts laughing again at the way Baxter is way overdoing it. I get it, his point is made. I wonder if I should save him from himself or let him keep going.

Deciding to let Baxter off the hook, I say with a wide smile, Salem's laughter and gaiety becoming contagious, "Sorry for assuming wrong. You can calm down now. You're obviously not together, I get it. Such a shame though because you two are cute together."

I look at Salem, and he nods in agreement and Baxter, now smiling, slaps the back of his head. "Yeah. I went over the top, didn't I? I feel like a right ass now. Forgive my outburst?"

"It's already forgotten. So tell me, have either of you been interested in any of the ladies that have come through so far?"

They both get uncomfortably quiet all of a sudden, and I look between them. "I'm sorry, was that rude to ask?" I'm quite certain that the change in atmosphere has to do with my question somehow.

Salem does a deep inhale and exhale with his eyes closed and then gets up and sits next to me instead, taking my hands into his. His actions make my stomach flip, and I tell myself that it's not what I think and to calm down.

"Do you remember when you came to the medical centre at Threshold after you had an accident with Summer?" Salem asks, and I frown wondering why that has anything to do with what I asked, but I nod anyway. "Well, when Baine carried you in, my heart stopped and started again, and I knew why immediately. I also knew why I couldn't say or do anything about it."

He pauses, and so does my brain. *No way!*

Baxter adds with a chuckle, "You might need to be a bit blunter. Alice's eyes have glazed over."

"Alice!" Salem's voice is louder and gets my full attention. "You're my Kindred, and I'm sorry that I've been keeping it from you, but back then it was too early for me to say anything and then when you came here I knew that I couldn't just bombard you with it. It didn't seem fair."

"We actually had a coalition meeting after you and Mischa went to bed," Baxter interjects. "It was important that your Kindreds came forwards to prevent any fights within the village. So, everyone was very clear from the first day who your Kindreds were and to respect that."

I pull my hands back and stand up, needing space. "Everyone but us, apparently!" I know I'm justifiably angry because this is a massive thing to keep from someone, but on the inside, I also know that I wouldn't have been able to handle Navy, Ture, and Salem all coming up to me on the first day and declaring their undying love. I'm still mad, though. I've been here for quite some time at this point, and I had no idea that Salem felt this way. I've considered him my friend, and it feels like a blow to the stomach that he's kept the way he feels for me hidden for so long.

Salem stands and steps into my personal space. "Please don't push me away. I see the anger on your face, but I didn't want to force you to accept me before you were ready. Please tell me I haven't ruined everything?"

"What... what am I supposed to do now?" I stutter, feeling lost and taken back.

"Whatever you think is right," he tells me, his eyes open and vulnerable. "I don't have a grand gesture or a handmade gift to bestow upon you, I only have my heart and my future, but it's all yours if you'll accept it."

How am I meant to say no to him? Especially when I've developed feelings for him and even Baxter that I've been trying to hide because of what I thought their relationship was. Fuck it. At this point, I've already come this far.

"Okay. Let's do this shit, but if you lie to me ever again or keep anything important from me, I'll be so pissed at you."

Baxter clears his voice and stands up, shuffling his feet awkwardly. "Is this a good or bad time to let you know that I'm your Kindred, too?"

"Oh, for fuck's sake," Mischa shrieks from the hallway. "You've got to be kidding me. I can't get laid here, but fatty gets a whole harem of hot guys. Where is the justice?" She storms to her room and slams the door.

We all stare after her and her temper tantrum before looking at each other and bursting out laughing. It may very well be hysteria. *How the fuck is this my life right now?*

CHAPTER TWENTY-ONE

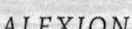

ALEXION

Once again, I look around, the distinct feeling of being tracked rising the hair on the back of my neck. Nothing seems out of place, and I don't catch a whiff of anything unfamiliar on the wind when I raise my nose, inhaling. I contemplate shifting to my Cheetah because I know my senses are heightened in that form, but something inside me tells me that I need to leave, and I never ignore my instincts.

Still in my male form, I speed up to a pushing run, whipping through the trees, my eyes focused before me while my other senses keep a vigil on my surroundings for any possible threat. It's not often that I run away from anything any more, not since... my thoughts drift away from that time, needing not to get stuck inside such a visceral memory.

With graceful movements, I glide through the woods until breaking the tree line next to my cabin. I stop instantly, not wanting to draw anyone's attention to me by making any sudden movements. I live out here for a reason, I don't want or need anyone in my life. The only reason I came back into a coalition was because of my beast's need to be part of one.

Luckily, the other Cheetahs here have given me the space I require and have never tried to encroach on my privacy or past too much. I know they've heard the rumours of what happened to the village where I'm from, and I wouldn't have blamed them if they'd turned me away, but for Gods know what reason, they didn't.

With a driving need that I can't deny, I move quietly along the border, my eyes focused on the cabin I know that *she's* in. I tell myself I'm just making sure that the females are safe, and that I'm not going to act on anything. But not even I buy my own shit.

The undeniable pull I have to Alice is nothing like I've ever experienced. I fought so many things in my life, but this might very well be the hardest fight I've ever come across. I know I can't have her, I don't deserve her but tell that to my body. I remind myself as her curvaceous form comes into view that if I let myself go near her, she will die. They all die, it's my curse, and she doesn't deserve that fate just because I was selfish.

Alice giggles sweetly as Baxter tickles her ribs. She tries to hide behind a pole, but he catches her and a laughing fit ensues. Watching the carefree exchange squeezes my heart. I'm torn between being relieved that she has other Kindreds to bring her happiness and furious that the universe would expect me to share her. Alexion doesn't share!

Shaking my head, I push off the outrage at Baxter's hands on what's mine and make myself step back several feet. I need space between us before I jump out and rip his fucking face off.

I must have moved too fast because Alice's gaze moves to mine, locking us within a stare that I find almost impossible to tear myself from. Her small hand rises to wave, and it snaps me out of my trance.

Running away from something for the second time in under an hour, I bolt to my cabin, slamming the door behind me. The depths of my cowardice, mocking me.

I close my eyes and am transported to a past I can never escape.

* * *

SIXTY YEARS AGO

"WHY ARE WE HERE?" Jamal's small voice asks me, his hand holding onto my uninjured arm like a vice. "I don't like it here, Alexion. Can we go home?"

Home. The only home we've ever known is gone, and as I look down at his wide green eyes, I have no idea how to tell him that. Instead, I simply say, "Don't worry about it Fluff, Kessar said that this is a safe place, and we need to trust him, alright? Show me what a big boy you can be."

With a big exhalation, Jamal lifts his head higher, and pulls his shoulders back, being a brave little soldier for his big brother even though he trembles all over, but I don't remark on that. "Great job, Fluff." I ruffle his unruly hair with my bandaged and sore hand, knowing he needs the contact. It's in our nature to be overly physical, especially when we need comfort.

I look around the dingy dungeon that we've been placed in by Kessar's so-called friends and wonder what on Rathe he's gotten us into. My own fears are dangerously close to the surface when surrounded by shackles, dried blood stains on the floor, and no windows to escape from. It's enough that I don't even feel my own horrific pain.

My heart clenches at the instant thought of the rest of our family that was trapped regardless of windows. Their screams are on constant repeat in my head. Phillis's desperate plea for me to save her will haunt me every single day until I die.

The door suddenly opens, and four large males enter, with various shades of scowls on their faces, and Jamal shifts his body so close to mine that he's practically a part of my leg.

"Come on, kid," one of them says, his hand out for Jamal. You're coming with us." Jamal's arms wrap around my body, and he starts to shiver uncontrollably. "Please, don't let them take me," Jamal pleads with a trembling voice.

Ignoring the pain in my lower back and hands, I pull Jamal behind me. "Where's Kessar?" I ask, letting my voice boom loud and braver than I feel. "Jamal's not going anywhere without me or him, and that's final."

Kessar chooses that moment to pop his head inside the door. "Come on, Fluff. We've got a nicer room for you to rest in while these guys fix up Alexion's injuries." His eyes rise to mine. "Don't act like a child. You're too old for that shit."

My gut instinct tells me not to let Jamal go, but it's Kessar after all, he wouldn't let anything happen to our little brother. I tell myself while trying to calm my urge to hold him behind me until we're out of here.

Jamal makes the decision for me and runs to Kessar, holding him tight around the waist. Looking back at me with hope, he asks me, "Will you be alright, Alexion? Or do you need me to stay and make you feel better?"

My little fluff, the name that mama gave him after he was born because of his fluffy hair, is the sweetest of kids and has always done what he can to make others around him feel good. He will be a great male one day.

"You go. I'll get all fixed and meet you out there after. Do what Kessar says and behave, okay?" With a nod, he follows Kessar out.

One of the guys moves over to close the door behind him, and the four of them surround me. I have a sinking feeling they aren't here to kiss my boo-boos better. "What's going on?" I don't bother pretending that I don't see the malice aimed at me.

The biggest of the group steps forwards. "You were meant to be watching the girl, but you let her go back!" he growls at me, fury evident.

The girl? My sister, Phillis? Why would they be concerned with the loss of my sister?

I already know she's dead because of me. If only I hadn't let her run home before me. Why didn't I keep her hand in mine, keep her safe beside me? My heart squeezes and I try not to retch as I once again hear her screams echoing inside my fractured mind. "Alexion."

Without warning, a hammer-hard punch smashes against my skull, and I land hard on the ground with a heavy thud. My head ricocheting off the solid stone floor.

My eyes peel open, and I groan, trying to lift my hand to my head. The male's face bends low to be right above mine, and I moan out, "Why?"

They laugh in unison, and it gets cut off by another scream in my head again, "Alexion." It sounds so real that I wonder if I have a head injury, but another piercing scream renders the air from beyond the walls. *What? That's not Phillis.*

"Alexion help me." Screams out from Jamal's voice, and my gaze whips to the door before a foot crashes down on my head, sealing the terror for my little brother in darkness.

* * *

PRESENT

A HOT TEAR rolls down my bearded cheek, and I let my head drop with the constant screams that rip apart every second of my every day from the two people I was meant to protect. They should be here, laughing and living their lives the best that they can, but instead, I'm here trapped inside my own mind, trying to stay away from anyone that can be hurt just by knowing me. Never ever do I want to hear Alice's scream. I will do anything to protect her from me, from the death and pain I bring.

As if I conjured her from the darkest corner of my mind, her soft voice breaks through my dreaded memory. "Alexion, what's wrong?"

I practically jump, and I instantly scold myself for not being aware of my surroundings. How did she get inside my home without me hearing or smelling her? Her floral scent is so strong that I can't imagine how she got this close to me. *How far gone was I inside my own memories?*

Yet as I look at her innocent blue eyes looking up at me, a hand frozen halfway between us as though she wants to touch me, I know I don't have the strength right now to push her away. The need to feel her skin against mine is uncontrollable.

"Touch me." I practically beg, the sound of my voice another reminder of that dreaded day.

CHAPTER TWENTY-TWO

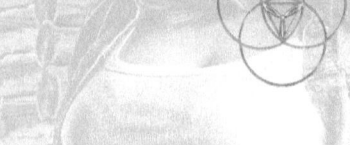

ALICE

Unable to help myself, when I saw Alexion take off running back to his cabin after sharing such a deep and intense moment from even that far away from each other, I had to follow him.

Baxter warned me against going, but after reminding him that he should learn to trust me since he's my Kindred, and what a mindfuck that is, he reluctantly let me go. I'm not under any illusion that he isn't really close by, but I appreciate he's giving me the space I asked for.

At the door to Alexion's place, I go to knock but hear what sounds like a pained moan. My hand pushes the already ajar door open. I know I shouldn't just walk in, but he sounds like he's hurting, and I don't want him to run from me again if he needs help.

I'm not prepared for what I find when I walk inside. Alexion's massive frame is pressed hard against the back wall, hands clenched at his side, with his muscles and veins straining to the max. A rogue tear slips down his fully bearded cheek, getting lost within the rugged mess, and I unconsciously step forward, the need to comfort him too loud to ignore.

Reaching out for him, I croon, "Alexion, what's wrong?" and it's like I shot him the way his body jerks in surprise and I freeze, regretting my decision to just let myself into the poor guy's house. I didn't want to frighten him.

Holding my breath, his voice rasps two words, and I don't know who's more stunned by them, me or him. "Touch me."

Unsure if he meant them, I keep still for a second but the vulnerable way his good eye looks at me has me inhaling and stepping forwards, letting my now shaking hand rest softly on his chest and Alexion shudders under my touch, his own hand rises and holds my hand tighter to him.

I look between his two eyes, one a dark forest green and the other like a fluffy cloud rolling over the forest green hidden behind. It makes me wonder how he got such a horrific injury, if this is what keeps him hiding in the shadows, or if his real injury lies much deeper.

The thudding of Alexion's heart beats fast and hard under my hand, and I rub my fingers softly over the spot, his hand still covering my own, and he moans, closing his eyes. Clearly, savouring such a simple touch.

How long has it been since another person touched this man? Is he so alone in this world that he is so starved for attention? It makes me feel bold, and I lift my other hand wordlessly to flutter softly against the tough skin of his cheek. The whole time, Alexion stares down at me, letting me touch and look my fill.

I go to pull my hand back, but his other hand shoots up and

grasps my wrist, not hard enough to hurt, but hard enough to stop me from taking it back. "Please, don't stop."

His voice, even though raw and deep, is so fucking sexy that I have to rub my thighs together, imagining what his purr would feel like against my most private places.

Alexion's eyes darken, and he leans forward, sniffing the air deeply. I lick my lips and do something that shocks me, too. Leaning up on my tiptoes, I softly peck his lips, wanting to see how he'll react while feeding my curious heart. The pull I feel towards him is so similar to the others that I have to know if it's just me, or if he is what I think he is.

In a split second, I'm off my feet, my back smashed against the wall, my legs around his waist, skirt up and his mouth hard and hungry on mine. Alexion's tongue plunges into my mouth, and I meet it stroke for stroke, everything primal inside me feeding off his energy and lapping it up greedily.

Alexion's hips grind against me and his rock-hard, clothed cock pushes against my now exposed core in just the right spot, ripping a moan from my throat and into Alexion's mouth, who growls in response.

The friction between us builds up, and before I know what's happening, an orgasm is torn from me just from this movement alone. With frenzied, clumsy movements from us both, Alexion tears his pants down and pushes inside me, my orgasm still spasming my insides, but with unrelenting need, he pushes his wide girth all the way to the hilt before pulling out and pushing in even harder.

"Fuck," I cry out at the fierce pressure it puts against my swollen g-spot, and he uses it as fuel, pistoning hard and wild inside me, my back smashing against the wall, and my thighs shaking around his waist from the intensity building between us.

Alexion fucks me so hard that I can't catch my breath, his face bobs to my neck, and he nips and licks at it, tasting me as much as he can. "Harder," I moan, even though there's no possible way he can fuck me harder at this point.

To prove my brain wrong, he turns with me in his arms, still pistoning furiously. We reach his couch, and he pulls me off him without a word and turns me, bending my body over the arm of the chair and pushing my head down so that my ass is in the air and totally exposed.

Before I can protest, his mouth latches on to my pussy, and he purrs in deep satisfaction, tasting against my sensitive nub. His ministrations are hungry, the longing he's had for wanting to taste me is obvious with every lick and suck.

He's unrelenting with his mouth until I cry out as I cum again, just before he stands back up and shoves his cock back inside me so hard that I jolt and cry out again, maximising the orgasms I was already having.

The pleasure is so intense that I feel like I might actually die from it. My whole body shakes with the severity of it, and he just fucks me even harder. The smacking of our bodies together and the wetness growing between us reverberates throughout the room, with our moans and grunts of ecstasy.

When I think my heart's sure to give out, Alexion leans over me, biting hard down on my shoulder, and uses all his strength to get as deep inside me as he can and growls low and deep against me. His cum fills me so much that I can feel the heat and pressure of it.

We lie like that, trembling together and catching our breath, my head heavy from being mostly upside down, but I couldn't care less. If this is how good sex normally is, I've been severely missing out. *Omar, wherever you are, you're shit and your dick is tiny.*

Alexion lets go of my neck and starts licking it tenderly, and I close my eyes. *Man, I'm gonna hurt tomorrow.* It looks like I'm going to need to get used to being bruised and bitten. Totally worth it.

I let out a deep sigh and relax my body, if I wasn't sure before, I am now because the moment Alexion came deep inside me a piece of my soul felt like it clicked into place. He *is* my Kindred, and I *am* his. I don't know why I was so scared of this feeling. It's amazing.

Like he's been electrocuted, Alexion suddenly freezes, his breath sucking in.

"Are you alright?" I question, worried about his abrupt change.

Without a word he withdraws his still-hard dick slowly, cum pouring out of me the instant he's gone, and I feel empty, wanting him back inside me. I turn my head to see him stepping back with his hands up and his eyes wild, shaking his head.

"What?" I sit up and turn around, looking for whatever it was that's startled such a big guy so badly. Seeing nothing unusual, I ask again, "What's wrong?"

When I step forwards, he steps back and looks absolutely disgusted, his face twisted and freaked out.

I instantly pull my skirt down and fold my arms around myself. *Did I do something wrong? Is it because of how I look?* Regret is plain to see all over Alexion, and I want to vomit. It's like Omar, all over again.

"This never happened," he growls at me. "Stay away from me and my house." His tone demands compliance, and for the first time since I came here, I feel frightened.

Stepping back, my voice breaks with my heart, "I - I don't understand. Aren't you my Kindred?" I know I look and sound pathetic, but I'm confused and scared, and I don't know what to do. He claimed me. He fucking claimed me, and now he's going to break me down.

Alexion pulls his shoulders back and stands taller, his features hardening. "Get. Out. Of. My. House." He punctuates every word like a bullet to my soul, and I feel another piece of my self-confidence die.

What did I expect? It's me, after all. Who would want me the way I am?

Without my permission, tears roll unchecked down my cheeks as I step back. The flood of rejection is a mighty one. It's the kind of hurt that digs itself into your centre, clamps on tightly, and gnaws away at the very essence of who you are. When a person you think cares about you, rejects you on such a primal level, the hurt is forever.

I turn and barrel out of the house, tripping over myself in the front garden and falling to rip up my knee on a rock. Ignoring the pain and blood, I get back up ungracefully making my way back to the safety of my room, ugly crying the whole way.

Concerned eyes turn and watch me as I stumble along, but I ignore their questions and stares, needing to be alone to wallow in my own self-pity.

When I get to the house, I fly past Mischa and down the hall, slamming my bedroom door behind me. I dive onto my bed and cry even harder as I feel the remnants of our union running down my thigh.

Navy bursts through the door unceremoniously, "Alice! What happened to you? I smell blood and..." He stops and growls so low and mean that I have to turn around to see why he changed so suddenly, and then his words register. He must be so disappointed in me for sleeping with Alexion when I haven't even slept with him yet.

"I'm s-s-sorry," I cry, curling into a ball, with my head in my hands.

The growling stops as quickly as it starts, and Navy crawls onto the bed and pulls me into his arms, encircling me as tight as he can without hurting me. He coos and soothes me with soft words of love and affection, telling me that I have nothing to be sorry about.

He lets me fall apart in his embrace without judgement and then helps me put myself back together again until I feel raw and exhausted until there's nothing left inside.

I don't even realise that Baxter's in the room with us until I turn in the bed, finding him lying right behind me with unshed tears in his own eyes.

"My queen, why are you crying? What can I do?" Baxter's voice comes out desperate and tense, my pain seeming to hurt him as well.

With no illusion, they can both smell what I did with Alexion, I bury my head in Baxter's chest and explain what happened and how it ended.

"I don't know what I did wrong," I sniffle, trying to wipe my face with the blanket below me. Snot, tears and utter destruction is a mess all over me.

Why can't I be a pretty crier? I bet Mischa cries pretty.

Baxter smooths my hair, as Navy rubs circles on my back. The former whispers to me, "You did nothing wrong, and I'm so proud of you for letting yourself be loved. We aren't going anywhere, and you take as long as you like, but I guarantee you that something like that would never happen with any of us. You are the stars, the sun, and the moon for us, and we will cherish you forever, the way you deserve to be."

I listen to his words and let them settle on my heart, trying to heal my fresh wound, and I slowly start drifting off to sleep. The last thing I remember is Baxter handing me to Navy and telling him he's going to take care of business.

I hope Alexion's ready to run again.

CHAPTER TWENTY-THREE

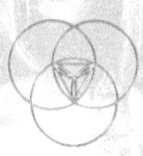

MISCHA

I shake with rage at the audacity of Alice for taking another Kindred. How many does the fat slut need? Leave a little meat for the rest of us.

As I eavesdrop on Baxter telling Ture and Salem about what Alexion did to Alice, my mood considerably lifts. Serves her fucking right for not keeping her legs closed.

Baxter takes off to go and find Alexion, and I walk in the opposite direction, needing to get away from all the love-struck fools of this village. The sooner I can get away from here and on to the next place, the better because clearly the men here are pathetic and don't know a good thing when they see it.

Grumbling to myself about Alice and her Kindreds and walking through the trees, I eventually look up and realise that I have no idea where I am. I turn on the spot, but it all looks the same in every direction. *Where's a Starbucks when you need one?*

I'm so sick of being stuck in this mother fucking shithole. I want to go back to Earth where my beauty is appreciated and worshipped as it should be. I didn't fight to get away from the low-rent life my Russian single mother brought me up in, get out of the reach of her drug habits and nasty pimps of Los Angeles, and work myself up to be able to spend this much money on making myself utterly perfect just to be left out in the wilderness with beast men that would rather fuck a repulsive pig.

Trying to retrace my steps, I stomp around unhappily until a distant hissing has me pausing. It must be one of those cat people. Putting on my nicest accented voice, I call out, "Who's there? I'm lost, and I need help."

Hurry up, you nasty thing. I'm getting tired.

No one answers me, so I shrug it off and keep walking, but I get a bad feeling that has my hair standing on end. Is something stalking me out here?

I look around again but still don't see anything out of the ordinary. Just then I turn back and a massive, and I mean massive, guy is standing right in front of me, naked as the day he was born and scowling so ferociously that if looks could kill, I'd be beyond deceased. A mean-looking jagged scar on his chest.

"Hello, little female. So, you're lost, are you?" he growls out through clenched teeth. I have definitely never seen this guy before, and I step back in fear. "Yes. Run. I love a good chase."

My body freezes, and I almost wee myself at his dark look. "What do you want?" I squeak.

He steps forwards, a hard dick tapping my stomach, and I instantly think the worst, but he surprises me by asking, "You know Alexion, yes?" I nod quickly. "You don't like the round female, do you?" I agree, shaking my head. "Good. Then we have much to discuss."

The big guy starts walking to my left, and I think for a moment that he's going to leave me, but he calls back without turning, "You'd better follow me if you don't want my Cheetah to hunt you down."

Deciding that it's best not to make the Neanderthal angry, I follow him, keeping a decent distance between us until we reach a large tree with scratches all along the bottom as if it's been used as a giant cat scratcher.

He swivels and nods to a fallen trunk. "Sit." It's a demand and I do what I'm told, looking around for any sign of someone else, but there isn't a trace.

"It seems we have similar interests, smelly one," he starts and I sit up straighter.

"Who are you calling smelly? You're the one that looks like you need a shower." I clamp my mouth shut at his look and tell myself to keep quiet.

His top lip curls in distaste and he growls out. "Your scent burns like freshly squeezed lemons. It's fucking terrible. That's why no one here will go near you." Positioning himself in front of me, his dick way too close to my face for my comfort, he talks. "I am Kessar, Alexion's older brother. That son of a bitch killed my whole family and gave me this scar." Pointing to his chest and now that I take a closer look at him, I can see the similarities with his large build, green eyes, and hard planes. "He doesn't deserve a Kindred or to even breathe in this world. Just like your chubby friend doesn't deserve to steal all of your males. Am I right?"

If he's going to talk with such good logic, who am I to brush him off so quickly? "So, you've been watching?" I ask. "She's so fat and gross. I don't know what she's done to turn them against me, but she has to be stopped."

Kessar smiles wickedly, his eyes glinting with intelligence. "Exactly my point. I can't go into the village because Alexion will turn them against me, and they won't see you for the beauty you are with her in the way. I propose a truce between the two of us that will settle things for both of us."

My mind goes to the image of those gorgeous men drooling over the fat pig, and my anger rises again. "What do you need me to do?" I refuse to come second to someone like that. Not now, not ever.

"All I need from you is for you to bring the female to me during the mid-summer festival. I will do the rest, little one." His hands are outstretched as he explains, but a piece inside me niggles that something about this feels wrong. I don't like her, but I don't want to kill her or anything.

I bite my lip in thought, can I really do something like this? "What exactly are you going to do to Alice?" I need to know that it's nothing too heinous, I'm not a monster after all.

Kessar steps back with a smile. "I won't kill the human if that's what you're worried about, and I have no interest in forcing my body into hers. My brother has touched her, it would be like fucking a pile of shit."

Oh, I like that analogy. I chuckle at that and cross my legs, feeling much more confident and interested in the idea now that I know Alice is in no real danger.

"How will you having Alice help you get back at your brother then?"

"He will follow her here. I only need her to pull him away from the others. I owe him for all the pain he's caused, after all. Then I'll just take her to the next village over and give her to them to keep." Kessar turns and starts walking away. "Time to go, female, follow me and I will point the way out."

I get up and run after him, following about three steps behind because I'm not an idiot and wouldn't trust him with my life, only Alice's. I giggle again at the thought.

Kessar points to a clearing ahead and tells me it connects to the lake, and I can easily get my way back to the village from there.

"See you during the festival, female. Bring her right here and I'll take over. Don't worry about a thing. Both our problems will be over soon."

With that, he disappears back into the brush and I smile wide, whistling my way back, a renewed skip in my step.

CHAPTER TWENTY-FOUR

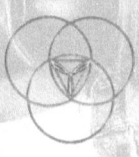

BAXTER

$\mathcal{A}$bsolute fury burns and boils my insides at the very thought of Alexion disrespecting Alice in such a gut-wrenching way. How dare he take advantage of my Kindred like that. I don't care that she's his Kindred as well, it doesn't give someone the right to behave that way. When I find that son of a bitch, I'm going to show him why I'm the lead warrior of our coalition. It's about time he was put in his place.

Alexion's cabin comes into view and my footfalls speed up, the desire to have my fingers around his neck pushing me into a run. It's a shame I can't kill him, but now that he's claimed Alice, their lives are irrevocably linked, and until she claims another one of her Kindreds, if something happens to him, we will lose her too.

I can't believe Alexion is Alice's Kindred. How did I not see that coming? Especially after that weird thing at the lake. I feel like an absolute idiot when it seems so obvious looking back. Hindsight I suppose.

There's also a selfish part of me that is hurt by Alice choosing Alexion over me. I've been nothing but a good male to her, and I would do anything in my power to make her happy, but instead of running into my arms, she ran into his.

Every time I see the heart-stopping beauty of Alice and hear the lyrical lilt to her soft laughter, my dick gets so hard that I'm worried I'll embarrass myself accidentally by jizzing in my pants.

My thoughts are selfish, and I am ashamed that I'm even having them when my queen is in her room broken down and needing my support more than ever. I brush my traitorous thoughts away and focus on what's truly important. Bashing Alexion's stupid head in.

As I come across his house, a loud smashing pulls me short. Has someone already beat me to it? Not wanting to give away my presence I round the side and peer into the window that opens into his family room.

The room is trashed, with crumpled-up and destroyed furniture littered all around. A distraught and unkempt Alexion is in the centre, his long hair in all directions as if he tried to pull it out in clumps.

The visual is so shocking that it settles my own anger considerably. What has happened to this male in his life that he's reduced to this?

Alexion picks up a dining chair and smashes it against the wall, a shard bouncing off and embedding in his arm. Without missing a beat, he rips it out and picks up the next chair, throwing it before collapsing onto his knees, his head back in a primal roar of pure agony.

I feel his cry to the very core of my being and know without a doubt that this situation isn't as cut and dry as any of us realise. Something so much deeper is going on within Alexion, and my beast whimpers inside me, wanting to soothe his pain.

He collapses forwards as his large body is wracked with sobs, his shoulders shaking from the strength of it. Alexion cries so hard that his breaths come out broken and severed, his body closed in on itself on the floor.

Knowing that he's already in so much pain, I take pity on him and decide that he's clearly punishing himself enough for the both of us and nothing I can do to him will hurt him worse than he's already feeling. I truly hope that whatever his personal journey is, it brings him out on the side of us, so we as a Kindredship can help him through it.

He will have to choose that for himself, though, so I step away from the window and leave Alexion to bathe in his own agony. Agony that I believe he deserves after what he just put Alice through because no matter what his own issues are, he had no right to lay them at the doorstep of her heart.

Walking away, I head straight back to the love of my life because my own beast needs soothing after all the turmoil we've seen today and I won't feel at ease again until I hold her close to my heart once again.

I step inside and find Navy talking to Ture, they both stop and turn to me with questioning gazes. No doubt wondering why I'm back so soon. It wasn't exactly hidden that I was about to gift Alexion with an ass whooping of grand proportions.

"Not now," I tell them, needing to get to Alice. "Let's just say he's taken care of and leave it at that for now."

Excusing myself, I open the door to Alice's room and see her curled up against Salem's chest, fast asleep but with the odd whimper still making an appearance.

Salem looks at me solemnly, and I slide onto the bed behind Alice, wrapping myself around her warm body, nuzzling her neck, and kissing her shoulder tenderly. There isn't anything I wouldn't do to keep my queen safe and happy. I never want to see or hear that kind of anguish coming from her ever again.

Alice wiggles in my arms and a tired voice asks, "Is that you, Baxter?"

"Yes, my queen. Just rest and know that we have you, and you're loved." I kiss her cheek this time. "So much."

Salem adds, "By all of us."

"Are you both mad at me?" she asks with a sniffle, sounding like she's going to cry again, and I squeeze her tight.

I tell her honestly, "We would never be mad at you for claiming a Kindred. That's what we're here for, and it's not like we were very forthcoming about what you were to us. So, if anyone's to blame, it's us. You deserved for us to be truthful with you the moment you walked into our village, but we weren't, and I can never take that mistake back. That doesn't mean we aren't happy for you to claim your other Kindreds."

"It's not going to change the way we think of you or how much you mean to us." Salem tenderly moves the flyaway hairs sticking to Alice's moist face. "There's no hurry because we aren't going anywhere. Not without you by our sides, and as for Alexion," he growls low. "He's obviously not worthy of your love and attention, and I'm not going to pretend that I'm okay with his actions. He's got to answer to every single one of us for the way he's behaved, most of all, you."

Alice shakes her head, hiding her face under Salem's arm. "No. I don't want to see him," she mumbles, and it breaks my heart again.

"I know, baby, and you don't have to," Salem assures her, then looks at me, his eyes filled with all the feels, I'm sure that I'm mirroring.

I hate seeing her this way, but I vow to make her smile every day from now on. Fuck Alexion and his issues.

CHAPTER TWENTY-FIVE

ALICE

Overwhelmed doesn't even begin to describe how I'm feeling right now as I hear Navy saying goodbye to the others for the night. It's been such a full day between the intensity of the sex I had, the heart-wrenching feeling of rejection from Alexion, and the devoted expressions of love by Baxter and Salem.

I breathe a sigh of relief when Navy comes back to our room, closing the door behind him and joining me on the bed. His strong arms envelop me tightly, and I let my cheek rest against his chest, focusing on the soft rhythm of his steady heartbeat.

"I love you." My words are simple but painstakingly true. "Thank you for never making me feel less."

He kisses me softly on the top of my head and strokes my hair tenderly before whispering back to me. "I love you too, Alice. Thank you for not making me feel less."

Aren't we a pair? The two of us not quite belonging anywhere before now but perfect in each other's embrace, never to be alone again because I know without a shadow of a doubt that Navy will never leave my side and will always put me first for the rest of our lives together and if I have anything to say about it, it'll be a long time.

Everything falls into place inside me and all doubts are gone as I lift myself up, raising my lips to his. I refuse to wait to commit to this man, my own insecurities need to be put aside for this. For once, I'm going to let my heart choose courage. I could have let today defeat me and pull me even further down into myself, but Navy doesn't deserve it, and neither do I.

"Claim me, Navy, I'm yours," I breathe into his mouth, with gentle pecks along his lips. "I don't want to wait any more."

Navy groans quietly, kissing me harder before pulling back to look down at me. "Are you sure Alice because I can't take it back when it's done, and I don't want to be a mistake you made because of Alexion?"

For someone who's been fighting for this moment, he's being surprisingly understanding of my potential inner turmoil. It just makes me love him even more that he would step out of his logical comfort zone to make sure that I'm truly alright with this decision, and I pull his head back down to me, kissing the living hell out of him, showing Navy just how confident I am about giving him my all.

He gets the hint and rolls us over so that his body is above mine, sliding himself between my thighs, and I open them willingly, my skirt riding high with the movement.

Navy's hand slides between us and his fingers slide across my pussy, one digit slipping deep inside me. Then I remember why I am so wet down there already.

"Oh my gosh, I haven't showered yet. Give me a second." I try to push him off me but instead of budging, he starts to pump his finger slowly inside me, slipping in a second one, with his palm rubbing blissfully against my clit with each movement.

With another half-hearted push, I moan, opening my thighs wider at the torturous pleasure building between us.

"Do you really want me to stop?" Navy asks huskily in my ear. "Because I want to fill you with my cum, too. I want to be the one to wash him away, take his place, and remind you of how much I want to be here."

He never stops pushing me further and further, his incredibly effective movements have me panting at this point, and I no longer give a shit, wanting him inside me. Filling me up and getting as close to me as possible.

"Please, more," I moan embarrassingly loud, but I'm pretty sure Mischa is used to it by now. If I've found anything out about myself since I moved here, it's that I'm a screamer, and I don't feel the slightest bit bad about it.

Withdrawing his fingers, Navy removes his pants, his impressively long manhood on full display. He slides his body between mine again, his hand lines his cock up with my entrance as he looks into my eyes, a question there that I appreciate. In answer, I grab his ass, wrap my legs around him and pull him in closer to me, the head of his cock breaching me and we both moan.

Navy guides the rest of himself inside me, a purr rolling in the back of his throat and his head nuzzling the crook of my neck until he's fully seated, stopping there and letting me adjust to him.

Instead of moving his hips, Navy rolls his fingers the way I love against my nub, and I squeeze him in response. With a hiss, Navy sucks in his breath and groans, "I think this might actually kill me. It feels so good to be inside you, I don't think I'm going to last long."

He keeps moving his fingers, and I shudder at how close I am. "Fuck Navy, I'm gonna cum, don't stop."

With a deep primal growl, Navy pulls out and slams back in while moving his fingers, and I explode around him with loud cursing and my hips tilted as much as possible.

Navy moves his hand to grab my hip and keeps a steady, tortuous momentum, taking my orgasms to dizzying heights and moaning sweet words of love into my neck as he goes, his voice breaking more and more with the obvious strain of not cumming too fast.

"Give it to me, Navy. Give it all to me." My words push him past what he can handle, and his movements become fast and erratic before he slams into me one more time hard, his whole body convulsing with the magnitude of his pleasure, my name softly on his lips like a prayer.

After a moment to get his breathing back, the whole time with his arms holding me tight, Navy rolls to his back, not ever leaving my body.

Worried about squishing him, I try to get off, but he holds me close to his body. "Sleep there. I need to have you close." Navy's voice is barely audible.

I hear his breathing slow down and hold a steady rhythm as he falls straight to sleep, his grip still strong around me, even now. Letting myself relax, sleep comes to me easily with a serene smile no doubt on my face.

This is right.

Humming happily, I make a pot of tea for the men in my life, the four of them chatting in the lounge about the festival. The mood was alleviated dramatically this morning when they came over and found out that I'd claimed Navy last night, and twice more this morning.

My cheeks heat at the memory of him ploughing into me from behind and the many, many orgasms that have left my legs feeling like jelly today.

"What's put that beautiful pink on your cheeks?" Salem asks me with a smirk as I walk in with my tray of tea. He gets up and takes it from me, kissing me softly on my neck, making me even redder than I was, for sure. "Let me do this. Take a seat and relax. I'm sure you'll need to get your energy back."

"Ha ha ha. You're so funny." I roll my eyes at him as they all laugh jovially. "What were you guys talking about anyway?" I ask, hoping to change the subject and cool down my ears and cheeks.

Baxter takes pity on me and says, "Well, Ture was saying that there was something he wanted to talk to us all about but wanted to wait until you were in the room too because it concerned you."

I sit next to my saviour on the couch and pat his knee in thanks. Baxter takes the opportunity to entwine his fingers with mine, and I let him, still silently shocked that this gorgeous guy wants me.

Ture clears his throat. "Well, I've been thinking about it and because of everything that's happened lately and the things that hopefully are yet to come, I'd like to propose a change. One I hope you will agree with." His eyes focused on me as he talks, but I know this is for everyone.

"Hit me with it," I tell him, interested in what Ture might want to say. Thankfully, since our date, his foot-in-mouth condition seems to have reduced dramatically.

"Move in with me." *Say what?* "Hear me out before you freak out. I have the largest cabin here with five bedrooms and all of them are unused except for mine, and the master suite has a massive built-in bed for future days, but for now, I think it would be a great way for us all to spend more time with each other and see how we work as a Kindredship."

"I know that it's optimistic of me to assume that you'll accept all of us at some point, but I'd like to think that I'm not reading the signs wrong that you like us and might want a future together as well. Am I wrong?" Ture's eyes search mine, fear not very well concealed within the depths of his gaze.

I roll my lips in nervously, thinking about what he said, and try to ignore my rapidly beating heart. I choose my words carefully, nervous but wanting to put his mind at ease. "I would like a future with you guys. You all feel like family to me now, but it seems like a big step."

Ture nods, his shoulders relaxing. "I agree with what you're saying which is why I would like to recommend that we all have our own bedrooms until a time when you are comfortable. I'm not in any hurry because I'm not going anywhere, but I know I would sleep better just knowing you're under the same roof. You can have the master bedroom, which has its own bathroom, and it will be your own space which we wouldn't ever enter without your permission, of course."

He pauses, and I look at all the large men in my small lounge and their matching looks of nervousness and excitement.

"Will you think about it at least? I think it's a great idea, but you need to be comfortable with it," Salem adds, breaking the thickening silence.

I really think about what it would mean for me. Being away from Mischa - major bonus. The guys would make sure I'd be safe and looked after - always a plus. I would never feel alone and sad - a nice change. Honestly, I already love these men and can't imagine my life without them - a surprising admission. I'd also have my own space, and they wouldn't push me into anything I wouldn't want - game changer.

"What would my parents say?" I sigh dramatically but then smile at them. "Fuck 'em. When do I move in?"

The guys jump up excitedly and whoop loudly, fist-bumping each other and laughing ecstatically. It's freaking gorgeous, seeing grown men behaving like kids in a candy store just because I agree to live under the same roof.

Navy cracks me up when he turns to me with a straight face and worried features and says. "I'll be in your room though, right? You're not gonna make me sleep somewhere else, are you?"

Baxter groans and tells him to shut up and be happy with the win, but Navy grumbles about it not being fair and plonks down on the couch like a child.

Wanting to put his mind at ease, I tell him, "How about you guys move to my room as we claim each other? That way it's not too overwhelming, but we can eventually all be together."

Navy's mile beams again and pokes his tongue at the others. "Ha. I won."

How is anyone equally as adorable and sexy as this man?

CHAPTER TWENTY-SIX

SALEM

I pour the three of us some more drinks, humming to the music in the background that Ture hooked us up with before he and Navy left town for coalition business. Apparently, there were some shipment issues that needed to be sorted out, so Baxter and I happily volunteered to chill out with Alice tonight. Drinks and music were a definite plus.

With an appletini for Alice, beer for Baxter, and neat scotch for me, I make my way back to find those two rolling on the floor in laughter.

"You should have seen her face?" Alice rasps out between laughing fits. "You would have thought I'd stolen her precious looks by the horror on her face."

"What's that?" I ask, handing out the drinks.

Baxter takes his and guffaws before answering. "Mischa, when

Alice told her she's gonna be moving in with all of us. Apparently, she can't handle someone else being happy."

I chuckle, and the front door opens, Mischa walks inside and looks at all of us, me on the couch and the other two on the floor. When she screws up her face in distaste, Baxter and Alice start laughing hysterically, and I try my best not to do the same.

"What's with them?" Mischa stiffly asks, scowling at them both.

I try to keep a straight face and say, "They've just had too much to drink. Don't pay them any mind. Can I get you something to drink?" I don't want to be rude, even in my half-trashed state.

Mischa looks between me and them but shakes her head. "I don't think so but if you want a break from them, you're more than welcome to come and hang out in my room instead."

Baxter throws his head back on an even harder laugh, and Mischa shakes her head, storming out with heavier footfalls than someone that small should be able to make.

When the door slams I let out my own laugh, I know it's kind of mean, but I can't help it. She's been so mean to Alice, especially lately. I'll be happy for her to be out of here where we can smother her in the good vibes that she deserves.

We decided to move into Ture's place the day after the festival when all the hype has died down, and we can put time and effort into just focusing on each other. Plus, it gives Alice another day or two to wrap her head around it and change her mind if she's not ready. None of us want her to rush into something that will make her uncomfortable, regardless of how ready we all are.

We slow down on the drinks after that, focusing more on the company than the entertainment and refreshments. With all of us squished on one of the couches, Alice squarely between us, it's not at all a surprise when she accepts a kiss or two from the two of us, her confidence is growing, and I try in vain to keep my hope in check. Her sexy curves pressed up against me and her rounded bosom heaving against the fabric of her shirt as she starts to make out with Baxter, her hand on my knee the whole time.

There's no way that we're going to be *that* lucky, I tell myself over and over again, and I swear my heart stops for a full five seconds when Alice gets up and walks down the hallway, turning back and asking us if we're coming.

Yeah. I almost just did.

* * *

ALICE

Embracing my moment of confidence, I decide to just go for it. Thank god for liquid courage. I've had enough to be brave but not enough to not be aware of what I'm about to commit to. In fact, this is kind of why I recommended having drinks tonight. I knew what I wanted, and I knew what I'd need to have the ovaries to go for it.

I get up and walk towards the room, with my heart in my throat, and turn with the most sultry look that I've ever tried for and ask if they're coming. *Holy shit! I can't believe I'm doing this.*

Baxter gets up so fast that he trips over his own feet and falls super ungracefully to the ground. It's got to be the first time any of them have ever looked physically awkward before.

Salem chuckles and pats Baxter as he steps over him, coming to me with a massive smile. "You don't have to ask me twice."

In a heartbeat Baxter is on his feet and running at me, with a swift move he picks me up and throws me over his shoulder, never missing a step with a low growl in his chest that excites me.

Salem follows close at our rear, closing the door behind us, and I squeal when Baxter throws me on the bed. These guys really do act as those I don't weigh any more than a feather, it's super weird but great for my self-confidence.

The two of them join me on the bed, one on each side of me, as I scoot right back to the wall. Baxter grabs my foot and drags me down the bed again until my head hits the pillow and Salem grabs my chin for me to face him, his lips pressing soft but needy against mine.

I let him devour my mouth as Baxter kisses up my leg, purring as he goes, and the anticipation of his purring lips against my greedy core has my legs opening.

"Fuck," Baxter growls. "Look at how wet and soft you look. I need to taste you. So fucking bad."

Salem's hand rises to pull down the top of my dress, freeing both of my breasts, just as Baxter's hot mouth connects with my pussy, and I arch my back with pleasure. Salem's mouth leaves mine, and he looks down between Baxter devouring me with his tongue and my heaving breasts.

"Of all that is holy, Alice, you are so beautiful." Salem's words are a husky prayer before taking one of my pebbled nipples into his mouth. The intensity overload is almost too much for me to take.

Baxter uses the distraction of Salem's mouth to slip a large finger inside me, curling it the way I like, and I gasp in shock at the feeling, and he increases the tempo of his purring against my nub. I cum immediately and scream way too loud. Again.

Salem moves to my other breast, vibrating my nipple with his tongue from his own thick purr. *I love Cheetah Shifters.* I've definitely won the Kindred jackpot.

"Navy was right. That does work," Baxter chuckles as he kisses my thigh. "I'm nowhere near done with you yet. Get on your hands and knees, my queen. I want my dick so far inside you that you don't know where I stop, and you begin."

I get an idea of my own as Salem gets up to let me move, both of their eyes heavy with lust and a hint of desperation. Facing Baxter at the end of the bed, I get on my hands and knees in front of him, my mouth right in front of an impressive twitching dick.

Looking up into his confused eyes, I smile before licking him from his balls to the tip of his cock. The taste of precum is salty and delicious. Baxter's hips jolt, and he cries out in what must be pleasure.

"What are you doing?" he rasps down at me, but instead of answering, I suck the tip of him into my mouth and roll my tongue around it at the same time. "Alice! Gods, that feels incredible. Don't stop."

Having no intention of stopping, I work my mouth up and down his shaft, enjoying the act way more than I thought I would as he rocks and moans, lost in ecstasy.

Not prepared for it, when a different mouth attaches to my sex, I shove my body forwards, groaning and sucking Baxter down even further. Salem sucks my clit and slides a finger inside me, purring once again, and I use all of my focus to keep sucking on Baxter's dick, but the feeling is so intense that before I can grasp how good it feels I cum again, Salem sucking even harder as I do.

I scream with Baxter deep down my throat, making him curse at the feeling. I pull my mouth off and take in a deep breath, looking back and telling Salem, "I need you inside me. Please."

Salem rises straight away, licking his lips and sucking on his finger as he lines himself with my body, the tip of his cock sliding between my folds and making me shiver.

"Put Baxter in your mouth and suck him hard, beautiful. You're so hot, swallowing him down the way you do," Salem tells me as he teases my entrance.

Turning to face Baxter, I grab him with one of my hands again and run it up and down his length, loving the way he trembles at my touch. I pull it towards my mouth, my eyes on his as I lick the tip seductively, his eyes rolling back in his head at the contact.

Putting my hand back down for support, I suck him deep into my mouth as far as I can, and Baxter hisses out a curse. Salem takes that moment to shove his thick cock into its hilt, and the mixture of pleasure and pain almost makes me climax again.

The two of them start moving their hips in time with each other, and I stay still and take it from both sides as they fuck me hard and deep. I choke, suck, and moan, working up a sweat as my legs begin to shake uncontrollably. Their rhythms start increasing, and Salem bends over me with his hand finding my clit, rubbing it in perfect synchronisation.

Baxter pulls out of my mouth and sits back as Salem bites my shoulder hard, pushing me into a massive orgasm. It hits me so hard that I start squirting all over the bed.

Mortified, I move forwards so that Salem slips out of me, and I shudder as I try to crawl away, but Baxter is instantly behind me, thrusting hard and deep, and I shudder again. *So much feeling. Too much.*

"Oh God," I shout.

Baxter pistons hard into me, and Salem slides under me from the side, taking a nipple into his mouth and nipping at it hard at the same time as he squeezes my clit.

"I can't. I can't," I cry out, another orgasm trying to rip free from me. "Please. Oh, fuck."

Salem and Baxter increase their movements and just as Baxter yells out my name, Salem pinches me again and another stream of pleasure comes out of me. My mouth opens wordlessly and my back arches, unable to take the level of ecstasy I'm in. A level I didn't even know existed.

"That's it, baby. I knew you could take it," Salem coos, moving and letting me collapse onto my face with zero grace.

Baxter follows me down, turning us on our side, not leaving my body. I reluctantly open my eyes to find Salem on his side, looking at me with pure adoration, and I smile back weakly.

"You're mine now," he chuckles. "There's no getting away from me now. I'll follow you to the end of the world and further." Salem leans over, wipes the hair off my face, and kisses me on my forehead. "Love you, baby girl."

Baxter's hand comes around and squeezes my boob. "I love these," he chuckles. "You should never ever wear a shirt, these are too beautiful to hide." He tweaks my nipple and I jump, making them both laugh.

Closing my eyes, I relax into Baxter's arms. But before I fall asleep, I have to ask. "What's going to happen with Alexion?" It's the first time I've brought him up since the incident.

I've seen him watching me from the treeline almost every time I leave the house and sometimes through my window. He never comes close to where I am, seeming content with just being within eye view, but he's never too far away.

Neither of them answers. My eyes are still closed, but I know they're both giving each other *the look*. I try again to ask the question I really want to know. "Why won't he come near me?"

"Don't you worry about Alexion, my queen. He's got his own stuff to work through right now, but I believe everything will be alright with time," Baxter says softly in my ear, kissing my temple. "Sleep for now and let us worry about that. Sleep and know how much you're loved."

Too tired to argue, I decide to let it go and smile into Salem's chest when he sandwiches me between them, his hand on my hip.

CHAPTER TWENTY-SEVEN

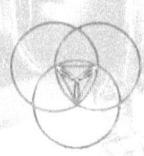

MISCHA

I'm so over this shit. At this point, I just think Alice's mocking me. No one screams like that during sex. Talk about faking it a bit too enthusiastically.

I roll my eyes at the thought and pace my bedroom trying to think of a way to make those stupid men see the light. It doesn't seem right to let them be stuck with someone like her when they could have someone like me.

Pausing in my steps, I hear Alice's bedroom door open and close. With no loud steps, I know that it's not the heifer leaving the room. I walk to my door and open it slightly, curious about what's happening, and I'm delighted to see Baxter's exposed body, covered only by a small towel around his waist, walking into the kitchen.

Deciding that this is my chance, I slide my clothes off and

leave them in a pile on the floor as I silently step out of my room, my sexy body fully exposed for his viewing pleasure.

I tread quickly but lightly into the small room behind him and drop to my knees with my legs apart and rip his towel off. Baxter turns and looks down at me with wide eyes, but before he can come up with unnecessary excuses, I lean forward and pull his cock into my mouth and suck hard and deep, humming the way I know guys like.

He's still flaccid, but I increase my efforts, knowing I'm an expert at blow jobs. I meet the job with extreme enthusiasm, sucking harder and harder, hoping that once he gets hard I can choke on his cock and he'll pull my hair.

Baxter grabs my hair, and I clench my pussy in anticipation but what I don't expect is when he rips me off him and tosses me right out of the kitchen.

He growls viciously, and I scream, "What the fuck?" Rubbing my sore scalp. "What did you do that for?"

His large body heaves with his heavy breathing, and I remember how much I want him. If he wants to play rough, I'm all for it. Opening my thighs, my moist pussy facing him, I slide my fingers inside me, throwing my head back on an exaggerated cry.

I pump them in and out, "Come on Daddy, come show me how that big dick can tear me apart."

When he doesn't respond, I look up at him in the dark, his silhouette clear but his facial expression hidden. He steps closer, his features coming into view, I'm shocked enough to freeze my fingering at his furious expression and limp dick.

"How. Dare. You," Baxter growls out, his voice venomous. "What kind of female are you that you would put your hands and mouth on someone else's Kindred? Do you have no shame?"

Right then, Salem comes quietly jogging down the hallway. "What's going on?" he asks in a low voice as he puts the light on.

Salem's wide eyes go between Baxter's naked body and the fingers I still have deep in my pussy. His face is pure repulsion when he looks down at me and his head whips away, covering his mouth as if I make him sick.

Not willing to take this level of deprivation, I jump to my feet and put my hands on my hips. "What is wrong with you two? Don't you see these?" I yell, grabbing my perfect breasts, and squeezing them. "How about this?" I smack my tiny, taut ass. "I'm fucking perfect. How can you fuck a boar and then turn away from all of this?"

I'm bordering on hysterical at this point, and it doesn't help when Baxter picks up the towel I pulled off earlier, putting it back on before walking past Salem. "You deal with that. I need a shower, so I can scrub my fucking skin off."

Salem shakes his head at me and tells me in a low, predatory voice. "Get dressed and stay the fuck away from us. You had no right to violate Baxter like that. We don't condone rape here, and you're lucky he didn't kill you for it."

"Rape? *Rape?*" I scream. "What the fuck are you talking about?"

"What do you call it on Earth when someone sexually abuses another person without their consent?" he growls at me, looking angrier by the second, and fear begins to trickle into my heart at the terrifying look he's giving me.

Wanting to get away from him, I fake confidence even though my legs are starting to shake and start walking past him with my head high. "Whatever. You guys aren't good enough for me anyway."

Alice pops her head out of her door, with her hair a mess on her head, looking confused. "Is everything alright?" She yawns and I want to shove my foot down her fat fucking mouth, except for the fact she might eat me.

"Fuck off, Alice," I grumble, slamming my door and diving onto my bed to scream into my pillow.

To think I was starting to feel bad about taking Alice to Kessar, Not any more. It'll teach them all to treat me like anything less than *her*.

I hope he fucking kills the bitch.

CHAPTER TWENTY-EIGHT

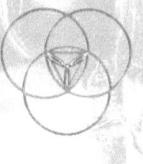

ALICE

Hands caress my ass as I sleep on my stomach, the firm strokes waking me up, and I moan as a leg squeezes between mine, parting them, and I lift my ass expectantly.

Within seconds, a thick penis slides between my folds, pushing inside my tender pussy. The night before has left me wet and swollen from overuse, but I moan at how good it feels anyway.

A mouth brushes against my ear and a familiar voice whispers. "I missed you." Navy. I should have known he'd wake me this way.

I open my eyes and see Baxter's perfectly chiselled face, watching me as Navy thrusts in again, deeper and harder. Looking down, I see Baxter's very hard dick in his hand as he slowly jacks off to Navy fucking me. And fuck me he does as he lifts my hips, sliding my pillow underneath, and pistons his hips rough and deep.

A groan sounds off on my other side, and I find Salem's eyes half-lidded as he moves his hand up and down his shaft. *Holy shit. They're both wanking to Navy fucking me.* My heart stops when I look at the door to find Ture standing there. His cock is still in his pants, but they're bursting at the seams.

I moan, unbelievably turned on at being watched, while dirty things happen to my body. Navy nips at my shoulder and neck. "Your pussy feels so good." Another low growl gets me even wetter, and I realise Navy likes to have sex with me when I'm filled with other guys' cum.

Baxter groans, and I turn to see his seed spurt all over his perfectly shaped abs, and I slip my finger in it before bringing it to my mouth and tasting it.

He moves his body closer and whispers something in Navy's ear. It makes Navy flip us over and then sit up, so I'm straddling him backwards, his cock never leaving me. I feel Navy lie back down, and he grabs my hips lifting me up and down on top of him and the change in position hits me in the right spot. I feel exposed though and vulnerable like this.

I put my hands over my stomach, but Baxter rips them away, placing his fingers over my clit, rubbing and circling until I see stars. "That's it, take what we give you and never hide from us. You're so sexy."

Salem kneels next to me as he keeps sliding his hand up and down his cock, groaning low, his eyes on where Navy's entering me and Baxter's strumming me.

Ture moves to the end of the bed, his focus on my eyes, and we get lost in each other's eyes as Navy sends me spiralling over the edge, my cry for all of them.

Warm liquid covers me just above my pussy as Salem leans over, cumming on me with a deep growl. Baxter reaches up and slides the cum all over my overly sensitive clit and around Navy's cock as he slides in and out, making both of us moan at the contact.

Navy speeds up, his hips jerking with the new sensation, and he empties himself deep inside me while holding my hips down hard on top of him.

Sweat drips in between my breasts as I sag in exhaustion, but Salem leans forward and licks it off me with a purr of appreciation. I open my eyes, not even realising I closed them to find Ture still standing at the end of the bed, adjusting himself. He must be so uncomfortable.

* * *

TURE

Of all the fantasies and dreams I've had about how sexy I thought Alice would be, it was nothing compared to the reality of it. The way she cries out, her soft curves, the way her body trembles when she cums and the way she looks filled with one of us is *everything*.

I try to move my straining penis confined in my pants as I watch her, not wanting to assume that I have the right to do more than that. Being claimed by a Kindred should always be the female's choice, and I will wait as long as she wants me to, but the second I'm alone, I'm reliving this in my head, and I have no doubt that I'll explode harder than normal.

"Ture." Alice grabs my attention away from my increasingly dirty thoughts, and I step forwards unconsciously, but I catch myself before I go any further. The scent of their mixed arousal filling the room is an overwhelming aphrodisiac, I don't have the full confidence I can overcome if I get any closer.

I swallow hard before I find my voice. "Yes, my darling?"

Alice lifts herself off Navy and crawls to the end of the bed. "Will you kiss me?"

Fuck yes, I will. Keeping a semblance of calm, I slowly approach her and lean down, caressing her cheek tenderly, and I place a soft kiss on her lips.

She looks up at me, her eyes filled with questions I'm not a hundred percent understanding, then she says, "I'd like a moment with Ture please." I love the way she takes charge. It's a piece of herself that she doesn't let out much, but I adore it. She should hold her power more often because we're hers to command, and we like it that way.

The other three males silently leave the room without any dispute, but our gazes never leave each other. When the door closes, her hand reaches out and grabs my hardness through my pants and lightly squeezes.

I exhale at how good it feels, and I keep very still, praying she doesn't stop touching me. To my absolute delight, she undoes my pants and when they drop to the ground, my cock springs free and her eyes dip to it hungrily.

"May I?" she asks me, or more specifically, my cock because her mouth is inches from it. Her warm breath brings pre-cum straight to the surface, and I almost have to close my eyes at the painful strain of it.

"Please," I beg, my hands by my sides clenching and unclenching.

Her hot lips kiss the tip and my hips jerk at the contact. I had no idea it would feel that good. She licks the head and circles it.

"I love the way you taste," she breathes over me before sucking me into her mouth and I shudder, my hands grabbing her head, unable to stay still any more.

With a bobbing head, she takes me in and out, so far that she gags on my dick and Gods help me, I love it. The feeling of her throat trembling and squeezing me almost makes me cum right then.

Not able to take it any more, I pull back and whisper, "Stop. I'm not going to last any longer."

Alice gets up on her knees and reaches her arms up for me, and I gladly lean down to her. Her hands wrap around my neck, and she pulls herself up to standing.

I chuckle and kiss her with love. "Now you're at my height."

She smiles back and tells me, "I want you inside me, Ture. Do you want me, too?"

Without a word, I pick her up by her thighs and wrap them around me, slipping straight inside her from all the cum she's already been filled with.

"Oohhh. You feel so good, so wet," I groan, licking up her neck, and tasting the salty sweat of her.

With my hands full of her glorious ass, I walk her to the wall and press her against it. "Hold on tight, my darling, this is going to be short but hard."

Alice moans when I start to fuck her relentlessly against the wall, I use the immovable force of it to slam deep into her, again and again until she screams out her release, but I don't stop. I push into her, all of my pent-up need and desire since the moment she stepped foot in the hub. I feel like I've been rock-hard ever since, and I want her to feel every pound of want I've had for her.

"Shit. Shit. Shit. Shit," Alice cries out, as she cums again and I follow her. The clenching of her pussy is so intense that there's no way I can last a second more.

She milks every drop of seed out of me as I roll my hips, my cock sensitive and twitching inside her. It starts to harden again, wanting more of this tight heat.

I push again and look at her face, exhaustion clear as day written all over it, and I know I can't be selfish. I have all the time in the world to show her how hard she makes me and how much I want her.

Lifting her off my dick, I turn her, cradling her in my arms, and carry her back to the bed. I take in the large wet patch and park her on the other side of the bed, tucking her into the bed and stroking the hair away from her face.

She pulls me down beside her, and I snuggle her under my arm and kiss the top of her head. "I love you, my darling. Today and every day. Thank you for deeming me worthy to claim. I will never let you down."

"I know. I love you too." She turns her head and looks at the closed bedroom door. "What's that?" Her little hand points to the gift I brought for her.

Nerves flutter in my belly like they always do when I give something to Alice. "I thought you might like something extra special for the mid-summer festival tomorrow, so I made you something new."

Alice squeezes me tight against her, and thanks me before going for a much-needed shower. Her voice tells me that she means every word because I could hear the love and appreciation. Now I just have to hope she likes it.

CHAPTER TWENTY-NINE

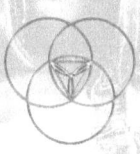

ALEXION

Paranoia has finally taken the last vestiges of sanity I had left. No matter what I do, I can't shake the feeling of being watched. Which of course is majorly hypocritical of me because here I am in the trees, staring at the only thing I want in this world like a complete psychopath.

I can't leave her. I keep walking away, but my beast just drags me back again, an overriding fear inside me that the second I look away something will happen to Alice. No part of me can survive if another person I love dies, just because being close to me is a death sentence.

The hair on the back of my neck rises, all the warning signs in my head going off. Turning my head away from the back of Alice's cabin, I raise my nose to the air and sniff, looking in all directions around me but once again I don't see, hear, or smell anything out of the ordinary.

What the fuck is going on?

Knowing this isn't helping my mental health, I take one more look at Alice's window and see Navy staring right back at me. He smiles at me and waves like we're old friends, and it's totally normal for me to be stalking his Kindred. Our Kindred, I guess, but it's still not right. Especially after the way I treated her. I did it to keep her safe, I tell myself over and over again, but it doesn't stop me from feeling sick to my stomach.

I remember when Navy was just a kitten. He was always wandering off and freaking Abel out. Little did he know, he was always at my cottage, following me everywhere. It didn't matter how gruff I was with the kid, he just kept coming back and prattled on all day long. He reminded me so much of Jamal that I didn't have the heart to turn him away. Instead, I would just torture myself with his company, and every time he'd laugh or play, I'd remember that Jamal could never do it again. Because of me.

Navy never got to know his parents because of his mother dying giving birth to him and his Dad following very soon after. One Kindred can not live without the other part of their soul. That knowledge makes me feel better now that Alice has claimed the others. If something happens to me, she will have them to keep her going.

Poor Abel ended up with the full responsibility of being a father when he was nowhere ready, particularly with a child like Navy. He was and still is cut from a different cloth, but I like him that way, not that I'd tell him that.

Most of us lose our parents because of the unfortunate luck females have on Rathe, with females being hunted, bred, and discarded by the other faction, and any claimed ones killed out of jealousy and their Kindreds following soon after from a broken heart. But for Navy to never know that kind of love and devotion, it just didn't seem right. I did what I could for him, but now he seems to think we're friends or something. I don't do friends or any kind of relationship. It's too risky.

Guilt eats away at me as I turn away without acknowledging him; my cabin, my current target. The need to run away from my obsessive behaviour is pushing me forwards. This isn't healthy for me or her. What if she sees me again? Alice must think I'm a stalker. I sigh deeply. I guess I am a stalker.

Closing the door behind me, I walk to my room and stare at my disfigured image in the full-size mirror. I've smashed so many things inside my home many times but never this mirror. My reflection reminds me of who I really am and all that I've lost along the way. I don't deserve to forget for even a moment.

I should never have left my village that day. I should never have let my little sister run back by herself. I should never have let Jamal out of my arms when he needed me. I should never have trusted Kessar. Because of all of my bad choices, every person I've ever loved has died a brutal death. A death that I relive every time I close my eyes.

With a regret-filled exhale, I rip my shirt above my head and storm towards my bed. The festival is today and the whole village will be overflowing with gaiety and laughter. It's the last thing I need right now, to see how much better everyone else's lives are.

If Alice will be safe then it's got to be today because her other four Kindreds will be all over her, making the day as special as she is. Today I will rest and they can protect her.

I'm so very tired.

* * *

SIXTY YEARS AGO

. . .

PAIN SLICES THROUGH MY HEAD, and I cradle it in my hand with a groan. *What happened?* It takes me a second but as I come to more, memories rip through me with painful accuracy. *No! My family!*

"You're awake." I hear the familiar voice of my eldest brother and crack my eyes open, the light between the trees slices my vision like a knife.

Ignoring the pain, I slowly sit up, wondering how I got outside and where Jamal is. "What's going on? Where's Jamal? I heard him screaming." My voice breaks as fear tightens its grip on my heart. *Please be okay.*

Kessar leaps across the small gap between us, and his heavy boot slams against my chest, sending me flying back onto my ass with a humph. "You wrecked everything, you fucking maggot. I should never have tried to keep you away from the village. I should have known," he kicks me again but in the stomach and I roll into a ball, my eyes burning with confused tears, "that you would destroy everything I'd worked for."

He leans down and grabs my chin, squeezing way too hard, and turns my head to face him. "They are all dead because of you. Pop is dead! Ma is dead. Phillis is dead. And Jamal is dead. All. Because. Of. You!" Kessar screams into my face, his spittle flying all over my face, but I don't care. All I care about is his harsh words, thick with hate, for me.

"I didn't do anything," I object weakly. How could it all be my fault?

"Ha!" He shoves my face down and walks a few steps away, shaking his head and facing the other direction. "That's the fucking problem." Kessar spins back around, pulling a long knife out of the waist of his pants and staring at me with scorn. "You should have done what you were told but no, you're too dumb to even do that."

Stepping towards me slowly, my eyes flicker between the knife he's holding and his hard eyes. "What are you doing?" I ask, scooting back on my hands along the dirt. *He wouldn't hurt me, would he?* "I didn't mean to hurt anybody." Tears start to streak down my cheeks unchecked, as I choke on pain mixed with fear. "You're my brother. I love you."

Kessar laughs maniacally. "You pathetic boy. Look at you, a grown man sobbing like a child. *I love you. You're my brother.* Stop embarrassing yourself, it's disgusting. Do one thing good in your life and just fucking die!"

With a quick move I wasn't prepared for Kessar swings for my head, and I only manage to move back enough to keep it attached to my body but excruciating agony slices through my face and I hold it, rolling to the side on instinct.

Jumping up I open my eyes, and instantly know something is really wrong when I can only see through one eye, but I don't stop to think about it, just push forwards and start running as fast as my feet will take me, using only my good eye for direction with blood pouring down my body.

Run. Run. Run. It's my mantra, and I am focusing only on my burnt feet slamming into the ground, one step at a time. Footfalls pound right behind me, Kessar cursing my name the whole time. *Why is this happening to me?*

Large hands grab me as I'm tackled into the ground, face first. My body is in so much pain, all over but all I can think of is I have to survive. His massive body rolls on top of me, straddling me, with the knife held high, but I shove my hips up just in time, knocking Kessar off.

"Stop this," I scream, pushing him away, but he just gets right back up again, coming at me like a wild animal.

Without thought, I smash my legs into him, fighting in any way that I can but Kessar just keeps coming, landing on top of me as we wrestle with the knife between our bodies. His blood drips on me from a cut on his hand, and I use the distraction to headbutt his face, needing his bigger body to get off mine.

It gives me enough momentum to roll on top of him instead, both of our hands clasping the grizzly weapon but my desire to survive gives me a strength I wouldn't normally have, and I gain the advantage.

The knife is turned towards Kessar's chest, and he scowls up at me, his arms starting to shake. "Please," I ground out between clenched teeth. "Don't make me do this."

"Everyone you will ever love will die," Kessar spits at me. "Painfully and cruelly because you are death."

"No," I yell, but before I can pull the knife away to make my point that I'm not like that, the knife slips between Kessar's fingers, delving into his chest, where his heart is.

A splutter of blood fountains out of Kessar's mouth and all over my face. The taste of his life on my tongue as I watch as the life leaves his eyes, a grimace of hate still frozen on his face.

The body of the last person I had in this world lay beneath me with a knife protruding out of his chest with my hands wrapped around it. I can't move or breathe. *What have I done?*

"Kessar?" I whisper, unbelieving what I can see. Numbness takes over, and I push up to my feet, looking down at my last brother.

My body takes over, going into survival mode. My feet start walking away from the horrific scene with my mind in a daze, my limbs shaking uncontrollably as I go.

He was right!

It's all my fault.

I'm death.

CHAPTER THIRTY

ALICE

Navy waves out the window as I unwrap my newest gift from Ture. "Who are you waving at?" I ask, only half interested because I'm excited to see what he's made me.

I used to be so nervous when Ture made me clothes, but I learnt very quickly that he's a master at it and every single piece he makes is a perfect fit and suits me more than anything I ever wore back home.

"Alexion," Navy says, as a matter of fact, garnering my attention straight away. "He must be very lonely. I wish he would come inside already."

Alexion is a strange subject for me, but Navy is the only one who doesn't tiptoe around it, and I am grateful for that. I will never forget the way we burned perfectly together, but I also can't forget how he made me feel afterwards. He's a conundrum that I'm not sure if I want to figure out.

"Is he standing outside again?" I've noticed him watching even more than he used to, his gaze always seems melancholy.

Navy shrugs, then sits on the bed next to the package. "He was. What's this?" He grabs it off me and opens it up for me. "Oh, clothes. I take it this is from Ture."

He pulls out a wide-brim straw hat and a large piece of floral pink material. I snatch it off him with a mock scowl. "Mine." I unfold the material to find a long sleeve, country-style maxi dress that has a drawstring under the breast area. It's so pretty, and I can't wait to try it on.

I let my pants fall to the ground, taking off my shirt too. As I reach for the dress, Navy's hands cover the globes of my ass, and I turn around to look at him with one eyebrow up. "Aren't you meant to be somewhere, Mr Committee?"

With a pout, he reluctantly steps back. "Fine but we're not finished here," he complains, leaving me to get dressed.

Navy volunteered to take over most of Ture's duties today, so I could spend the majority of the day with Ture. We never get to take time to be with each other alone. Today he is my date, and I'm really excited about it.

I pull the dress over my head and tighten the tie, looking at my reflection in the mirror, I'm pleased with how it looks even though I'm still not a hundred percent comfortable walking around without a bra. I found out it was Navy who got rid of all my bras and underwear, and he openly warned Ture that he'll destroy any he attempts to make me.

At the time I was a bit pissed about it, but I know Navy does everything out of love in his own way, and it's his way to show me how much he loves my body. It's hard to have self-hate around these men, that's for sure.

I open my cupboard to find my slip-on shoes, but a pair of light brown cowgirl boots are sitting in there wrapped in a bow. With a wide smile, I take them out and try them on and of course, they are once again a perfect size. I have no idea where he finds the time and materials to do all of these amazing things for me, but I adore it. It makes me feel really special. Maybe one day I can give him a special gift that *I've* made.

My hand smoothes along my stomach and the idea of being filled with a child of theirs makes me smile. I know the deal about being here and honestly, I can't wait. I never really gave myself the time to think about the possibilities of being a parent until we moved here and when we were told about why we were taken, my hope soared.

With my self-confidence so low, I still feared I might not be lucky enough, but now I dare to dream because I want to be a mother, and any child who gets to grow up in this village with this much love and affection will be lucky. I'm going to give them all the affection I wish I'd been given.

A knock sounds on the door, and I giggle quietly. Only Ture knocks on the front door at this point, the others just walk in without warning, much to Mischa's distaste.

I walk to the door and open it with a flourish, doing a spin for effect. "Ta-da," I say happily, showing off his beautiful design. "It's beautiful, Ture, thank you so much."

He steps inside and takes me into his arms, kissing me softly on my cheeks, forehead, nose, and then my mouth. When Ture tries to pull away, I pull him back in for a deeper kiss, enjoying the taste and feel of him.

"You look stunning, my darling," he whispers against my mouth. "As usual."

Heat suffuses my cheeks and ears as I pick up the hat I'd put down to open the door. Placing it on, I reach for his hand, excited to see what the festival is all about.

The day is hot but beautiful with fun stalls filled with games, food, and gifts. We play and laugh together without a negative thought between us, holding hands and stealing kisses like teenagers.

I check up on the stall that I filled earlier with iced tea and see that it needs topping up with more tea and ice. We walk back inside to see Mischa sitting on the couch, her knee jiggling and chewing on her usually perfect nails.

"Are you alright?" Worried because of her unusual behaviour, but she smiles up at me wide. Which of course really gets me worried because the only smiles she's ever given me are malicious ones.

Getting up, Mischa says, "Of course, I'm fine. What are you two doing?"

I explain that we needed to pick up some tea and ice, and she instantly tells us she wants to help and starts carrying a large jug I'd made earlier out towards the stall. Ture and I get two more jugs and a large bucket of ice, and I give him a '*What the fuck*' look, to which he shrugs.

We follow her out and set up the new jugs, topping them all up with fresh ice to help keep them cool on such a warm day. Mischa even takes the old, empty ones back to the cabin without me having to ask.

"Do you think she's a changeling?" I ask Ture as a joke, but he gives me a serious look.

"No. Of course not. She's too old."

Okay! The fact that he thought I was serious really freaks me out. Note to self, watch your kids closely.

Abel walks over to us, rubbing the back of his head nervously. "Hey, guys, sorry to be the bearer of bad news but Ture we kind of need you. There's an issue at the meeting, and it's getting a little out of hand."

"Let me guess, Navy told them to get over it?" Ture laughs and gives me an apologetic smile. "I'm sorry, my darling. Do you mind if I just run over for a second? It shouldn't take long."

Mischa comes back at that moment and puts her arm around my shoulders. "You go, us girls can hang out together and have a glass of this delicious iced tea. Does that sound alright with you?" She gives me a beaming smile, and I'm reminded of how stunning she is when she smiles.

Not seeing an issue with it, even though Mischa is being super weird. I figure she wants to talk about something woman to woman. I am the only other one here, after all.

"Sounds nice. You go and sort whatever it is out and tell Navy I said to behave himself." I know full well that whatever has happened is probably because of his bluntness. Not everyone appreciates how honest he can be.

The men walk off and Mischa pours us both a nice cold glass. "I wanted to have a chat with you without an audience," Mischa starts. "I know I haven't always been the best person to be around." She stops and watches the Cheetah Shifter walking by. "Do you mind if we go for a walk together? I don't really want to pour my heart out with so many sensitive ears nearby."

Totally understanding, I nod, and we walk towards the lake together, with her leading the way. Comfortable silence gathers around us as we start to walk down the private path, and I look around, realising she must want to go the whole way. I suppose it would be a nice place to have a talk.

"What did you want to say?" I ask, figuring we're far enough away to at least start talking.

Mischa licks her lips and takes another sip before saying, "It's hard for me to admit this, but I've been jealous of you and all the love that's so easily been bestowed upon you since we arrived. It's lonely being on Rathe without anyone I'm familiar with, and I haven't handled it with grace at all."

Her honesty surprises me, and I don't interrupt her, in case she stops or takes it back. It's hard to line up this person talking now with the one that's been doing everything she can to make my life as difficult and miserable as possible.

We get to the water's edge but instead of stopping, she walks along the edge, continuing to speak. "I know it's probably selfish of me to ask you to forgive me, but I'd really like to start fresh, and maybe we can even become friends."

Misha's gaze flickers around the treeline, and I try to see what she's looking for, but I don't see anything out of the ordinary. I suppose she's just nervous being so far away from the village.

"Anyway," Mischa stretches out the word. "What I'm trying to get at is that I'm very sorry for being a bitch to you." Her eyes become more frantic as she searches for something before she smiles coldly, then looks back at me with what seems like some kind of twisted triumph.

The bushes behind me rustle, and I turn to see a very large man coming out of them. Face stoic but eyes hard as granite. "Very good female. You can go now."

Is he talking to me? He's looking at me as he approaches. I turn to see if Mischa knows him, and she cocks her hip out, attitude all over her features.

"Not so fast, big man." She turns to me and suddenly shoves me back. "You pathetic swine. As if I'd want to be your friend, or be sorry. What am I meant to be sorry for? That you're a gluttonous cretin or that you're so pitiful that you would walk away from everyone who could protect you with someone who obviously despises your very existence."

She scoffs before laughing cruelly. "How about this? I had Baxter's cock in the back of my throat last night while you slept. That's right. That's what you walked in on when we were both buck naked in the kitchen."

My chest constricts at the memory, my brain now putting two and two together. Why would he do that? Of course, he would. Who wouldn't choose someone like her over someone like me?

"He tasted so good, and I licked up every drop of him. Then he roared as I pleasured myself for him. He almost came again just watching me." Mischa started stepping backwards from where we came from, and two strong hands grab my arms, yanking my body against a hard chest. I was so heartbroken that I didn't even notice the stranger coming in behind me. I try to pull my arms free, but his grip is like a vice.

"Keep still," he growls in my ear, his voice is malicious and scary, and I freeze. My stomach is so sick from what Mischa just told me that I'm not suitably scared of the situation I'm in. All I can focus on is the pain in my chest.

I look up at Mischa as she starts to turn the corner to get back on the path. "Don't worry piggy. My cunt will keep them all nice and warm tonight. I'll make sure to soothe their pain and suck out any lingering thought of you."

Her dark laugh dissipates as she heads further away, and the man behind me lifts me up and carries me into the woods. Away from safety and my Kindreds.

Opening my mouth to scream, a knife gets placed at my throat. "Go for it. I don't need you alive for what I have planned." I seal my lips together, a sob escaping me. "That's it. Cry for me." The frightening guy licks the tear off my cheek, but I feel so broken all I can do is turn my head and close my eyes, visions of Mischa sucking Baxter's cock clear in my imagination.

"Who are you?" My devastated voice is barely audible.

"I'm Kessar, your Kindred's brother and the last thing you, or he, will ever see."

CHAPTER THIRTY-ONE

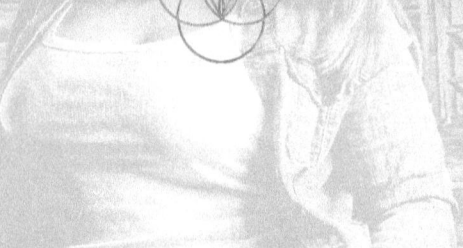

SALEM

bel and I sit in the back of the room, laughing quietly between us at the ridiculous squabble that Navy and Ture are having over small, petty council issues that shouldn't even be a thing. Apparently, Navy has decided to reorganise the way our village orders, categorises, and keeps the stock coming in from the neighbouring village.

To be fair, Ture never should have told him that he was in charge of it all today. Navy has a way of taking over when his own brand of logic kicks in. It's going to be one hell of a fight trying to convince him that it was fine the way it was.

"We're going to be here for ages, Salem," Ture groans, facing me while rubbing his temples. "Do you mind keeping Alice company for me until I've convinced this maniac to step back?"

Navy flings his hands in the air for dramatic effect. "Maniac? Who are you calling a maniac? I'm simply fixing your primitive system to a more efficient, and frankly, better way of doing things. It's not my fault you're so old that you can't learn new tricks. Get with the times, Grandpa."

"You little shit," Ture growls, diving for a too-fast Navy, who easily jumps out of the way.

I smirk at Abel and say, while watching the two grown Shifters run around the room like cubs, "I'll leave these two with you and go check on my female. Good luck."

Both Navy and Ture cry out at the same time, not missing a beat. "Our female."

Laughing loudly, I walk out, leaving crashing sounds behind me. It serves Ture right for not knowing something like this would happen.

I head towards the stalls, greeting my friends as I go, and stop at the iced tea station. Looking around I don't see any sign of Alice or Mischa and Ture did tell me when he came over to the storage room that he had left them together.

Grabbing the first few people I see, I ask if they've seen either of them but to no avail. No one has seen them for ages.

Figuring that they probably went back to their cabin and away from the heat, I head over there and am instantly relieved when I see Mischa sitting on the patio on the rocking chair having a drink.

"Good day, Mischa," I greet but not as nicely as I would have in the past.

Baxter pulled us aside this morning and explained the terrible thing that this female had done last night and warned us to be wary in her company. Poor Baxter showered three times this morning and said he still felt dirty. We all agreed that it would be in the best interest of Alice, to keep it from her for now. The last thing she needs is to feel anything other than happy, besides it's Baxter's story to tell, and I know he's not ready to talk about it with her.

Keeping my head focused on why I came, I ask, "Have you seen Alice at all? I've been looking for her, I thought it would be nice to take her to play some of the games."

Mischa smiles widely, and it looks so terribly fake that I wonder why I ever thought she might be a decent person in the first place. I guess females can be bad people too.

"Yes, she asked me to tell you guys that she was feeling a bit tired and overwhelmed, needing a little bit of space," Mischa tells me, and I frown, worried about what's wrong with my Alice. "Don't worry, she's fine, just tired. Alice was asleep the last time I checked on her. Let her rest. I'm sure she'll be up before dinner. It must be all of those extracurricular activities the four of you have been pushing on the poor girl. If you know what I mean." Mischa's eyes twinkle and I have to hold back a shudder. After what happened with Baxter, she just seems like an evil sexual predator now.

I feel really uncomfortable leaving when I know Alice is so run down, but Mischa seems like she doesn't want me to go inside, and I don't want to be rude and push it. It is her house too, after all.

Turning with a frown, I slowly start to walk over to the hub but run into Ture halfway there. My face must have given away that something was wrong because Ture grabs my arm and demands to know what happened, his eyes wide with worry.

After explaining what Mischa had said, Ture agrees with me that it doesn't feel right to leave her on her own without checking on her first, and we decide to head back. If she doesn't want us there, she can tell us herself, and we'll respect her choice, but at least then we can see with our own eyes that she's alright.

Mischa sits up in the rocking chair as we approach together, halting the swinging motion with her feet. "Is something the matter?"

Ture smiles at her politely, but without any warmth. "Sorry to intrude, but we need to speak to Alice. I know she's tired, don't worry, we won't take long."

He doesn't even wait for a response and walks right by her and into the front door. I follow him trying not to laugh, as I watch Mischa splutter for what to say, but instead, she just looks like a fish out of water.

I'm right behind Ture as he knocks gently on her closed bedroom door. "My darling, are you awake?" he calls out, softly but loud enough for her to hear.

When we don't hear a reply, he knocks again but a little louder. Silence is the only response we get, and worry takes over my manners, and I open the door carefully to peek inside.

Straight away I can see that the bed is made and looks like it hasn't been lain on at all, so I swing the door open the rest of the way, showing Ture what I see, and step inside.

"Alice?" I call out, much louder, with a tinge of fear in my tone that I don't hide very well. "Are you here?"

Nothing. Not a sound other than Mischa's footsteps leaving the porch.

Where is she?

Ture starts to frantically search the whole cabin, even Mischa's room, but I can't move from the spot, staring at Alice's open window and fearing the worst. *What if she sneaked away? Has she left us?*

I turn and run from the room. Out the front door and after Mischa's retreating footsteps. Catching up to her only takes me seconds, and my hand grabs at her shoulder, spinning her to face me.

"Did she leave us? Did Alice tell you where she was going? Are you covering for her?" I shoot questions at her one after the other, panic setting in at the idea of Alice wanting to run away from us without a word. It took me so long to win her heart, I can't lose her now.

Mischa pushes my hand off her shoulder, and I realise that I was squeezing it too hard. Rubbing where I held her, she replies with a grimace, "What are you even talking about? I told you she's in her room."

Turc steps up beside me, his face mirroring my own panic. "Where could she have gone?"

* * *

ALICE

We don't walk for too long before Kessar drops me on the hard ground with a violent thud. My lower back screams out in pain, but before I can even protest, a large hand collides with my face, sending me sprawling across the twig-covered dirt.

Crying out, I roll into a ball with my hands covering my face, hoping to avoid being hit again, but his foot kicks my back with such force that a scream tears out of my mouth.

Kessar grabs my hair and lifts me off the ground with it, the burning pain makes me use my feet to help him pick me up, wanting to ease some of the pressure.

He glares at me with hate that I don't understand. I've never done anything to anyone in my life to deserve that level of disdain and fury.

"Why?" I sob out, my body shaking with an equal mixture of pain and fear.

Forgotten is the betrayal of Baxter for now, a healthy dose of self-preservation kicks in, and all I can focus on is staying alive and unhurt.

Between sobs, I ask, "What do you want from me?"

Kessar drops me to the ground with a deep huffing laugh. "From you? Nothing. From your Kindred? Everything and unfortunately for you, that means your life is forfeit. So while we're waiting for the idiot to figure out where you are, you get the pleasure of my winning personality."

With the last word, he kicks me in my chest and I fall back, smashing the back of my head on the solid floor. For a moment, all I can see are black spots, and there is a high-pitched ringing sound in my ears. Confused and hurt I lie still blinking wildly and trying to catch my breath, the land on my chest winded me badly, and I can't breathe properly.

A blurry face hovers over me, and I moan, clutching the front of my dress in desperation for air. Kessar's laugh echoes over the screaming inside my mind, and my eyes flood with the sudden knowledge that I'm going to die here today, and there's nothing I can do about it.

"After all that little shit has taken from me, it's going to be my pleasure to take even more from him," Kessar says, to himself I think.

My breathing slows down as air flows better, the pain still there but my fear of imminent death receding. I make a point to lie still with my eyes closed, hoping that Kessar will leave me alone. I know I can't outrun him, especially while I'm so injured, and I definitely can't fight him. What else can I do, but freeze?

"Do you know, female, that I had an endless amount of power and status within my reach?" Kessar keeps talking as I listen to his heavy footsteps pacing all around me. "All I had to do was deliver them my little sister, Phillis. I had it all worked out, and even made space for my younger brothers to follow me but no! Alexion had to be his useless self, letting Phillis go back to the village. I gave him one fucking job. Take care of the kids for me."

What the fuck? He's Alexion's brother? I hope he's not relying on him coming after me when he can't even be anywhere near me.

"It was the perfect plan. Real genius. The fire started exactly the way I planned it, and I knew everyone was selfless enough that they would all run inside to help each other. I locked them in and when it was completely aflame I headed back to my siblings, ready to make the trade."

My eyes snap open at an enormous smashing sound. I turn my head carefully to see Kessar breaking a massive branch in two, a rage-filled scowl on his face, his teeth clenched painfully.

With a roar, he yells, "How was I to know the little bitch was inside? She was meant to be with Alexion." He smashes it again against a thick tree trunk, pieces of wood flying everywhere from the collision. "When I saw that dumb cunt lying in the fire after hearing Phillis dying, I almost left him there to burn, but I thought maybe I could still use him somehow. Should have fucking left him there!"

Kessar looks down at me, seeing I'm watching him. He takes long strides before kneeling next to my head, a twisted smile on his face. "Don't worry, I won't kill you. Yet. I need you alive to give him hope, just so I can rip it from him when I pull the head off your body and bathe in your blood."

I shudder, and he grabs my chin hard when I try to turn away, making me give him my full attention. "Only then will I kill him and burn down his new village. I don't care if I'm the last Cheetah Shifter alive, as long as I get my revenge."

CHAPTER THIRTY-TWO

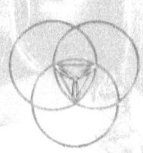

BAXTER

Can you believe him? This is the thanks I get for fixing the abhorrent system that was in place," Navy repeats, again, clearly annoyed by the altercation he had with Ture earlier.

Abel got me from my game stall to come and talk Navy down while he fixed up the storage room. Apparently, some things were thrown before Ture stormed off, refusing to be a part of it any more.

"I know buddy but how about we focus on what's important here," I start, attempting to calm him down. He looks at me questioningly, and I smile at the fact that he's open to what I have to say. "Don't you think the serenity in the village and our ability to work together, so fluently as a coalition, is more important than fighting over stock?"

Navy sighs deeply. "I guess."

"And isn't it also more important that we get along as a

Kindredship?" I continue seeing his stubbornness waver. "What do you think Alice would think if she saw the two of you fighting like that? Especially when we're about to all move in together. You don't want to make her sad or worried, do you?"

His eyes widen in realisation, and I know I have him. With a nod, I put my arm around his shoulders. "That's what I thought. How about we go find Ture and you guys can make up?"

We turn and walk down the path but within a few seconds, Ture and Salem come bolting towards us at full speed, terror is written all over their features and my stomach drops. *Alice!*

"What's wrong?" Navy shouts way too loud, making everyone around us turn and stare in worry, obviously picking up on what I did. "Where's Alice?"

"She's gone," Salem cries out, distraught. "Mischa said she went to her room, but her bed was made, and her window was open. I tried to pick up her scent there, but I couldn't find it. Not a recent one, anyway."

Mischa's name makes me instantly suspicious. "Did you ask the female?" I question, not wanting to use her name ever again after what she did to me. My mind blocks it out straight away, I can't think about that right now.

Ture nods. "She didn't seem to know anything but someone would have to help her escape."

Navy shakes his head furiously. "No. She didn't leave, Alice would never leave us. She loves us." His voice comes out slightly hysterical, and I don't know how he will cope if she really did leave. It would be impossibly hard for all of us, but Navy would never understand, and I fear his response. "She needs us. We need to see Alexion, she must have visited him, or maybe she went for a walk to the lake. She didn't leave. She didn't!"

Salem pulls him in for a tight hug. "Of course, she didn't, let's walk around and have a look together, mate." He looks at me over Navy's shoulder, as worried as I am.

"Let's try Alexion's place first," Ture adds, patting Navy on the back. "That's a great idea. I'm sure she's just over there."

Our fast-paced walk to Alexion's house is fast but silent, all of us in our own heads thinking the worst, I'm sure.

The cabin is as silent as we are, but his scent is strong here, and I know he would never go to the festival. He's never been before, and I doubt today is the day he's decided to be social.

Stepping up, I knock on the door, very aware that I can't smell any trace of Alice, but I refuse to give up hope.

We hear small crashes inside and Alexion steps approaching us. He rips the front door open with a heavy scowl, staring each of us down. "What?"

Navy pushes past him and starts running through the house, wildly calling out Alice's name. Alexion doesn't tell him off, but his face does change from anger to confusion to worry.

His gaze snaps to mine. "Is Alice missing?"

With a simple nod, I look behind him to the carnage that is his home. The once well taken care of cabin is now in shambles, some of it from when I saw him break down but a lot of it new. Maybe I should have been more of a friend to Alexion and not let him push me aside. It's clear that he's going through something, and no one should ever feel alone with their dark feelings.

"I knew this would happen," he growls, garnering all of our attention, including Navy who runs back to the room, his eyes wild.

Navy grabs Alexion's hand. "What do you mean? Knew what would happen."

Alexion rips his hand back and steps away from all of us. "People near me die. It's unavoidable. I tried to stay away."

His words hurt my heart. There's so much more to what he's

saying and decide from now on he'll never be alone whether he likes it or not. We're family now. I hope one day he'll feel comfortable enough to tell me his story.

Navy scoffs at his words and goes to the back of Alexion's house to resume his search. I don't know what he's planning to find exactly when it's clear she's not here.

"What the fuck is this?" Navy yells out, bringing the four of us running to the back door, where he's holding a small note, his face ashen. He looks up at Alexion, "Who's Kessar?"

Alexion stumbles back, clutching at his heart. "W - what?"

Navy steps up and passes him the note, and as Alexion reads it, it's like watching someone die on the inside and be born again in a pool of fury.

A massive roar rips from Alexion as he dives onto his knees, pulling at his hair like a madman and frankly scaring the fucking shit out of me, and I'm a seasoned warrior.

The piece of paper flutters to the ground like a harmless thing, seemingly unable to cause such chaos, and I stare at it for a second, not wanting to pick it up in case the madness spreads.

Alexion jumps up, rips his shirt clean off, and then speeds out the back door faster than I've ever seen anyone move. Fuck, this male would be lethal in a fight.

With a sharp exhale, I lift the piece of paper and read the words I'll never forget.

LITTLE BROTHER,

You took what was mine, now I have what's yours. Next time you kill me, make sure to take my head!

Kessar

. . .

MY MIND REELS with the implications of this letter. Alexion has a brother? He tried to kill him? This male has my Alice, and it insinuates that he might kill her if he hasn't already. *What the fuck?*

My Alice!

CHAPTER THIRTY-THREE

ALEXION

I run. I run hard and fast, the rhythm of my feet on the ground my new heartbeat as I pound into the woods. I don't know where he is, but I know I will find him. I know it as clearly as I know that today, one of us *will* die, for good this time.

Kessar is not only alive but wants revenge for trying to kill him in the past. I don't know how he could have survived the knife I clearly saw piercing his heart so long ago. I was sure he breathed his last breath and all this time his death, along with too many others, has been weighing heavily on my heart. He wouldn't really kill Alice, would he?

He must have been out here watching me for a long time to know that Alice was my Kindred, and probably waited for the perfect moment to take her from me. Why didn't I stay watching her today?

Alice must be so frightened, being taken again. I heard that she was kidnapped by the other faction in the past and that's why she was brought to our village because we are such strong predators and could easily keep her safe.

How did I let this happen? And how did he get this close to her without me scenting him? I almost trip at that thought. I have had the feeling of being watched many times and Kessar must have been at my back door to leave the note, but why haven't I scented him, even once? There's no way he could have gotten this close without me knowing he was there.

I smell magic afoot. Kessar must be in touch with some very powerful Sorcerers to be able to procure a spell like that. I haven't seen one before myself, but I have heard about it. In the past, I'd always presumed it was just a rumour, but not now.

My feet pound in the dirt, and I jump falling logs as if they are nothing. I may not have much going for me, but over the last sixty years I have done nothing but hone my physical skills until I have passed out from the very pain of it. Pushing my body to its limit every day is a type of torture I use to punish myself for the past choices I've made. If those I love don't get to live pain-free, then neither do I.

A fast and heavy breeze pushes by me from the south and I freeze. Jasmine, gardenia, and ylang-ylang. Even in this form, I could smell her a mile away. *Alice!*

With a swift, smooth movement, I change my direction to where the alluring scent of my Kindred is coming from. A renewed ache of hope hits me until I scent the blood in the air. Her blood.

Roaring loud with a lingering snarl, I tear into a clearing with my sweet, battered and bruised Alice lying in a bundled ball at the centre. Before her is the towering form of Kessar, looking exactly the same as the last time I saw him, but this time he is very much alive.

"Ah, brother, you did decide to join us after all," Kessar says in greeting, his arms wide in a fake welcome, while his eyes burn into me hard. "I guess this belongs to you?" He kicks her whimpering form.

I step forwards with a growl. "Tut tut, little brother. I can kill her before you make it two steps and you know it. If I were you, I'd take a step back." He pulls a familiar knife out of the back of his pants and points it towards his hostage.

Worried about what Kessar is willing to do in the name of vengeance, I take a step back, my eyes on her small dirty bundle. "Alice," I call out. "Are you alright?"

Please be alright! I think to myself, fear for her burning a hole in my chest. I won't be able to handle the pain if anything has happened to her, especially after everything I've put her through, but my nerves tamper down as she croaks out. "I'm okay."

Alice turns her body to face me, and I suck in a breath at the state of her face. Blood drips from her split eyebrow, and one of her eyes is swollen shut from what must have been a violent hit. Her one good eye pours tears down her cheek. Her jaw on that side of her face was already turning black from another painful injury.

"Just let her go," I plead, taking a step forwards again but this time coolly and without threat. "This is between us and has nothing to do with her."

Kessar laughs and steps over her. "That's where you're wrong. It has everything to do with her. You want her, and therefore we won't be even until I take her away."

I assume he's talking about our family, but I lost them too. I grieve for them, too.

"Do you have any fucking idea how long I had planned that?" he asks me, and I'm confused. "It was all going perfectly until you wrecked everything. Argh! I could have had everything, power, territory, and my own army and all I had to do was give them a useless little girl. I knew they wouldn't let me take Phillis without fighting for her, so I had to set fire to the village, there was no other way."

He watches me carefully as I take in every dirty word coming out of his mouth. My stomach turns, and my throat fills with bile. He did that to everyone? Our family? Kessar wanted to sell our little sister to mercenaries for power?

"That's it, big boy." Kessar grins menacingly. "Get angry because you're going to need it. I made a deal for her, but I was going to let you and Jamal help me rule our new territory. I figured that you were weak enough that I could train you and Jamal was just a kitten, what did he know?"

A low rumbling growl vibrates up my body from the very centre of my being. "You killed our parents." My voice is as raspy as ever but with the deep, fettering rage inside me, my words come out like those of a demon. "They would have raped and caged Phillis and you wouldn't have cared?"

Kessar starts flipping the knife in the air in a show of complete confidence and comfort that he won't feel for long. I take notice of Alice slowly and quietly crawling away from behind Kessar, and I know I have to keep him distracted and away from her. If she can get far enough away, I'll be able to safely attack him without worrying about her being hurt.

"What do I care? She was an annoying little brat anyway." My brother chuckles like the thought of my sweet little Phillis screaming through the fire for me to save her was nothing.

Kessar looks like he's about to turn, so I take a big step forwards, instantly getting his attention. "What about Jamal? What happened to him after you took him away?" *I don't want to know. I don't want to know. I don't want to know.* I keep the mantra in my head, but I know Kessar will stay focused on me.

He huffs and shakes his head. "When I went back to my

contacts, they were so pissed off with me losing their little female that they demanded blood. Of course, I wasn't going to let them have you because you were mine to kill after fucking up my life. So, I gave them Jamal. You should have seen it, Alexion." Kessar actually laughs, shaking his head at the memory. "While you were knocked out, he pleaded and screamed for you to save him as they stripped his skin off one line at a time until his heart gave out, and he died from pain and terror. Not once did he give up on screaming for you until he couldn't scream any more. Just another child dying with your name on their lips."

My knees buckle, and I land hard on the dirt, emptying the contents of my stomach all over the ground. My mind is ringing with the last screams of Phillis and Jamal I ever heard. The screams that keep me up at night.

How can the brother I looked up to be the same monster in front of me now? Laughing at our little Jamal crying out in pain as he had the skin ripped from his body. How does a person turn out like this? Phillis deserved for me to be smarter and stronger, so I could have saved them.

"If it wasn't for you," Kessar starts with a more violent tone, backing up my current thoughts. "They would both be alive. Phillis as the pet she was meant to be and Jamal standing by our side in power, but you only bring death to those you love, don't you? I guess Alice is next?"

"No. You are." My head is still down, but I am paying close attention to the fact he's taken a few steps closer to me, I lift my head carefully and see Alice get silently dragged out of the clearing by Salem. His eyes are on me and with a nod, he slips her away to safety.

The full focus of my good eye lands on Kessar, and I sit up and pull myself back up to a standing position, using the back of my hand to wipe away the spittle from my mouth. "You will be the next person I love to die, and the last one for a very long time."

Kessar laughs, not at all noticing that Alice is gone or that we're not alone. My hypervigilant senses have picked up Baxter and Navy beyond the treeline.

"Oh, you love me, do you? Do you want to snuggle first?" Kessar mocks me but I don't care.

Standing up to my full height with pride, I tell him. "I love the brother you were before you became what you are. For the memory and respect of our parents, I will love you the way you were forever because they loved you too. The male before me is not my brother, just a villain wearing his skin. I will give you peace, my brother, in this world and the next."

I feel the love of all of those I've lost to this monster fill my heart, and I know that no matter what happens in this fight, he will be no more, whether by my hand or the hands of my new brothers, today is Kessar's last, and I'm at peace with that,

Kessar takes that moment to look behind him with an eyebrow raised, and he turns back to me. "Ah, I see. You think you're going to win. Don't worry, I'll catch the bitch soon."

Without warning, he dives for me, the knife from my dreams coming at me at a fast speed.

Goodbye, brother.

CHAPTER THIRTY-FOUR

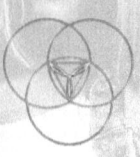

NAVY

My heart breaks for Alexion, for the tale his brother spins makes the pain he has been dealing with all this time clearer and clearer with every word. It feels wrong for us to be hearing something so personal and utterly devastating, but we won't leave him or Alice.

Salem retrieves Alice safely, but she promptly passes out from her pain. Both he and Ture rush her back to the village for medical care, leaving me and Baxter here to back up Alexion if he needs it.

Baxter is a clear choice as his fighting skills in both man and beast form are exceptional, but I look up to Alexion like a second brother, and not hell or high water will take me away from his side in his time of need. I will fight to my death for him if I have to because I know he'd do the same for me.

I can't imagine someone being evil enough to kill their whole family and sell a little girl to the black market. My brother is such a good male and has done so much to help me understand who I am and how to find my own place amongst our people, and right now I wish I could give him a big hug to say thank you. It goes to show that good siblings that love and care for you are not guaranteed, they're a blessing.

Baxter and I watch patiently as Kessar pounces on Alexion, a knife brandished in his hand. They fight violently together, with Kessar on the full brutal attack. I'm surprised to find Alexion calm and focused instead of wild and frenzied like I would expect after such a barbarous confession.

They tussle and Baxter grabs my attention with a soft touch, nodding silently that he's going to go around the other side and pointing with his fingers for me to stay here but watch in case I need to jump in. Nodding in agreement, I concentrate on the movements of the two males in the clearing, waiting for any sign that I need to get involved.

Knowing I'm a better fighter in Cheetah form, I slide my clothes off quickly but quietly and shift. My beast prowls low in the brush, my eyes focused on the weakest areas of my prey, mouth salivating with the idea of a hunt.

I notice Baxter closing in on the opposite side just as Kessar slices across Alexion's front. He jumps back with a howl of pain and without a second thought I sprint out into the clearing and pounce on the feral Mhanu named Kessar, my beast hungering for his demise.

Biting down hard on his thigh, I use my claws to rip open his Achilles' tendons, and he drops like the sack of shit he is. Kessar's wild eyes meet mine in shock, he was so unaware of our presence that he should be ashamed to be called a Cheetah.

Baxter runs out and helps Alexion up before turning on Kessar, kicking his head so hard it sounds like a pop, and I do a premature bounce of excitement. Premature because a split second later white-hot pain sears through my stomach, and I look down to see my innards fall outwards. Kessar used my moment of distraction to slice my stomach open and for a full few seconds I can't feel anything but shock but reality always comes knocking in the end.

My body slumps to the ground unceremoniously, the pain as prevalent as my mind's numbness, and I know death is politely knocking at my door.

I lay my head back and watch the fight crashing before me because there's nothing else I can do as my warm blood pools around me, sticking to my fur, the smell of it so thick I can taste it.

Kessar howls as Baxter rips open his chest, pushing him against the ground, now in Cheetah form as well. Alexion looks down at him bloody and panting before ripping off his own clothes and shifting into a half-scarred beast of a Cheetah, terrifying to view.

He prowls to his brother's face, ignoring Kessar's pleading, and rips out his throat, not stopping the tearing and biting until his head is severed completely. The wet gurgling sounds don't last long, but I relax the last bit of my tension, happy to let go now that I know my family and my Kindred are safe.

I use the last of my strength to shift slowly, the pain almost unbearable, but I don't want to be in Cheetah form when Alice sees my body later. She'll want to hold me.

Alice. I close my eyes and think to myself, picturing her beautiful pink cheeks and the way her curvy body fits against mine. My whole life was perfect, and I wouldn't change a thing other than to make it longer. Alice gave me all of her and accepted all of me, and that alone will forever bring me peace.

"Navy." Alexion's panicked voice has me opening my eyes, heaviness thick in my lips as weakness begins to take over. "Where do you think you're going?"

Baxter starts to put my intestines back inside my body carefully as Alexion holds my hand tight, his eyes wet with unshed tears and face smeared with the blood of his brother.

I smile weakly at him. "It's alright. You have to stay with Alice now, no more running away." I get out slowly between pained breaths. "Tell her I love her, and I'm sorry."

"No. No. No. No." Alexion starts to shake me as my eyes slip closed again, and I can barely make out what's happening any more. Hot, wet drops of his own pain land on my face, and the knowledge that he is crying for me is my last thought before the darkness holds me close and calls me home.

CHAPTER THIRTY-FIVE

ALICE

My eyes open at the same time that pain slaps me in the face. Oh, good morning, injuries I forgot about. I moan and roll over, my whole body sucks balls right now, including my face, and not in a good way.

Salem squeezes my hand right beside me, and I squint at him with one eye because apparently the other one is currently owned by Satan, and he's using it as a footstool. I'm shocked to find his eyes flooding with tears and his cheeks wet from what looks like hours of crying if his swollen eyes are anything to go by.

"Baby, it's okay. I'm safe now," I tell him, pulling him close. With a sniffle he rolls onto the bed beside me, pulling me close in his arms, wrapping me up until I can't move an inch. It actually hurts a little, but I don't mind.

Kisses rain over my face softly so as to not hurt me, along with soft words of love and devotion, and it touches my heart to know that he adores me this much. Nobody's ever been this upset on my behalf before. Yes, I'm injured, but it'll be alright. Plus, I have excellent pain tolerance, and it won't bother me half as much as it probably should.

I let him keep me secure in his embrace until my bladder informs me that lying there is no longer a choice, and I slowly wiggle out from beneath him, letting out a pained moan from my back. *That asshole.*

Getting up very carefully, with Salem assisting me with support, I look down to the floor and find Baxter and Ture asleep in each other's arms. It's so freaking cute, I wish I could take a photo.

Salem comes around to my side and lifts me up in a bridal hold, being gentle on my bruised back. He kisses my cheek softly and whispers as he walks me to the bathroom, "I was so worried when I couldn't find you, and when I saw you lying on the dirt like that, I think my heart stopped."

He puts me down on my feet softly, and I remind him again that I'm safe now and use the bathroom in privacy. When I'm done, I wash my hands and stare in shock at the reflection looking back at me. I mean, I knew I was in pain, but I didn't know I looked this pretty. *Ouch.* I wash my face with warm water, trying to not let the stinging stop me.

With a deep breath, I go back out and Salem is still waiting for me patiently with a small smile on his face. "How can you resist all of this?" I ask over dramatically, but when I try to smile it hurts too much, and it turns into a groan and pained grimace instead.

"You're beautiful, even with a face only a mother could love," he jokes back to lighten the mood, and I swat him playfully before grabbing his hand and leading him back to the room.

Both Baxter and Ture are sitting up with their backs against the wall now, their gazes filled with worry for me, and I appreciate it. It's weird that Navy isn't here, though. I figure if anyone was going to be all over me, it would be him. Maybe he's checking on Alexion.

I sit on the edge of the bed and lean back on my hands. "What happened anyway? I didn't mean to pass out. Is Kessar gone?"

The guys seem to simultaneously fidget and look away from me, but finally, Salem says bluntly, "Kessar is dead and won't ever bother you again." I guess they were worried about how I'd feel about a death, but I'm not perfect. I'm glad he's gone, and I don't care if that makes me a bad person, he's a horrible man.

"Did Alexion kill him?" I ask and he nods. "Good. Fuck that guy. Is Alexion alright? Did he get hurt?"

Salem starts to look me over physically as I ask my questions, obviously checking my injuries, and I appreciate his attention to detail. Baxter talks for them all, "He did get a little sliced, but he's doing a damn sight better than you are, that's for sure. Well, at least physically anyway, I can't say much for his headspace at the moment."

I can't even imagine how hard it must have been for him to not only have to fight his brother but to have to kill him just to save my and his lives.

"Oh yeah, for sure. Poor Alexion. Can we go and visit him?" I ask standing up again, but Salem just sits me straight back down. "Oh, and what happened to Mischa? Did you know that bitch sent me into that trap?"

"Don't worry about her, she was sent away the second we got back, and she saw what had happened to you. She told us everything out of guilt, but we couldn't even look at her. As for Alexion, it's not that simple right now, Alice. There's something else you need to know," Baxter says, rising and sitting next to me on the bed, and takes my hand in a comforting gesture.

My stomach tightens and I look between the three of them.

Three. Oh no, Navy. "Where's Navy? Why isn't he here with you?"

The silence in the room is eerie and my heart clenches. I get back up to my feet and look between them more frantically, "Where is he?" I practically scream.

Baxter sighs and pulls me back down beside him, wrapping an arm around my shoulder and into the crook of his hard body. "My queen, the fight was quite bloody, and Navy fought so bravely for someone who's never been in a fight before. Unfortunately, the battle was more than he could handle, and he was gravely injured."

What? Why the fuck is he so calm?

A sob rips from my chest and I fold into myself, feeling like a piece of my heart is dying. "No!" I scream gutturally. The kind of scream that can only be rendered from deep grief.

"No. No. No. Baby." Salem rips Baxter off me and pulls me into his lap. "He's alive, calm down."

"Oh shit." I hear Baxter cursing. "I'm so freaking sorry, I didn't mean to make it sound that way, I just wanted to be clear about how bad his injuries are."

I try to focus on their words as Salem rocks me, and Baxter rubs my legs vigorously. Ture comes around to my head and kisses my temple with tenderness as my sobbing slows down.

"Is- is- he okay?" I sniffle and hiccup out, "Navy isn't dead?" It hurts even saying those words, but I need to be clear that I'm hearing them right.

Ture kisses me again. "No my darling but he is in critical condition at the moment. The healer Dr Orion is with him right now, and Abel and Alexion are by his side."

Alexion suddenly rips open the bedroom door, his eyes and hair wild and his beard more unkempt than usual. With a growl, he searches every corner of the room. "What's happened?" He shoves Baxter aside roughly and kneels at my feet, looking up at me. "Is she alright?"

My scream must have brought him over, and I feel equally guilty for scaring him and delighted that he was scared for me.

I reach out and palm his cheek. "I just found out about Navy and I thought he died," I explain through my still lightly flowing tears. "Were you just with him? Are you alright?"

Seeming to realise what he'd done, Alexion stands up and steps back, with my hand dropping from lack of contact. "He's still unconscious, but he's healing fast." His raspy baritone sends shivers down my spine, and his words give me a small amount of relief.

"Take me to him," I demand, standing up. "Don't bother arguing because if he could, he'd be by my side."

I start walking out the door and Alexion quickly passes me but then slows down without looking back so that I can follow him easily. My body hurts all over as I move, but it's worth the pain to be with Navy, and I know Baxter, Salem, and Ture are right behind me, ready to catch me if I fall.

Surprisingly, we walk into Baxter and Salem's house right next door. No wonder Alexion was at my house so quickly when I screamed my grief out.

We walk through the house and down to the last room, I take a moment at the closed door to collect myself before I open it and let myself in, Alexion now behind me with the others, obviously wanting to give me the time I need before I'm faced with the harsh reality of what my injured Kindred will look like.

When I enter, Abel stands up at the side of Navy's bedside, his face swollen with the tears he's no doubt shed on behalf of his little brother. He nods at me mournfully, and we both look down at the still figure, Navy's breath comes slow and even. If I didn't know better, I'd think he was sleeping if it wasn't for the IV beside him and the Dr in the corner of the room sitting solemnly still, reading a book.

Dr Orion, whom I remember from Threshold, takes that moment to close his book and place it on the small table at his side. Standing up, he says, "Alice. It's good to see you again, although I do wish it was under different circumstances." He moves to stand beside Abel, and I step into the room further, standing on the opposite side of the bed and taking Navy's hand. "He is doing a heck of a lot better than when I saw him yesterday. I've placed a healing spell on him as well as added something a little extra into the saline IV, courtesy of the Fairies. I had a little of it left over since my last exchange with them, and it's working wonders."

I'd forgotten there were Fairies here, nobody really talks about the Fae much in Rathe. Or at least none I've been hanging around.

"Thank you so much, Dr. Will he make a full recovery?" I ask, hope littered in every word.

With a confident nod, he replies. "Absolutely. It won't take long, either, I'd wager. It's lucky that I was in such close proximity when it happened. Nasty business this all was, it could have been a much worse outcome, and I'm glad you all came out of it alive."

I look down at Navy's sweet face and stroke his cheek. "I don't know what I would have done without him. Thank you from the bottom of my heart."

"My pleasure," he replies, his eyes twinkling happily. "I must be off now, Salem is more than qualified to continue with the remainder of Navy's medical care. I guess I'll see you when it's time to bring new Cheetahs into the fold." He laughs heartily, and I swear it sounds like the Dr off of the Simpsons.

Dr Orion leaves us alone, and I sit on the edge of the bed, leaning down to kiss Navy. I breathe him in. Is it weird that I've already missed the way he smells? "Love you," I whisper to him quietly.

Abel comes around and puts his hand on my shoulder. "Since you're here I'm going to go and sleep for a couple of hours, I've been by his side all night, and I'm running on fumes."

I happily agree, and Alexion takes his place across from me. He reaches over and takes my hand in his, getting my attention. His raspy voice breaks the silence building. "I'm so sorry this happened. It's all my fault. I knew something would happen if I stayed near you, but I couldn't stay away. It was selfish and because of me you both got hurt."

"Don't be ridiculous," I snap harder than I mean to, but I'm not letting Alexion take the blame for something Kessar did. "You are as much of, if not more of, a victim as we were. Kessar is a piece of shit and his actions have no reflection on you, and I won't hear otherwise."

He lets go of my hand and steps back. "I've decided to go with Dr Orion to the other village." The other guys in the room gasp from shock at his words, and I feel as though I've been kicked in the chest again. "No matter what I do, the people I care about get hurt, and I don't want to do that to any of you. You don't deserve it." Alexion can't even look me in the eye as he tells me these things, and I'm mad as hell.

"No, and that's final," I tell him bossily, and I'm not sorry about it. "You are my Kindred, and I love you. You are going to stay with us forever because I don't want to live without you. Any of you."

Alexion doesn't seem to hear me as he steps away again, making more space between us. "I'm sorry, but it's for the best." The resignation and finality in his voice break my heart as a tear rolls down his cheek, and I don't know what to do to make him stay.

CHAPTER THIRTY-SIX

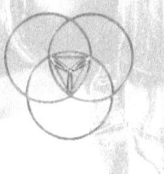

NAVY

s I lay here listening to Alexion feeling sorry for himself and disrespecting my Alice, I know I can't fake sleeping any more. My stomach freaking hurts badly, and I would have liked just lying still for a while, but I can't hear this crap any more.

"Stop being a baby, Alexion," I say croakily, my mouth dry from disuse. I pull my heavy eyelids open to find my Alice looking down at me with one good eye wet with tears but the other one and her jaw are so bruised that I growl low at the sight. "That motherfucker. Look at your face."

Small chitters of laughter fill the room and Ture steps forwards, standing next to Alice, and says, "And they say I say stupid shit. You're meant to tell her she looks beautiful."

I scoff and it hurts my stomach. I wrap my arms around my middle with a groan. "You're always beautiful, Alice, but I don't like you to be hurt."

She pretends to hit my shoulder, silent tears falling down her face. "Look who's talking. You scared me so much, I thought you'd died."

"Me too," I admit. "I was sure I was a goner, but it's weird, this Goddess came to me and told me that I had stuff to do. I honestly figured it was some kind of dream, but I'm pretty sure I did die."

Alexion comes closer and squeezes my hand. "You did. Right in front of me but then all of a sudden you started breathing again, it was a miracle. What Goddess was it?"

I shrug slightly, "Fuck if I know. I wasn't really listening, but she said something about our kids being important and some sort of war or something."

My Alice looks pale, so I tell the others to leave me with her and that I want to talk to Alexion next because I have something important he needs to know.

All my new brothers hug me with feeling, showing me how grateful they are that I'm okay, and I've never felt more a part of something than I do now, and I know I will never take what we have as a Kindredship for granted. We are a family.

When they leave me alone with my love, I take her hand, ignoring the thumping pain in my middle for now. "You know I love you more than anything in the world, right?" I ask rhetorically because we both already know the answer. "Well, I need you to do something for me. I need you to have patience with Alexion, the way we had patience with you. Okay, yes, the others had more patience than I did, but you get what I'm saying, right? You seemed a little broken when you got here, and we helped to pull you back together the way you deserved to be, am I right?" Alice nods quietly, hooked on my every word. "That's what Alexion needs now. He needs our family more than he'll ever admit, so it's your turn to help build him back up. He deserves it too."

Alice sniffs back more tears and leans down with her head in the crook of my neck. "You are such a good man, Navy. I hear you and I agree. Let's make this family strong and help each other when we need it. I love you, just the way you are. Don't you ever change."

"I'm too stubborn to change," I tell her, stroking the back of her hair. Fatigue and pain start bearing down on me, so I tell her. "As much as I want to cuddle you, I also really want to taste you right now." She laughs and swats me playfully, sitting back and looking down at me with a small wet smile. "I'm running out of energy and still need to talk to Alexion before I pass out again."

With a deep kiss before she leaves, Alice swaps over with Alexion, the male looking as grumpy as ever when he returns. I guess some things will never change.

Alexion grumbles a half-assed "What?" and I just look up at him until he properly looks back at me.

"That's enough fighting us now, big brother. You've taken your time as a nomad, but you are a part of our family now, and you're old enough to know better than to leave your Kindred," My voice is harder than I've ever used with him before, but he needs to hear how serious I am. "Do you hear me? You are my family. Our family and we need you. We don't expect you to change or suddenly grow a bubbly personality, but we do expect you to stay with us."

Alexion shows me enough respect to not leave the room in protest, I can clearly see how uncomfortable my declarations of affection are for him.

"I love you. You have been as much a brother to me since I was born as Abel has been. Whether you like to admit it or not, you have taken really great care of me and made me feel accepted even when it was hard for others because I'm so different." I sigh deeply, my pain increasing the more I talk. "I can never replace your little brother or sister, but please let me love you and look up to you the way I know they would have if they were here."

I know it's a lot to ask Alexion, but I'm asking anyway. I'll never forget the way he treated me as though I was any other Cheetah Shifter growing up. I was never less in his eyes. Not once.

"Thank you, brother." I reach for his hand and squeeze his hand with mine. "But it's time to move on from your past and focus on your future, and Alice is your future. Let us help you get through your healing together, as a family. What do you say?"

He doesn't pull his hand out of mine, but he doesn't look at me either, his eye firmly on the blanket. I watch patiently as his features flutter with different emotions as he goes through what I've said, but I have faith that he'll stay with us. I have faith in him.

As Alexion seems to come to a decision, he looks up at me. "What if I'm not enough?" His voice breaks and the vulnerability of his words chokes me up.

"Are any of us enough in this world?" I counter. "Maybe Alice has five Kindreds because all of our broken pieces fit together perfectly and if even one of us is missing then we all stay broken. Ever think of that?"

I see his resolve crumble further. "I'll be hard to be with. Sometimes I can't stop the screaming," Alexion tells me honestly, pointing to his head, and I can't help trying to lift the mood away from his dark thoughts.

"Easy fix, fuck Alice often and hard, and all you'll be able to hear are her screams after that and trust me, they're memorable as fuck," I joke. "Tasting her helps a lot too, she loves that, and she's fucking delicious."

Alexion chuckles low and shakes his head at me, taking his hand away. "Way to make it weird."

"Just telling it how it is. Now go out there and make the most of every second you get with that gorgeous creature we have the privilege to be tied to forever and let us all love you the way you deserve to be loved. Your old brother might have been shit, but we're awesome as fuck, so get used to it. We're not done with you yet."

In a shocking move, Alexion bends over and hugs me tight, careful not to hurt my middle when he does. Just as quickly, he retreats from the room, and I close my eyes as the rest of my family comes to stand around me.

"Thank you," Alice whispers in my ear, hopping onto the bed beside me and gently snuggling into me.

I know that we have plenty of rocky roads ahead of us, but I also know that we can get through anything, as long as we're together, and I can't wait to see where Alice will take us.

CHAPTER THIRTY-SEVEN

ALICE

NEW YEAR'S DAY, SIX MONTHS LATER

fist wraps around my now much longer hair and yanks me back into a very large, very hard body, and I mean hard everywhere. I know who it is straight away because no one likes it rough with me except for Alexion.

His large, scarred hand comes around my stomach to gently rub circles around the area our baby grows. The contrast between the two movements is very much like the man, equally violent and filled with love and adoration.

"How's my baby doing?" he growls in my ear, his hardness pressed into my back.

I wiggle against him seductively, feeling extra horny these days, and reply, "Which one? Because if it's me you're talking about, I could really use some attention right now." I know the perfect way to spend the first day of the new year.

Dr Orion said that I'm about five months pregnant now and after doing several tests we are sure there's only one baby inside me. I couldn't care less who the biological father is because it doesn't really matter on Rathe as it would on Earth, we will all love it equally regardless.

We all live in relative peace these days, the way it should be, except for the random disagreement between Ture and Navy over whose idea is better or Alexion's propensity for stealing me away from everyone else with the excuse he doesn't share. It makes me laugh and reminds me of Joey from 'Friends' saying, "Joey doesn't share food."

Speaking of Alexion, he picks me up as soon as Baxter enters the kitchen and carries me down the hallway to our combined bedroom. Thankfully, the room and bed Ture set aside for us are big enough for all five of us, even though some days Alexion will sleep alone or kidnap me in the middle of the night to sleep with him in the room he claimed for his own.

"The fuck, man," Baxter shouts, coming after us. "She's mine too."

Alexion slams the door in his face. "Fuck off. I don't share." His gravelly voice grinds out, carrying me to the gargantuan bed. He lays me down carefully on my back and spreads my thighs open. "Mine." His growl makes me instantly wet, and so does the way he feasts on my pussy with his eyes before lowering himself down to taste me the way he does.

Between Navy and Alexion, I don't know which one's worse about going down on me, they treat it like a religion they worship day and night, and let me tell you, I. Am. Not. Mad! I've cum more times over the last seven months to outnumber a normal chick on Earth during her entire lifetime.

With a deep growl and expert roll of his tongue, Alexion has me screaming his name as I hear a disgruntled Baxter growl outside the door that it's not fair, but I'll make it up to him later, of that, I have no doubt.

The large man between my thighs crawls up my body, licking his lips with a cheeky side smile lighting up his face. "Delicious," he rumbles, pulling his shirt over his head before kissing me senseless, my taste all over his mouth.

Alexion's body is covered with more scars than I ever knew before the incident with his brother. The bottom of his hands, feet, and back are so badly burnt that I can't even imagine the pain he must have faced. Not to mention the scar across his face and the newer ones on his abdomen, but even with all of that, I find this man unendingly sexy from head to toe.

Within seconds, we are both completely bare, and his impressive cock slides into my already soaking pussy, both of us moaning together at the feeling. Normally Alexion likes to fuck me pretty hard and fast, biting, slapping my ass, and pinching my nipples until I beg but since my stomach has started growing rounder with the little being inside it, he's become more cautious with his movements, and his hand is almost always caressing the new life.

Alexion uses his arms to hold his body above mine to not put any pressure on me as he moves in and out in a slower motion than I want from him, so I grasp his biceps hard and beg, "Please, fuck me harder. I want you deep inside me. Please, baby, I can take it."

At first, he looks uncertain, but when I bite my lip and squeeze my large aching breasts, his control slips, and he pulls out, turns me over fast, and pulls my ass up.

With a move so quick I wasn't ready, he spears me deep and I cry out. His thrusts don't falter as he pumps me hard from behind with one hand holding my hips high, and the other slides around and flicks my clit.

"Holy shit," I groan, clenching tight around him, and he uses his fingers to work me even closer to the climax his thrusts are urging me towards.

Deep, hard, and fast, an unrelenting pace that makes me cum so hard my limbs begin to shake, but he doesn't slow or change in any way, fucking me until I see stars and cum again, twice before wrapping his large hand around my throat and using his grip to pull my body up and against him, his hips still pistoning against my ass.

He tightens his grip around me and bites down on my shoulder, hard, and I fucking love it. I crave it. His other hand pinches my nipple, and it pushes me over one more time, the tight clenching of my walls milk him dry as he fills me with his hot seed.

His grip lets go of my neck, and he tenderly licks my shoulder. "You alright?" he gruffly asks, lowering me back onto the bed and slipping out of me, but before I can reply the door jimmies, and a naked Navy strolls in with a big smile on his face.

"My turn." His eyes light up at the sight of me all sweaty and freshly fucked, just the way he likes me. "Damn you're sexy." He practically pushes Alexion out of the way and slides between my thighs and straight inside me. "Oh, fuck yes, that feels so good."

Alexion drops beside me and turns away, pulling the blankets up. "You're a sick fuck, you know that, right?" he grumbles to Navy, dissing his little fetish, which I happen to love.

"Fuck you, bro, I like what I like, and I'm not sorry." Navy thrusts deep inside again with his last word, ending it with a groan. "You want me, don't you, Alice?"

I wrap my arms around him and pull him down for a deep kiss as he continues to thrust into me, slowly but with purpose, his body grinding against my clit the way he knows I like. "You know it," I say between kisses.

We rub our sweaty bodies together as we make love. The whole time, he's careful not to put any pressure on my stomach, and I love him all the more for it.

After we climax together, Navy picks me up and carries me to the shower, carefully washing me down as if I were made of delicate china and the most precious thing in the world to him, but I suppose I am. Alexion surprises me by jumping in the large five-person shower with us, at the other end of it mind you, but still with us.

The three of us dry off and return to the bedroom to find Ture and Salem making the bed up while Baxter changes all the pillowcases. Which is a lot for one bed.

"What are you doing?" I ask them, confused.

Ture comes and takes my hand, kissing it with adoration. "Taking care of our Kindred. What else would we have to do but that? I made some new sheets out of extra soft cotton. I hope you like them?"

This man, will he ever stop gifting me things? Probably not, will I stop being grateful for the time and love he puts into spoiling me? Never.

Salem puts more logs in the fire at the end of the bed to keep the room warm for me. They don't really notice the cold as much as I do, but they do whatever they can to make me comfortable. It's a very cold winter, with snow coming out of my ass and after the Christmas we all spent with Summer's pack having a big celebration together, I've felt chilled to the bone.

It was a lovely Christmas holiday with all my old friends. Summer with her growing clan, Havana and hers, as well as Bell, Shylo with her son, and Nateesha. Nateesha came back to stay with us for a few days, and it's been nice having them around.

Unfortunately, Janice and her Bear Shifters couldn't make it for Christmas because her daughter Lemon has been very difficult, and the trip was just too much for her right now.

I slide into the middle of the massive bed and get comfortable, my mind on the lovely time I had with my old Threshold friends and their kids, and my hand unconsciously caresses my tummy and the baby I can't wait to meet inside. Seeing everyone's kids laughing and playing made me even more clucky than I was before, and I know my men feel the same way by how much they were watching all the little ones.

It makes me think about schooling. "Do you think we can get together with the other mums and set up some kind of schooling for the kids? Maybe somewhere in the centre that Sorceress can pop them in and out of, so they can grow up together and learn properly?" I say my idea out loud, but I don't get a response as the guys hop into bed on both sides of me.

On my left Alexion lies next to me with Navy next to him and on my right is Ture, then Salem and Baxter. It's definitely a cosy setup, and I have no doubt Alexion hates every second of it.

To back up that statement, Alexion grumbles loudly, "If you don't stop spooning me Navy I'm going to throw you in the fucking fire and use you as kindling."

Navy laughs and snuggles in more. "Don't be silly, I'd roast if anything because there's too much liquid inside me to use as kindling. It needs to be dry and help the flames not put them out as I drip."

Baxter and Salem start laughing really loud, and Ture chuckles beside me.

"You're impossible," Alexion grumbles, turning and shoving Navy off the bed with a heavy thud. "I mean it, hands to yourself, or I'll throw you in the fire to drip on the flames." He rolls his eyes in exasperation and cuddles into my side.

With an absolutely serious tone, Navy states getting back into bed. "You do realise that I'll just get out? I'm not going to just lie in the flames, that would be stupid."

"Oh shut up!" Alexion growls, over Navy's logical shit.

The guys all roar in hysterics at how serious Navy is and his nonchalant tone to Alexion's frustrations. I love my life, and I love these men.

* * *

THE NEXT MORNING, we all gather at the edge of the village to farewell Nateesha and Derryn. It was nice having them stay. While we'll see Derryn again for sure, I'm not so certain that I'll ever get the chance to see Nateesha after today.

After searching for her Kindreds all this time, Nateesha's loneliness has gotten the better of her, and she has decided to throw in the towel and go home, and honestly, I don't blame her. I was pretty ready to do the same not long ago. I just wish I could convince her to stick it out a little bit longer, you never know what might be right around the corner.

"Thank you for letting me stay with you lot," she says in her soft English accent. "It's been an absolute blast, but I'm ready to get back home now."

I give her a warm hug and Ture hands her a thick woollen scarf he knitted for her. "This will keep you warm and remind you of us back here," he says to her kindly.

"I truly appreciate that. It'll come in handy back in England, of that, I have no doubt." Nateesha's smile lights up her face, and I'm reminded of how naturally beautiful she is.

They start to walk away, and I can't help myself but to call back. "If you see Mischa back there, give her the finger for me." We laugh and wave to each other, and I stand there with my loves by my side until they both disappear down the path. I'll miss her, and I hope we meet again one day.

Baxter swings me into his arms and starts running with me back to our place, calling back, "Salem? Ture? How about a threesome?" My cheeks flame red as we pass other Cheetah Shifters. "Alexion? You can get fucked!"

Salem catches up and fist-bumps him as Ture beats us inside. When we reach the front door, Baxter turns around, gives Alexion the one-finger salute, and slams the door in his face with a laugh. "Payback's a bitch."

I giggle along with their antics and lose it when I see the bedroom window open and Navy lying sprawled along the bed with a gerbera in his mouth. Pulling it out, he asks with a smile, "How about a foursome?"

EPILOGUE

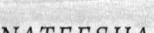

NATEESHA

Rathe is gorgeous. I think to myself as Bubba and Derryn take me to a clearing that looks upon a beautiful forest littered with pristine snow. I wonder if my heart will remember this place when I go home.

I'm a bit nervous about my memories being wiped, but I can understand why they need to take that kind of measure with all of us if we choose this path, or in Mischa's case get booted out of the world. Talk about an extreme eviction.

"Are you ready, lass?" Derryn asks me, patting my back with kindness. "It's nae too late to change your mind, you ken?"

I nod, sucking in a deep breath, "Let's get this over with."

Bubba starts to form the portal that will take me across the land to the Fae and explains, "A Sorcerer named Twist will meet you on the other side and will escort you to the Fae border where a Fairy male will let you through their portal. It's safer for you than the trek to the Bermuda Triangle, and it goes directly to Derryn's father's station in Ireland which is a heck of a lot closer to where you're from, so I've been told. Do you have any questions?"

"No. Thank you kindly for your help." My voice trembles slightly with my nerves, but I was taught to be confident when times get tough, and that's exactly what I'll do.

The portal fully forms and I step forwards, ready to go to my next destination and also kind of excited about seeing a real-life Fairy. I wonder if they're small like in the tales?

Derryn and Bubba wish me well, and I step right through, out of the snow and into soft lush grass, a warm breeze wisping along my skin. A completely different season, interesting.

A guy a little taller than me steps forwards, and I'm shook. This lad is well fit, and I do my best not to drool openly at him. His warm brown skin is smooth but muscled, his biceps and abs on full display from his open, hooded vest jacket. His low-slung leather pants hug his well-defined thighs and don't leave a lot to the imagination in the front department. I quickly avert my eyes and take in his long dreadlocks, barely hidden by the hood he's wearing, despite his shirt being open.

"You must be Twist?" I ask, taming my hormones and stepping forward with my hand out to shake politely. "I believe you're going to help me get back to Earth."

Instead of replying like I assumed he would, he stares into my eyes and then takes me in slowly from head to toe, his eyes flaring with a magenta hue.

Twist pushes his hood off his head and steps right into my body, his face only inches from mine, my hand now trapped between our suddenly close bodies, and he says seductively, "You must be my Kindred, and you're not going anywhere."

BOOKS BY ALEXANDRA K. MARTIN

<u>Series</u>

Rathe Chronicles (Epic Fantasy Paranormal Romance)

-Summer's Confine, Book One (RH)

https://books2read.com/summersconfine

-Janice's Entanglement, Book Two (Menage)

https://books2read.com/Janice

-Havana's Hell, Book Three (MF)

https://books2read.com/HavanaRathe

-Alice's Coalition, Book Four (RH)

https://books2read.com/AlicesCoalition

-Nateesha's Awakening, Book Five (RH/Coming 2024)

<u>Standalones</u>

-Broken Faun (Paranormal RH)

https://books2read.com/brokenfaun

-Hidden Fate (Urban Fantasy Menage/Coming Soon)

<u>Collaboration/Standalone</u>

-Lust: A Golden Bird Retelling. Sinners Fairytales Collaboration, Book Six (Dark Contemporary RH)

https://books2read.com/Lustsins

-Charity: A Beauty and the Beast Retelling. Virtue Fairytales Collection, Book One (Dark Contemporary RH, Coming 1st September 2023)

<u>Anthologies</u>

-Hidden Fate (RH), featured in 'Rebirth of the Dark Hunter' (Urban Fantasy/ No longer available)

<u>Soul Sisters Co-Write</u>

-Dom X (MF Erotic Standalone Novella/ Coming May 2023)

-Releasing the Beast (MF Paranormal Horror Romance/ Coming 2024)

Visit my Linktree for more information on me, the characters, Rathe and other novels:

https://linktr.ee/alexandrakmartin

THE SINNERS FAIRYTALES SERIES:

Book 1 - Gluttony by Kira Roman, a Red Riding Hood retelling
https://books2read.com/SFG

Book 2 - Sloth by AJ Blackburn, a Cinderella retelling
https://books2read.com/slothsins

Book 3 - Wrath by Jay Leigh Brown, a Sleeping Beauty retelling
https://books2read.com/wrathsins

Book 4 - Greed by J. Kearston, a Rumpelstiltskin retelling
https://mybook.to/GreedSinners5

Book 5 - Pride by Kris Butler, a Rapunzel retelling
https://books2read.com/pridesin

Book 6 - Lust by Alexandra K. Martin, a Golden Bird retelling
https://books2read.com/Lustsins

Book 7 - Envy by Jade Thorn, a Snow White retelling
https://mybook.to/SinnersFairytalesEnvy

THE VIRTUE FAIRYTALES SERIES
COMING 2023

Book 1 - Charity by Alexandra K Martin, a Beauty and the Beast retelling

Book 2 - Temperance by EJ Everette, an Ugly Duckling retelling

Book 3 - Diligence by Jay Leigh Brown, a Peter Pan retelling

Book 4 - Chastity by Kira Roman, a Swan Maiden retelling

Book 5 - Patience by Mia Z Staysails, a Goldilocks retelling

Book 6 - Kindness by Kady Monroe, a Bears retelling

Book 7 - Humility by Brooklyn Cross, an Aladdin retelling

ACKNOWLEDGMENTS

Thank you to my family, friends, editor, designer/Formatter and street team. You are all amazeballs and appreciated so much.

To my alpha/beta team; your time, support and friendship has helped me to become a better writer with every story and I am forever grateful to each and every one of you. Thank you.

Lastly, but just as importantly, my incredible readers. Words can't describe how much your support has meant to me over my journey. I wouldn't be here without you and everything I do is for you.

MY BOOK RECOMMENDATIONS

'Serpentine' by J. Kearston

https://mybook.to/Serpentine